Workshop 'Til You Drop

E. Sabbag

ISBN: 098355062X
ISBN-13: 978-0-9835506-2-4

DEDICATION

To all the writers that I've met along the way. Don't sweat the small stuff. Be relentless. And don't forget to laugh.

We are already writers; some of us simply aren't getting paid yet.
Sean McGuirk, 2013

DISCLAIMER

While Young's Dairy, Bonadies, Ye Olde Trail Tavern, Haha Pizza, the Sunrise Café and Glen Helen and the Antioch Writers' Workshop are all real, thriving venues, Mrs. Winthrop's Boarding House and the host of characters that populate these pages exist only in my mind. As far as I'm aware, there has never been a Dallas McGuire or "The Roach's Dream" and there has certainly never been a murder at the workshop. If you happen to find yourself in southern Ohio, I highly recommend visiting one or all of these places. Just don't piss off the creative types…

1.

Death can be extremely inconvenient. Or, more likely, friends can be.

I scrutinize Angelica's face to ferret out her thoughts. Voice-overs are much more helpful than ESP. I can almost hear Morgan Freeman's kindly baritone rumbling from the ether as he explains what is going through that inscrutable head.

"Angelica's cheeks flush scarlet; a scarlet that precedes spontaneous combustion. Ditto the brilliance in her sapphire eyes, sizzling from the rage that boils just below the surface."

In the decades that I've known her, her cheeks have never flushed scarlet and her eyes, actually a Hershey's Kiss brown, have never sizzled. Even her knuckles don't have the decency to drain white as she grips the steering wheel. No, she is calm and controlled, her attention focused on the deserted streets.

But this quiet serenity bothers me more than any emotional display. The complete absence of emotion terrifies rather than soothes. A strong man would meet this conflict head on, but that's not me. Not even close.

"Your hair looks – interesting…" A couple of months ago she'd been a sultry brunette with long wavy hair. This new blond razor cut does nothing for her—or me.

"Derek hates it, too," she snaps. "Says I look butch. Give a woman a strong look and the *stronger* sex is terrified."

As I mentioned. Not the stronger sex. Doesn't seem like a good time to point that out. Also doesn't seem to be the best time to announce that I finally agree with that arrogant lout she's married to...

"I didn't say I hated it."

"You didn't have to."

Silence. A sideways peek. Nope. Cheeks not flushed. Just stark blond hair glowing above pale skin and colorless lips. I wait. And fidget. Wait some more. And fidget some more. Finally, I crack.

"What are you so pissed off about? I'm the one who was arrested."

"Hmmm... Let's see. It's the first time I've seen the sunrise in years, I have to be at work in three hours and I should be in bed curled up next to my husband. Instead, a phone call shatters my dreams, infuriates my husband and makes me look like an idiot to my lawyer whom I call for advice at three AM. Then, there are the inestimable joys of contacting a bail bondsman, showing up at a police station and admitting an accused murderer is one of my oldest friends. You're right. I should be thrilled at the opportunity to pack so many new things into so few hours. Most people go a lifetime without encountering such a diverse array of experiences."

At least two bright red spots appear on her cheeks. A flush at last! She glows in the first rays of dawn, which softens her forty-year old face. Luckily, some hidden fragment of intelligence takes over and this observation stays in my head.

"All right. Tell you what. It won't come close to paying you back, but what if you let me buy you breakfast?"

"Can't. There's not enough time if I want to salvage the day and make it to work at a decent hour. Remember work? Some of us still have to. I have to shower, fix my hair, my makeup..."

"C'mon. You look great. Really. After we eat, you can drive straight from there to the office. Please?" Hard to tell if it's the compliment, my powers of persuasion or that she's just hungry, but her mouth softens. "It will give me a chance to explain."

"There can't possibly be enough time, this morning, this week, or even this year for a good explanation." Her tone belies the biting words.

"Maybe not, but it's a start. And, Young's Dairy is open. Fresh cinnamon rolls. Mmmm…" The last is cruel but effective. A hesitation then a tight nod. She continues towards Route 68.

A triumphant glow warms me as I settle into the bucket seat and watch the village of Yellow Springs give way to open fields. The sun hasn't appeared, but rosy streaks trickle across the sky, heralding its imminent arrival. We ride with the top down and the air feels fresh and cool, in contrast to the August heat that rises with the sun. Ohio summers are as hot as the winters are cold, and this one is no exception. The soothing engine hum coupled with a lack of sleep and an excess of alcohol, overwhelm me and I slide into unconsciousness.

There probably isn't a gentle way to wake somebody up when they're in a really deep sleep, but Angelica could have slammed her door a bit quieter. By the time my head clears, she is already across the parking lot to the restaurant. I sit for a few more seconds and listen to the gentle sounds emanating from the original and still working section of the farm.

Directly ahead of me is a barn. Traditional Midwest farm red. It exudes the soul of the land. Goats of all sizes and colors cavort in the dirt yard to the side of the building, where inside I know there are pigs and sheep and dozens of Jersey cows. At this hour, the automatons are gathering the butterfat rich milk used to make the best ice cream in the State and probably the whole Tri-State area. For a brief moment, I consider ignoring Angelica and the past few days and losing myself in a bucolic dream. But then my head clears and I scurry after my angry savior.

3

Even at this ungodly hour, the restaurant bustles with activity. While waiting for our turn in the cattle run, we have plenty of time to look through the menu posted above the grill. Especially since Angelica isn't talking to me. My normally large appetite is gargantuan due to the stress of the last few days and the lack of anything edible during the same timeframe. It is nearly impossible to choose from the enormous selection. Eggs over easy, home fries cooked crisp in bacon grease and thick slices of bacon nestled against flaky biscuits, finally wind up on my neon red tray. The biscuits pose a serious problem—what to slather on them? Sausage gravy? Fresh churned butter and raw honey? Not wanting to play favorites, I get both, hoping one or the other will neutralize the shakes that ripple through my body.

For a moment, panic sets in when Angelica is nowhere in sight, but then I catch sight of her blond thatch at an outside picnic table. At her feet, an orange monster of a Tomcat is ingratiating himself. The animal sits motionless, knowing from experience that social propriety gains more than caterwauling. And it works. Angelica doesn't notice my approach, engrossed as she is with bacon gifts. The cat sniffs the offering, licks it and then daintily takes it in his teeth. Then he purrs, his body motionless and eyes narrowed in delight until the process repeats.

"What happened to life without carbs?" My tray clangs onto the table and I gesture towards a cinnamon roll the size of my head.

"I've lost ten pounds since being yanked from sleep. I deserve comfort food." She and the beast glare at me with identical expressions of fury. I shrink onto the bench and dig into my own comfort food.

Angelica is always on one diet or another—high carb, low carb, fat burning, in the zone, grapefruit, South Beach, peanut butter—and all are unnecessary. True, there's a little more padding on her hips and thighs than twenty years ago; soft curves that suit her better than the bony angles she'd sported in high school. My opinion is irrelevant, however. Since her mid-thirties, the war against excess flesh has escalated. Her declared truce is a testament to the depth of her concern, even if she won't admit it outright. Never worried that much about my physique, I have no qualms about digging into my bacon and eggs. But my attack stalls.

"Talk." The command slices the air.

"Can't I eat before everything gets cold?" My pitiful look is not forced – I am starving.

"You can eat and talk at the same time. I've seen enough half-chewed food to attest to that."

I gaze off into the distance, molding my face into a mask of long suffering despair. Contemplating the desolate air of the empty batting cages and miniature golf course. Immune to my tactics, Angelica's unblinking stare draws me back. I sigh.

"Where should I begin?"

"Saturday. When you were still allowed in proper society," she prompts.

I sigh again, but realize it sounds less world-weary victim and more punctured inner tube. Squaring my shoulders, I bite into a honey-drenched biscuit.

2

My mother was an obsessive fan of the hard-boiled detective. She couldn't get enough of Mike Hammer, Sam Spade or Nero Wolfe. As a result, she was a fanatical groupie to the Kings of the Genre – Dashiell Hammett and Rex Stout. Or, at least, that was her pitiful excuse for why she gave me such a god awful name as Dashiell Rex Barker. It could've been worse. A friend of mine went through life as Odysseus Neoptolemus Farthington because his mother obsessed over Greek epics. Both of us bemoaned the fact that our mothers didn't read *People* or *Cosmo*. I'm convinced it would've set us on very different paths. Odie majored in archeology at Wright State and is managing the meat department at Meijer's; I avoided the higher institutes of learning altogether, preferring instead to attend the school of hard knocks. Result: I tend bar at Sloopy's downtown and dream of writing my own epic. At least Odie gets discounted rib eyes.

Growing up in Dayton meant that the neighboring community of Yellow Springs was part of our extended world. But it was always an anomaly, a throwback to the psychedelic sixties, and never taken seriously. Even before it was fashionable, its denizens were tattooed, pierced and tie-dyed. For a conservative Midwestern boy, a Saturday afternoon spent wandering its streets was tantamount to a voyage to Jupiter. After high school, I discovered it had an intellectual side that developed luminaries known to the world as Leonard Nimoy, Rod Sterling and Erma Bombeck. It also sported a darkness that produced scandals such as a Death Row inmate delivering the commencement address via telecast. This dichotomy was Antioch College. Devine and deviant, this institution shaped Yellow Springs. It was also the home of the Antioch Writers Workshop.

After years of listening to me ramble on about what I would do if given the chance, Angelica gave me the nudge I needed. The Workshop was in my back yard and, for relatively nothing, which it had to be, given my salary, I could participate in a week of creativity and inspiration. It took five years of constant nagging, but she eventually wore me down. I signed up. All of this Angelica already knew, so I didn't waste time going over it. For her, I begin on registration day.

Images of finally tapping into my creative soul tumbled and danced through my brain. Not only will I be rich, but the prizes, Pulitzer, Edgar, Oscar, Nobel, will flock to me. I was refining the acceptance speech for my third Pulitzer while I scribbled my signature beside my name on the registration roster. The purple-haired girl manning (personing? it is Antioch after all) the table, grinned as if reading my mind. When she talked, a silver stud clicked against her teeth.

"Is this your first time in the Village?"

It was difficult not to stare at the metal that adorns her lips, ears, eyebrows and belly button. Her crop top barely covered an almost obscene bosom, and did nothing to conceal her flat, pierced stomach. Her bra-less torso allowed suspicious outlines to protrude through the thin fabric leaving no doubt as to what other body parts were decorated beyond social norms. A deep flush crept up my neck. I stared at her nametag—Katryna—but it was too late. She knew. Her bebaubled grin widened.

"N-n-no, I've been here before. But I'm-ummm-from-uh-

Dayton,"

She laughed. "That explains a lot, Mr.—" A quick peek at the roster, then another laugh. Louder. "This is a joke, right?"

The flush deepened as I shook my head.

"Let me guess. Poetry? Children's books? Self-help?"

Unable to speak, I ducked my head, grabbed the proffered packet and fled the building. Her laughter chased me down the sidewalk and abandoned me only when I reached the entrance to the boarding house that will be my home for the next week.

"Hold on." Angelica says. "The girl had purple hair and a tongue stud and you fixate on her tits?"

"They were pierced!"

"Unbelievable." She shakes her head as she sips her coffee.

On the outside, the house was exactly what I'd imagined after reading the brochure. *Quaint Midwestern charm at its finest. An inviting fusion of modern convenience and warm Americana.* It had been built in the mid-1800's with local stone that had weathered charmingly over the years. Verdant strands of ivy softened the walls and imparted a dream-like quality that hearkened to an earlier, gentler time. The fluffy granddame, Mrs. Winthrop, enhanced the image as she ushered me into my room.

"Now come right this way, Mr. Barker," she directed in a quavery sing-song voice as she sprinted up the narrow staircase at the rear of the house. Dozens of cats' eyes peered out of the shadows as I struggled after her disappearing form, my suitcase getting heavier with every step.

"…anything at all young man, anything, you just ask. I adore helping young writers. Why I could tell you stories…"

Her ramblings faded into paisley'd wallpaper as my mind wandered. The history, the solitude, the literary inspirations would fill my every waking moment. Staying here instead of commuting back and forth was the right decision. I was finally taking control of my destiny; shaping my future, striving for a goal instead of drifting from one minimum wage job to the next, acting instead of reacting. Gasping for air instead of breathing. Black spots danced in front of my eyes. Just as I was about to lose consciousness and tumble backwards down the hellish stairs, Mrs. Winthrop stopped at a slightly skewed doorway. She inserted an ancient key, jiggled it a few times, and then swung the creaking door open with a flourish.

Along with extolling the virtues of available lodgings, the workshop literature held a warning that truly modernized accommodations, i.e. air-conditioning, were at a premium. As such they would be reserved first, but I'd shrugged it off. Mainly because this was the North, and only a little because I'd waited so long that I didn't have a choice. *How hot could it get?* As I stood in the cell-like room and felt the sweat trickle down my back, that question was answered. *Hotter than the bowels of hell.*

Looking around, I took inventory. It didn't take long. The furniture looked like garage sale items, each coming from a different garage. Maybe not even from a sale. It was a distinct possibility that they were trash treasures. After watching Mrs. Winthrop trot up the stairs, I was convinced she would have no problem dumpster diving. A dresser with three drawers snuggled up against an ancient bed that Daniel Boone had probably slept in. Beside that was a scarred writing desk, which the pioneer might have used to write letters to his family back east. A wardrobe with a door hanging slightly askew took up one wall. As I scanned the furnishings built for a time when old age was thirty and 5' 6" was tall for a man, I was glad that the 6' reported on my driver's license was a slight exaggeration of my true height. I looked at the bed again. Okay—luckily it was a big exaggeration.

I continued to scan the room. A dingy wastebasket, a few forgettable landscapes created by local no name artists. The latter was confirmed by handwritten cards tucked into the cheap frames. I gave a low whistle. $150 for a primitive rendering of a meadow with cows and a red barn in the background. And not primitive as in Grandma Moses and I'd uncovered a hidden gem, but primitive as in "Look what your nephew Johnny made for you at daycare..." Much like whoever had written the description of this room, that artist was delusional. I dismissed it and the rest of the art and discovered the jackpot. Almost obscured by the wardrobe was the edge of what had to be curtains. Relief at hand, I dropped my shoulder slightly and shoved.

The wardrobe didn't budge. Panic set in. If I didn't get relief soon, a damp puddle is the only thing that would be left of me and my aspirations. Adrenaline gave me strength and the next shove succeeded, but not without protest. The shriek of wood scraping across wood sent my already pounding head to new heights of agony. Black starbursts pirouetted through the room. The wardrobe was now jammed against the dresser, which had pushed the bed under the edge of the desk, but I didn't care. Because, miracle of miracles, a window appeared. I pulled on the lower wooden edge, but it remained in place; its frame swollen from years of humidity. Making one last superhuman effort, I yanked on the window. It gave a little. I gave one last heave and, with its own piercing wail, the sash flew up. Blessed air poured into the room. And so did Mrs. Winthrop.

"What are you doing to my house?"

Did everything in this place shriek? "Opening the window. I didn't realize that warm Americana was this warm."

No sense of humor. Fluff turned to flint. "You've ruined the floor."

The only reason you could distinguish the new scratches from the old was their color. "Sorry, but this was blocking the window," I said as I made a vague gesture towards the wardrobe. Her eyes narrowed further.

I'm not trying to steal the ugly thing. I bit my tongue, not wanting to antagonize the little troll further. After all, she did know where I slept.

"It was there for a reason."

"To keep burglars out? Worried they might steal these lovely furnishings?"

"Before you leave I want everything put back exactly where it was before you got here." She was five foot nothing and, with her gleaming white hair and blackish brown eyes, it was as if a nasty little West Highland Terrier was yapping at me. A snicker escaped. She whirled on one heel and marched away. The slamming door shook the entire room.

"Bet I never get another clean towel," I muttered. The silent walls agreed.

"Way to make friends."

I shrug. "That was trivial compared to the lack of friends I made later…"

The earlier tranquility was gone, replaced by a desperate need for a drink. A strong one. But I had left alcohol and any other mind-altering substance at home in a noble effort to make the most of my sabbatical. Doubts and regret were crowding the limited space.

"Stop it," I admonished myself. The command cleared the air somewhat. "Do something productive."

Good idea, but what? Unpack? It wasn't a bad idea, but it was very unappealing. Last night the bar had been overrun with Bachelor and Bachelorette parties, which meant cleanup took an eternity. When I arrived home early this morning, I'd realized that every piece of clothing I'd planned to bring was filthy. I washed them but there wasn't time for luxuries like drying or folding. The assumption had been that upon arrival, the clothes would be rescued from their convoluted wad and hung in a closet. Since the pioneers obviously did not believe in closets, the remaining option was to fold everything and tuck it away in the wardrobe. Since I'd already put that job off once, the second time was even easier. Besides, there was plenty of time before anything started.

Or was there? I retrieved the registration packet and sprawled on the bed. In truth, I sprawled mostly on the bed and a little off, sharing the tiny mattress with the desk.

There was a lot of paperwork: instructor bios, Writing Life

topics, several pages of home addresses, phone numbers and personal information—attendees, I guessed, and the schedule. The schedule was easy to pick out from the stack – its fluorescent pink made my eyes ache.

Day 1 (tonight): Banquet 7 PM, keynote address and reception to follow. The name of the woman giving the keynote wasn't one I recognized. I hoped she was attractive. I could put up with anyone, no matter how boring, as long as she was easy on the eyes.

Day 2: Orientation and Village Walk 10 AM. Lunch. The Writing Life. Intensive with Dallas McGuire. I was dedicated, I was, but the heat and the last couple of days took their toll. I drifted away…

"The Writing Life? Doesn't that define the whole workshop?"

"Yeah, but this refers to sessions with writers, editors, agents—anyone that's ever done anything with the written word. They read excerpts or articles, share anecdotes, basically whip us wannabes into a creative frenzy."

"And what's an intensive?"

"That's a class focused on a single subject. Mine was long fiction."

"And McGuire, that's the guy?"

"Yeah."

Angelica takes a long sip of her coffee, which has to be ice-cold. And mostly dregs. She doesn't flinch. "You ever heard of him? Read any of his stuff?"

"No, his class was the only one that was still open when I registered."

She sighs. "Do you ever think how much easier your life would be if you did anything before the last minute?"

"Sure, but look at all the excitement I'd miss…"

She rubs her forehead and emits another sigh. "Keep going."

3

Weird, twisted creatures filled the room and advanced upon my prone figure. Sitting up too fast, my head connected with the encroaching desk. The clunk reverberated through the room and set my heart pounding. But it also brought the world into focus. The creatures faded into shadows caused by the dying sun.

"Damn it." Tender but not bleeding, my probing fingers discovered. Still rubbing the wound, I looked at the clock on the dresser.

Blood red numbers glared at me. 6:30.

"Impossible," I muttered and groped for my watch. 6:32. "Damn it."

Some writer I was. Great command of the English language. *Damn it* was the only phrase running through my head as I showered, shaved, brushed and dressed in world-class time. It was still echoing as I dashed towards the Antioch cafeteria.

Knowing first impressions are everything, I adopted an attitude of casual elegance as I strolled into the banquet at 7:10, fashionably late. Unfortunately, my polo shirt and khakis did not support my attitude. In fact, I closely resembled a sweaty Shar Pei puppy. The only item wrinkle-free were my loafers.

And it would have been nice if I could've found some socks. Then my feet wouldn't be squelching while I searched for an empty chair.

At the very back of the room, a table with only one occupant and a cluster of empty chairs beckoned to me. Ignoring the bemused glances that followed me as I crossed the expanse, I slid into a vacant seat and took stock of my surroundings.

The wall behind me must have separated the kitchen from the dining area because the bustle of food preparation vibrated against my chair. To the front and right, adorned with an elaborate centerpiece, was a long table set back from another two dozen tables crammed into the banquet hall. Although calling the fluorescently lit, linoleum floored room a banquet hall was like calling a fishing boat a yacht. It was obviously a school cafeteria dressed up for the Big Event. The people seated behind the lilies had to be small time celebrities and workshop hotshots. Servers darted hither and yon, yonder and here, depositing baskets of bread and carafes of wine. As crowded as it was, it would take a while for the wine to reach my table, but that was okay. Just anticipating its arrival buoyed my spirits.

"Are you a writer?"

I jumped. The voice—low, cool, fresh—emanated from my right elbow. I'd forgotten the table wasn't single occupancy. I examined my neighbor.

The woman—girl—examining me from behind glasses with coke-bottle lens, was a study in contrasts. Every feature was either softly romantic or seriously intense. Long, straight brown hair, parted severely and perfectly in the center, framed a heart-shaped face. Her gray eyes were dreamy, softened by those huge plastic glasses perched on her slightly pugged nose. Olive skin, kissed by the Mediterranean sun, intensified the full, ruddy lips...

"Give me a break," Angelica snaps.

I jump. My reverie drifts away like smoke on a breeze. "I'm a writer. I'm supposed to paint pictures with words."

"Do your pictures have to be X-Rated?"

I grin. "Think so? That's what I was shooting for. R at the very least."

"You're a pig."

"I said nothing about her breasts."

"The story's not over…"

Glancing around the room, I thanked the instinct that led me to this spot. Dumpy, chatty bores packed the rest of the tables. Their energy exhausted me just watching them. There was a sense of vulnerability about the young lady seated at my side and I wanted to protect her, shield her from whatever it was that kept her from smiling at the world. As a start, I poured her a glass of wine. An extremely full glass of wine.

My name's D D—Rex," I stuttered.

"Directs? Like in films? Do you write screen plays?"

"No, no. Just Rex. Sorry."

"Mmmm," she answered and her gaze drifted away.

"And you are?"

Without gazing back, "Chase."

"Just Chase?"

"Mmmm."

Luckily, long nights at the bar talking to drunks made this conversation tolerable. "My favorite author's Ed McBain. Yours?"

The gray eyes swam back. "Hemingway. Ayn Rand."

There was a South Park episode that mentioned Ayn Rand. Something about a chicken molester. Didn't seem like an appropriate icebreaker.

"Hemingway?"

"Mmmm."

My knowledge of Hemingway was a little deeper than what I knew of Ayn Rand, but just. I decided to change the subject.

"Where do you call home?"

"Antioch," she said, the word dying away to a whisper.

"A local, then."

Her huge eyes pitied my ignorance. "No. A student."

"Ah, then you attend Antioch."

A sigh.

Fortunately, the arrival of our salads interrupted the fascinating dialogue. And right behind them came an exuberant couple.

"Thank goodness. We were so late..." exclaimed a dumpling of a woman. Her cheeks were bright spots of red that stood out in vivid contrast to the drab English tweeds she sported. The costume was perfect, right down to sensible brown walking shoes. Her companion was a mirror image except his hair was straight and thinning more than the tight curls that clung damply to her head. Since her face was bereft of makeup, they were almost indistinguishable. Oh, and he wasn't wearing a skirt.

"We thought we'd have to eat standing up," the man declared with a grin.

In unison, the couple plunked down and tore at their salads. Invaded by Agatha Christie caricatures. I was tempted to encourage their first suggestion; they could eat standing up. In the kitchen. That seemed overly harsh so I kept that thought to myself.

"Are you writers?" Chase fixed on the new arrivals.

"Oh my yes." This from the woman.

"Are you published?" Lips parted and a pink tongue darted out, leaving behind shining dampness before disappearing. Her breathy tone was exquisite. Roly and Poly didn't notice.

"We've written and published tons of books. Tons. Mostly travel. Been everywhere," the man's turn to answer.

"How exciting..."

"Rose and Roger Culbreath. Maybe you've seen our work?" It didn't matter which one answered.

Feeling I'd been left out long enough, I broke in. "Anything on the best seller list? I only read best sellers."

Three pairs of eyes riveted on me. Three frowns.

Chase murmured, "How very limiting..."

Quick to recover, Roger beamed. "Not yet, but we've been close."

Suddenly verbose, Chase leaned forward and asked, "Why are you here? Why would you weigh yourselves down hobnobbing with amateurs?"

Before either could answer, entrees were deposited; chicken breast nestled atop rice pilaf and cozying up to a vegetable medley. Benign and safe. No surprises. My glass was empty so I topped it off and then noticed Chase' was in the same condition. With a flourish, I filled hers as well. She didn't notice. I was hurt. Deeply.

"Since you're being such a gentleman, Mr.——" Rose was holding out an empty glass and her original grin had disappeared, replaced instead with a smaller, almost coy smile. Warmed by the psychic bond, or maybe the vinegary wine I'd been sucking down, I beamed at her and filled her glass. And Roger's.

"Barker. But please, call me Rex."

"Like the dinosaur or the writer?" The question came from Roger and seemed sincere.

"The writer. Stout."

"How exciting," Rose gushed. "Not to seem stereotypical, but is your forte the hard-boiled detective?"

Ashamed to admit I hadn't written enough to claim a forte, or even a twente, I nodded.

"This is definitely fate, don't you think, Roger?" The couple stared at each other, then back to me.

"We've been doing the travel books for so long," Roger explained, "that we're burnt out. We thought murder might help."

Maybe I'd had enough wine. "Murder?" I echoed. I stole a peek at Chase. Her eyes were as big as mine felt.

Rose bobbed her head. "Murder."

"Mysteries," Roger added, bobbing in unison. "Of the cozy English variety. They might be out of vogue, but if well written..."

The dreadful image cleared and I laughed. "Oh, you and

your wife want to write mysteries."

A frown creased Rose's forehead then she giggled. "We're not husband and wife, we're brother and sister." The family resemblance was now obvious. I lifted my glass with a flourish.

"Here's to talented families."

"Here, here," exclaimed the rest of the table—even Chase managed to get into the moment—and glasses were drained. I signaled for another carafe, which appeared within seconds.

"That explains the tweeds," I said, seeing to everyone's glasses.

Roger mopped at his forehead with a napkin. "It just never occurred to us that it would be so hot. We always try to get into the spirit of whatever topic we're covering."

"Grass skirts after hula lessons on Oahu, dancing under the full moon at Salem, and you should have seen what we did for the article on the nudist colony," Rose said with pride. Roger and I both flushed and gulped our beverages.

"It's a shame the workshop doesn't offer a practicum in murder," Chase murmured. Her eyes were flat. Reptilian. The three of us turned to see what had caused this abrupt change. A tall man with brilliant white hair was approaching the head table. The celebs beamed and let him join their midst. A particularly bosomy woman laid her hand on his arm and said something to him, her mouth so close to his ear she looked as if she was going to whisper sweet nothings into it. Or lick it. Or bite it.

"Who's the Warhol clone?" I asked, pointing to the newcomer. The woman was still murmuring, but now red-lacquered fingers were rubbing up and down his forearm. "They need a room."

"Dallas McGuire," Chase said.

"A brilliant man," Rose interjected, oozing idolatry.

Chase nodded her eyes, now sad and a little distant. My heart broke for her. I realized she needed comforting, support. I poured more wine.

She tossed it back in one gulp and stood at the same time.

"I have to go," she announced.

"But you haven't eaten a thing," I said, pointing to her untouched plate. Funny. I sounded like my mother. Or a clucking hen.

"Food won't help," the girl sobbed and ran from the room. The three of us stared after her and then looked at each other, but nobody made a move to follow. Cheesecake had just arrived. Dark chocolate cheesecake. With white chocolate curls. And raspberries.

"Do you think she's okay?" I asked, not wanting to seem uncaring. Because of course I wasn't; I cared deeply about young women.

"She'll be fine," Rose assured me as she patted my arm. When she pulled her chubby hand away, it left a damp imprint in the hair on my forearm. "Young people, especially creative ones, are so mercurial."

"You sure?"

"We see this sort of thing all the time," Roger said. His heartiness warmed me to my toes. I filled everyone's glasses. Rose laughed and pushed hers away. Marvelous people. So full of life.

"I've had enough," she said. "If I have any more, I'll sleep through the speaker."

"Speaker?" I asked, looking around the room. There didn't appear to be anyone speaking. Actually, there weren't too many people left. Most were filing out a back door.

"The keynote speaker," Roger explained. "As a matter of fact, if we don't leave now, we may not get a seat," he said, extending a hand to his sister as he pushed his chair back from the table. I stood up then sat back down, caught my breath and stood up again. The crowd swept up the siblings like a welcoming tide and I trailed along behind. My mood matched the summer night. Warm and dreamy and buzzy...

4

Light blazed, pinning me like a bug. I blinked and stared into an impossibly high ceiling. My lips were cracked and dry and I ran an equally dry tongue over them. Something in my head was trying to escape and it was using a jackhammer to make its way through my skull.

It was a struggle to sit up. My head had fallen backwards, forcing my neck into an unnatural position. And the throbbing behind my eyes wasn't helping. While I worked on convincing my muscles to relax and release my neck, people moved around and past me. It wasn't difficult to figure out that the speaker was done and the crowd was proceeding to the next gathering on the agenda. I ignored the scathing glances thrown my way and joined the flow as soon as I could.

Even though the night was close and muggy, being outside cleared away most of the cobwebs. The day's itinerary drifted into my consciousness and the group's destination came to me. The reception. That meant refreshments. My mood lifted considerably and I was able to ignore the pounding in my brain as I sauntered along with the group. Thank god it wasn't far. Actually, it was next door in an extremely bright gallery.

Pictures that seemed familiar covered the walls of the

sparsely furnished room. A close look at the signature revealed that they were produced by the same artist that had decorated my room. It didn't seem possible, but these creations were even more tedious. Never that much of an art lover, I ignored them in favor of a much more beautiful sight.

Humiliated by napping through the keynote address, I'd vowed to drink nothing stronger than Pepsi. But my resolution wavered. The same wine that had graced the banquet created a surreal masterpiece of true art. Light shining through the ruby liquid produced stained glass shadows on the hard wood floors. People wove in and out, oblivious to the beauty lying below their feet. The effect was mesmerizing. I had no choice. Besides, the drums were still echoing through my head.

The first glass didn't have much of an effect, but the second helped. By the third I started to enjoy life again. I looked around the now crowded room and got my bearings. A shock of white hair caught my attention.

Up close, Dallas McGuire was a lot younger than I'd assumed. The hair was misleading but it was nothing Miss Clairol couldn't fix. I thought about mentioning it—ice breaker—then decided against it. Probably the wine thinking and it wasn't a good idea to let it talk. I pushed through a mob of chattering groupies, consisting mostly of pretty twenty-somethings, and extended my hand. "Mr. McGuire," I began.

"Call me Dallas," he said and gripped my hand. Piercing black eyes met mine and found me wanting.

"Name's Rex Barker. You have my manuscript."

"Ah, yes. Barker." The smile was not encouraging.

"You remember me?"

"Definitely. A most memorable piece of writing."

"Great. And you loved it."

McGuire's upper lip curled and the groupies snickered. The air became hot and thick, difficult to breathe.

"The critique will be delivered at its appointed time and not before." *Ask not for whom the hell tolls...*

"What did you submit?" Angelica still sips the same cup of coffee. My stomach roils at the thought.

"Can I get you a refill?"

"Oh, sure," she says, handing over the mug. When I return she is petting the cat and murmuring something to it. We both sip, then, "You never answered me. What did you send?"

"A chapter of my novel and a synopsis. For sixty bucks you could have someone read your stuff and give their opinion."

"When did you write it?"

I study my coffee, not sure how to defend the good solid hour I'd put into the manuscript. I'd honestly planned to polish it a little more, but somehow time ran out. My silence answers the question.

"Never mind," she says.

I wish she didn't know me as well as she does. "I work best under pressure…"

"Uh-huh."

Sweat trickled down my back. Before I could respond, a familiar voice erupted in my ear.

"Rex. There you are."

It was hard to believe that the Culbreath siblings could be such a welcoming sight.

"Sorry we deserted you, old man," Roger said. "But you were dead to the world. Tried our best but just couldn't wake you."

"Your snoring almost drowned out Ms. Hellstrom," Rose giggled.

"Who?" Too late I remembered the keynote speaker. My comment drew incredulity from strangers and louder giggles from the Culbreaths. *Et tu, Rogair?* "Last night was extremely tiring for me and the heat…"

"And the wine…" More giggles. Now guffaws.

Desperate to extricate myself, I glanced back at McGuire. He was having an intense conversation with a man so wrinkled he made my clothes look like they'd just come from the dry cleaners. There was no way a man that old could still be moving around on his own, much less writing. Seeing no escape via that route, I murmured something about mingling and moved away. Rose and Roger didn't seem to notice.

As I worked my way through the crowd, snippets of discussion pummeled me from all sides. "An American original…" "Fresh, innovative. Wish I had her courage…" "Can you believe she dared…" "There was a time…burned as a witch…"

Almost wished I'd stayed awake. Almost. Of course, now I felt fresh and alert, which I wouldn't have without my nap. My wanderings deposited me at the refreshment table, which I took as a sign and refilled. As I paused, scoping out my next destination, a shining brown head struck a familiar chord. Grabbing an almost full bottle, I hastened to an isolated bench populated by a diametrically opposed pair.

"Hey," I said, gesturing with the bottle. "Bench side service. Can't beat that with a stick."

Two heads looked me over, one unknown, one familiar; one blonde one brunette. The brunette, Chase, remained seated but the blonde rose to her feet in a swirl of skirts and White Diamonds. Unfortunately, she'd marinated in it and the smell brought tears to my eyes. I coughed and put out my hand.

"Rex. Rex Barker."

"Kandi. Just Kandi. Like Cher," she said with a grin and a grip that finished coaxing the tears out.

This close I realized my initial assumption, that she was a contemporary of Chase', was off. Way off. About three decades. The woman was a study in flamboyance, from her leather flip-flops and beaded hip belt to her brightly flowered peasant blouse and Tammy Faye dye job. Although I had to admit, the strategic positioning of the peasant blouse showed off some very nice attributes. Kandi's grin widened when she followed my gaze.

I flushed. "Sorry. Didn't mean to interrupt your conversation."

"Don't worry about it, sugar," Kandi said with a chuckle. "This isn't a healthy conversation; this is a fan club meeting. A losers' fan club. You did us a favor." And then she was gone, leaving me with the lovely Chase.

"Boy, I thought she'd never leave. What was that about a fan club?"

Chase considered me across the top of her glasses, which had slid down her nose, and shrugged. Then she returned her attention to a slender volume cradled in her lap. The ivory pages contrasted beautifully with her olive skin. As I topped off the plastic cup nestled beside her, I maneuvered to read the author and title. "The Roach's Dream..." by D. McGuire.

"Amazing. You know, I've never considered that."

"What?" Her resigned tone conveyed just how uninterested she was in my opinion, but persistence is one of my virtues. Vices. Whatever...

"Whether or not cockroaches dream. He is talking about the insect, isn't he?"

"It's a metaphor."

Eighth grade English flashed through my head and disappeared with about the same speed it had when I was in the eighth grade. Triumphantly I said, "Then it's not about an insect."

Chase sighed and put down the book. "He's brilliant."

"The insect?"

Her glare said more than all the words she'd voiced that evening. I decided to move on to other topics. "How about that Ms. Hellstrom?"

"What about her?"

"She shows a lot of courage. And such originality."

"You really think so? I think she spews a lot of commercial rhetoric that's absorbed without question by literary sheep." At least now her glare was directed at the absent Ms. Hellstrom. I struggled to remember the other snippets.

"Maybe, but at one time she'd have been burned for heresy."

To my amazement Chase not only smiled, she laughed. A

low, throaty chuckle that made goose flesh rise on my arms. "That's not a bad idea. And, speak of the devil, here's the witch now." The good nature was gone, replaced by the grave expression I'd come to accept as Chase' natural state. Looking across my shoulder, I recognized the woman from the banquet, the one with the scarlet fingernails, once more stroking McGuire's arm. Dallas threw his head back and laughed, immensely conscious of his projected image. Chase looked tortured. The object of her pain suddenly became clear.

"You can't be serious," Angelica cries. "It took you that long to realize she had the hots for McGuire?"

"There was a lot going on."

"How are you supposed to be a writer if you don't notice dramas unfolding under your nose?"

"I did notice; it just took me a little while. The only reason you picked up on it is because I'm leaving out useless details." She grows silent, but her lingering smile says everything she's thinking. "May I continue?"

"Please…"

"Sometimes things just don't work out between two people." It was lame, but the best I could do. Dr. Phil, I'm not. But it did the trick. Chase leaned close and looked up into my face. Her eyes were bright and owlish, huge in her heart-shaped face.

"He's not like other men. His genius doesn't allow him to partake of the simple joys that come naturally to lesser human beings." A single tear slid down her cheek.

My respect for D. McGuire jumped up exponentially. "A quote?"

She nodded and gave a little sob. Another tear fell. "He's a deeply unhappy man; incapable of returning love. Always seeking what others have and what he cannot understand. Doomed to leap from relationship to relationship."

Studying the object of her adoration, I agreed that he was doomed to leap, but doubted it was from relationship to relationship. That was out of his depth. But Chase had it bad. And she was young. And pretty. And it wasn't in my best interests to point out that she'd been naïve at best, used and humiliated at the worst. This was my opportunity to ease her sorrow.

"You didn't hit on that poor girl, did you?"

"What do you take me for?" The accusation wasn't worthy of reply, so I continued my story.

"You must be deeply hurt. You did have an affair with him, didn't you?" I kept my voice soft and low, both to show understanding and to keep curious bystanders from hearing the conversation. Several attendees were looking our way with more than casual interest.

Another choked sob. Another tear. She nodded. Without looking up, she murmured, "Surviving the pain will give me strength, character. Make me a better writer because I can empathize with the struggles of others."

"Sometimes it helps to talk to someone that doesn't know the involved parties. Someone who cares but doesn't have a history. Doesn't have a preformed opinion."

Conflicting emotions flitted across the grave face. Wariness, pain and—hope. "What do you have in mind?"

"The first thing is to remove the source of painful memories. Let's go somewhere we can talk. More privately. And maybe get a drink." The drink sounded positively inviting to me right then. Something real, even if I did have to pay for it. The ruby red vinegar I'd been tossing back all night was getting to me.

Her face closed down when I offered the drink. "No thanks."

"No. I'm not... It's just that..."

She held up a hand. "No explanation necessary. I've had a headache all evening and the best thing for me is sleep. Good night, Mr. Barker." With the poise of a supermodel, she tossed her head and strolled out of the reception, not favoring me or her ex-paramour with the tiniest of glances.

"At least she didn't say she had to wash her hair. What did you do after that, proposition a grieving widow?"

"I really just wanted a quiet place where we could talk and I could have a serious drink."

Angelica frowns.

"Honest. I went back to my room."

"Alone?"

"A bottle of wine came with me, but I don't think that counts."

Angelica is silent for a few seconds. "No, it doesn't count, but it does explain your condition the next day. You know, free alcohol doesn't mean you have to drink it all."

"I was lonely."

Angelica sighs and leaves the table.

5

The sun is blazing down on the tin roof that's shading us and I can feel the summer heat building. Still, I don't refuse the steaming cup of coffee Angelica hands me when she returns. Just as I continue my story, something on the bench beside Angelica trills. With a look of annoyance usually reserved for me, she snatches up her purse and peers at her microscopic cell phone.

"What?" she barks into the little device. Then, "You did what?" "Listen, you little…"

She pauses and takes a deep breath, her chest heaving with effort. "Yes, I know it's nine in the morning."

With a start, I look at my watch. Had that many hours really disappeared? The conversation fades back in.

"You are my assistant, not my keeper. If you can't find me, call me. Me. My cell phone is always on…"

Silence as a dull flush crawls up her neck.

"Okay, let me translate. A friend of mine had an emergency and needed me. Still needs me. Reschedule all my meetings and appointments. That is your job. Oh, and Andrew," pause, "you ever call my husband again to track me down, you'd better dust off your resume."

This is one of the times I miss the old-fashioned black

phones. It would have been great to see Angelica slam the receiver down and imagine Andrew hearing stars from the impact. Instead, she jabs at the OFF button, mutters, jabs again and then throws it into her purse.

"Do you have to go?"

"Not only am I not going, I've turned off my phone."

"Didn't you just say…"

"I don't care what I said. That little creep called Derek."

I cringe for her. "Was he pissed?"

"Don't know," Angelica admits. She stares at a spot close to my left elbow and gnaws at her bottom lip.

I give her hand a squeeze. She smiles—weakly, but still a smile—and squeezes back.

"It's okay," she says. "I meant what I said about a friend needing me. You've bailed me out plenty of times."

"Not as many as you have me…"

"Let's not get into who's screwed up the most, okay?"

Her sharp tone makes me smile. I'm a lot more comfortable with this Angelica.

"Okay. But let's go inside where there's air conditioning."

"Good idea," she says and we move into the cool interior.

To appease the hovering staff, I buy cookies warm from the oven and glasses of milk. Angelica doesn't argue. Instead, she bites into the molten chocolate chunks with enthusiasm equal to mine. I'm shocked that she doesn't even complain about not having skim milk. Of course, asking for skim milk at Young's Dairy is comparable to asking for ketchup on your filet mignon at Ruth's Chris. You could do it, but you'd be marked for life. Might even make one of those picture boards typically reserved for bad check writers. The sign above would read "Do Not Serve – Doesn't Appreciate the Finer Things in Life."

It didn't matter that I'd forgotten to set the alarm clock because at nine o'clock sharp, World War III broke out in my room. Pillows flew in one direction and I flew in another, sheets wrapped around my legs as I fell out of bed. Lucky that they had, as the bedding kept my knees from connecting too hard with the wooden floor. My head didn't fare as well. Although it was hard to say whether it was the floor or the wine from the night before that caused the bongos to echo in my head. And it really didn't matter. The only thing of any importance was to get Excedrin into my blood stream.

Once the life-saving tablets had been found and ingested—four of them—it was time to figure out what had attacked me. The thunder was fading, but its residue was enough to reveal its origin. Church bells. Squeezing between the wardrobe and the dresser, I leaned across the windowsill and could just make out a white church complete with a steady stream of god-fearing townsfolk entering solid oak doors.

"Damn," I commented—loudly—then jumped back from the window, smacking my head against the windowpane in the process. I grabbed it and held my breath. It quivered, but didn't break. I exhaled and stepped back into the room. It was bad enough that I'd used questionable language loud enough for the entire village to hear, but I had uttered it in my usual sleeping attire -- nothing. I didn't look half-bad for my age, but that didn't mean that all of Yellow Springs needed to have that information.

Sitting on the edge of the bed, I took stock. In spite of the self-inflicted head wound and the major hangover, the Excedrin were working. As a result, the Village Walk didn't seem nearly as repulsive as it had when I first got up. I selected a tee shirt that didn't show wrinkles too badly, likewise some shorts, and headed for the rendezvous.

There was a diverse group awaiting the tour. I expected to see the Culbreaths and hoped to see Chase, but recognized only strangers. We stood at an entrance to Glen Helen, a gorgeous nature reserve that fringed the Antioch campus. The villagers were extremely possessive of the Glen and their attitude got old after a while. I hoped one of the die-hards wasn't leading the tour. That hope died quickly and painfully.

A Norse warrior maiden was our guide. Big, blond and

strong, she didn't tolerate stragglers. I christened her Helga and made sure she didn't know it. There was no doubt that in a fair fight, she'd break me into little bitty pieces. Antioch was about a half mile from downtown—felt like twenty times that in the heat—and we covered it at a pace that would have stressed Jesse Owens.

"Yellow Springs has struggled to maintain its village status in spite of the influx of outsiders," Helga proclaimed as she marched us past buildings that were beginning to blur. There was a moment when a restaurant sign swam into focus and I considered stopping for a soda, but I knew I'd never find my way back. And, Yellow Springers, knowing that I was an outsider, would allow me to wander aimlessly until I passed out in some unnamed alley. This vision firmly planted in my brain, I tapped some hidden reservoir of strength and staggered on.

At one blessed point, I thought the death march was ending, but then Helga led us onto an obscure path that dropped into the Glen. The woods felt blessedly cool, offering relief from the shimmering sidewalks, until we met the first hill. Sweat poured off every inch of my body. The rest of the group had been chattering and breathing like normal human beings, now they became one with me. It would've been satisfying if I thought there was a chance in hell I would survive. Helga never quit rambling on and on, imparting to us the special brand of torture she'd honed from years of handling the enemy. By the time the Village Walk was truly over, I was ready to nuke the quaint village. And could probably have recruited more than one of my perspiring compatriots. I didn't even bother saying good-bye as I stumbled towards the sanctuary of my room and—more importantly—the bed.

"Did you make it to lunch?"
"Nope. And I missed The Writing Life."
"Now there's an understatement…"

The three-hour nap and a couple of Quarter Pounders with

fries did wonders for my disposition. Much more than dissecting the literary experience. That could wait until later. I felt refreshed and alive as I strolled into the afternoon intensive. Late.

"Mr. Barker, I presume," McGuire said with a dry smile. "So good of you to join us. Our lives are now complete."

Sweat beaded on my forehead, partly from humiliation, partly from yet another fusion of modern inconvenience and warm Americana. No air conditioning. Everybody else seemed cool and serene, unmindful of the stifling heat. I decided they were aliens. Possibly mutants. Mutant aliens.

The only seat available was wedged between a large, balding man and an equally large woman with turkey wattle arms. Both of them beamed as I pulled out the chair, maneuvered my way into the tiny space and tried to become as inconspicuous as possible. The woman looked as if she were sizing me up as either a food source—scary—or as a potential mate—scarier—so I turned my attention to the man.

"Rex Barker," I murmured. He encased my sweaty hand with a dry, rasping one. His handshake was firm and oozed testosterone. I attempted to match it.

"John Townsend," he said. I couldn't help but return his grin.

"Gentlemen, if you could let the rest of us know when you're through…" The sniggers cut deeper than the tone, which sliced to the core. The two of us flushed, dropped the handshake and took on identical expressions of intense concentration.

"Before we begin working on your skills—and I know that will be a formidable task—I'd like to find out a little something about each of you. After all, we are going to be spending quite a few hours together," said McGuire. "Since we've already struggled through the introductions, let's get into something really interesting. Why is everyone here?"

"To get published," I offered. Maybe it was a little loud, but it certainly didn't deserve the deafening silence and shocked expressions it received. Bewildered, I glanced at my newfound friend. Unfortunately, he was busy examining a blank pad of paper on the desk in front of him and didn't seem to understand my need for support. I continued to scan the room, but there wasn't a sympathetic face to be found anywhere in the motley collection of human beings that confronted me. There were only about ten, but it seemed like a hundred. And the leader, Dallas, had once again assumed that patronizing smile that I hated so much. Almost as much as the tone he used when he donned the smile.

"If you had come on time, Mr. Barker, you would know that *Getting Published* is something amateurs crave and professionals abhor."

Nope, not even close. I hated the tone a gazillion times more. "I don't understand…"

"That's obvious," Dallas sneered. Titters swept through the group then were hushed as the great man continued on. "You can be truly creative only as long as the lure of money doesn't tempt you into commercialism. Amateurs don't realize this because they're not yet in the fold—professionals only learn it after they're trapped. But don't feel bad; if you were a professional you wouldn't be here."

"Give me a break." Okay, now it was really loud. And I felt the red flush creeping up my neck. "Do you mean to tell me there isn't anyone here that wants to get published?" This time, nobody met my eyes. John was the only one that really hurt. I thought there'd been a connection.

"Do I assume you're not asking him to the prom?" Angelica asked with a flick of long lashes. She wasn't smiling, but her mouth was twitching in a suspicious manner.

"It's a guy thing. You wouldn't understand. Do you mind if I continue my story?"

"Wouldn't stop this for the world…"

"Calm down, Mr. Barker. Let me explain. It's not that publishing isn't a goal; it's just that it's not the primary goal. In fact, given the control editors force upon your creations, it can be the worse thing that can happen to an author. No, give me the creative freedom of a small literary press over a large commercial house any day. Why, John Grisham was just telling me..."

"You know Grisham?" In another second, drool would drip down Townsend's chin. I fumbled for a handkerchief, but must have left it in my other pair of shorts. He was on his own.

My attention wandered as I considered how different my goals were from those of this group. Or at least their publicized goals. My reason for attending the workshop was to find the magic lamp that would allow me to become disgustingly rich beyond my wildest dreams. Writing was the occupation I'd chosen as being the most fun with the least amount of work, but work is still work, even if it is creative. My real dream is to make money drinking parasol drinks on a beach surrounded by girls almost young enough to put me in jail. Almost. Unfortunately, nobody had come forward with that offer. So, here I sat. Wondering if the other intensives were this depressing. Maybe this writing thing was going to be harder than I'd anticipated. With this bleak thought, I tuned the conversation back in.

"Ummm, like, what would you say is a good number of words to target per day? And can you average them out? I mean, like, for instance, if your goal is five hundred a day, is it okay to write 3500 on the weekend and none during the week?" A stunning blond groupie that I recognized from the reception asked this question. I was surprised. I wouldn't have suspected she knew how to count, much less do complex math.

Dallas laughed. An ugly laugh that made the girl flinch. I wanted to hold her, comfort her, let her know it was all right.

"You're too caring..." The dryness in Angelica's voice was almost as ugly as Dallas' laugh. Almost...

"First of all, true creativity cannot be shackled to

quantification. Whatever you write in a day, as long as it is the best that it can possibly be, fulfills your goals."

"Can't you write a whole bunch of words, meet a goal, and then clean up anything that isn't good later on?" This came from an earnest young man with an unfortunate case of acne. He seemed to covet the abuse that was sure to follow. But the easy target didn't tempt Dallas. The answer was almost paternal.

"Think of every word as a paving stone in a road that leads to your ideals. If even one stone gets laid in the wrong direction, the entire path skews away from where you want it to go. It's much easier to fix one stone than to rip up an entire highway."

"I see," the boy breathed. His eyes shone with an intensity rivaled only by Hare Krishnas. Dallas warmed to his oration.

"Sometimes it takes an entire day to come up with one word. And, as long as that word is the perfect one, that's a good thing."

"Okay, but what if the word you come up with is 'a'? Wouldn't you feel cheated?" I asked.

The group, including Townsend, moved away from me as one.

6

"Did anyone talk to you afterwards?"

"No, everybody either scuttled away or stayed to brown nose."

"Maybe I shouldn't have talked you into this. Doesn't sound as if you're having a good time."

I squeeze Angelica's hand and grin. She doesn't. "Don't worry," I assure her. "It gets better. Until last night of course." As my grin fades, Angelica squeezes back and gently smiles. I feel a little better. "Dinner was fun…"

Since two days of the workshop were completed and I had yet to use my pre-paid meal ticket, I thought it was time the Antioch cafeteria enjoyed the pleasure of my company. Looking down at my plate made me question the sanity of that decision.

"Opted for the tofu stir-fry did you?" A hearty voice boomed in my ear at the same time a tray rattled onto the table beside mine. "A healthy choice. Not bright, but definitely healthy. You'll live longer. Or it'll just seem like it." It was impossible not to be engulfed by John Townsend's boisterous laughter. I laughed and took inventory of his dinner. It consisted of what had to be half a pepperoni pizza, spaghetti and a toppling slab of chocolate cake.

"Where'd you get real food?"

"There are two food lines, one vegan and one real world. You stopped too soon. It's not your fault; they've got the real stuff hidden well."

My mood rapidly disintegrating, I pushed the congealing mass around on my plate. The only thing worse than pure vegetarian fare was cold vegetarian fare. John took pity.

"Here, you can have the pizza."

He shoved a plate towards me and I started to object, then came to my senses. Before he could change his mind, I touched each piece under the guise of arranging them in a more appealing fashion. That way he wouldn't try to take them back. "How about the cake?" I said, trying not to spit as saliva filled my mouth. "Looks like there's enough for two."

"Last time I shared chocolate cake with someone, they gave me the best blow job of my life. Still want it?"

I backed off although the cake did look tempting... Anyway, the pizza demanded my full attention and, once the first two pieces disappeared, I started feeling human again. Even the stark antiseptic look of the cafeteria—no different from any other institutional cafeteria, strange for Antioch, though—became warmer, more welcoming. There was a peaceful glow coming from everything, including the bald spot on top of John's head. Then, memories came flooding back.

"After what you did today, pizza isn't enough," I said, but kept one arm curled protectively around the plate.

"What'd I do?"

A noodle hung from his lip, but I refused to laugh. "You left me to the wolves! I can't believe you swallowed that garbage McGuire was shoveling." I think I was mixing allegories or metaphors or maybe even left my participles dangling, but I didn't care. I was mad.

"I had to," John protested. "He knows Grisham."

"He *says* he knows Grisham," I corrected. "Besides, what's so great about that? It's not as if he knows Dashiell Hammett or Tennessee Williams."

The look on John's face could only be described as horror. It made me realize that I knew nothing about the man other than that one moment when I thought I'd recognized a kindred spirit.

"Grisham is a lawyer."

The reverence illuminated the situation. "And you're…"

"A lawyer. Pharmaceuticals. Going on thirty years."

Not only was he a lawyer, he was a boring one. I was fumbling for an appropriate response when a stranger plopped down at our table; her tray also loaded with pizza, spaghetti and cake.

"Sylvia," John beamed. The woman responded with an equally warm smile.

Feeling like a third wheel, or a Peeping Tom, I thrust out my hand and said, "Hi, I'm Rex Barker and you're?"

Sylvia gripped my hand with a firmness belied by her slight, almost skeletal build. "Sylvia McMahan." Her voice was disconcerting, rougher than it should've been. From my years as a bartender, I guessed it wasn't genetic but the result of too many years spent consorting with Joe Camel. A guess that was supported by the twitchy way she scanned the room. Definitely strung out on nicotine or, more likely, a lack of it since Antioch was smoke free, even outside. And the enormous cup of coffee on her tray didn't help.

"You're a lawyer, too?"

It seemed logical but John corrected me with the same reverence he'd used for Grisham. "Used to be. Sylvia was one of the partners in my law firm. Now she's a judge—Common Pleas Court—in Columbus."

The earlier smile flashed again, but this time Judge Sylvia included me in its warmth. Basking in the moment gave me an opportunity to study her in this new perspective. First, I had to revise my earlier impression of height. She conveyed a sense of presence that made her appear a foot taller than her scant five feet. That same presence must have stood her well in her professional life. It was easy to imagine her spending a weekend building a playground for underprivileged kids, then, on Monday morning, slapping thirty years hard labor on a man for stealing a loaf of bread. Note to self: Do not commit a felony in Columbus.

"But Yellow Springs is okay?" Angelica's voice is light, though her eyes are anything but.

"I didn't do it," I protest.

"Sorry. Anyway, about this judge. Any possibilities there? You could do worse than a judge; she might even get you to clean up your act."

"Talk about hard labor," I say. "No, the honorable Sylvia was wearing a wedding ring. A massive, gaudy, expensive wedding ring. Not only is she attached and out of my price range, she's too old."

"Sixteen?"

"No. Late fifties like John. Although it's hard to tell. She doesn't overdo her makeup like a lot of old ladies and her hair's this coppery red. Sort of sexy. Cut short, but curled around her face. Soft. Not like those real short buzz cuts that look as if they'd been cut by a weed whacker." The words were out before I could stop them. There was a vague hope that Angelica didn't take the comment personally, but the flare of her nostrils told me otherwise. Evasive action was called for. "She's sort of emaciated. Boyish."

"You mean no tits."

"Exactly."

"Pig."

Back on safe ground, I return to the cafeteria.

The judge took a few bites of spaghetti, nibbled at her pizza and totally ignored her cake. It was a shame to let it go unappreciated, but after John's comment, I didn't have the guts to ask. There was no telling what she'd demand in return. Although...

"God, I'd kill for a cigarette," she said and pushed her tray away. "Can you believe these people even dictate the Great-Out-of-Doors? What happened to the land of the free?"

"That's Antioch for you. Not only is it not free, it's not even reasonable," I offered. "What are you in for?"

The russet-haired judge gave a short bark that I assumed was a laugh and shook her head. "And to think I'm paying for this. Actually, I've always enjoyed Yellow Springs—in an inter-dimensional sort of way—but I'm only along because John convinced me this could be a nice, relaxing vacation. Which I need. Badly. And who knows? My memoirs might interest someone enough to dole out a few bucks; all I have to do is take the time to write them. Truth be known, John's the real writer."

John was grinning, so I had to bite. "What are you working on?"

"Suspense thriller. Based on my own experiences."

"As a pharmaceutical lawyer?"

"You bet. My stuff is a cross between Grisham and Cook."

"Are you any good?"

The grin got wider. "I hope so. I just shelled out sixty bucks to have someone confirm it."

Sylvia paused her twitchy surveillance of the room. "He let me take a look at his manuscript. It was a waste of money to send it in."

Her reaction surprised me. A judge, true, but usually friends are a little more tactful. "That bad, huh?"

"Not at all," she said, her brow furrowed. "It's great. John doesn't need to have some nobody tell him that. He needs to finish it and send it to a publisher. Have the income flowing in, not out."

"Nothing like an opinion from a totally unbiased source," John said with a self-deprecating laugh. Then his normally jovial manner changed to intensity. "Of course, that'd be great. I'm counting on this novel to supplement my retirement. Got wiped out and I don't have many years left."

"Stock market?"

"I wish. That's a lot more forgiving than what I just went through."

Both John and Sylvia began to study the table. Fascinating

as it was, I failed to see the attraction. "And that was…"

Without raising his eyes, John mumbled, "Divorce. She got everything."

The laughter burst out before I could stop it. "But you're a lawyer."

"Pharmaceutical," Sylvia snapped. "Lawyers specialize. Just because someone can fight a sprawling corporation—and win—doesn't mean he can successfully combat the woman he once loved."

I backed off. "Who's critiquing your manuscript?"

"Dallas McGuire. That's why it's good that he's a friend of Grisham's. That means he understands the genre."

"From my observations, the only thing McGuire understands is that once you get a book published, you have your pick of nubile young groupies. And you get paid to pontificate."

John looked horrified, but Sylvia laughed. "Aren't you being a little harsh, Mr. Barker?" she asked. "After all, he *has* been published. Can you say the same?"

"Mind if I join you?" a welcome voice interrupted. Chase stood with a full tray, looking as if she might bolt at any second. Before I could react, John hopped up and pulled out a chair. Chase glanced side to side and then sat down, allowing the lawyer to push in her chair. I noted—with a small sense of satisfaction—that she flinched away when he let his hand brush against her shoulder. "I couldn't help but overhear your conversation. Have you been published Mr. Barker?"

It could have been the wistful admiration that shone from her face or Sylvia's admonition or just pure, unadulterated testosterone. "Not exactly. But I do have a manuscript being given serious consideration by a major publishing house."

"Which one?" John asked.

"I have so many works in progress it's difficult to keep track." The tone was perfect, breezy and confident; befitting of an author who's seen his name in print so often it's old hat.

"Not the manuscript. Which publishing house?"

"Not allowed to say. Could mess up contract

41

negotiations."

It was hard to tell whether Sylvia and John believed me or not, but Chase did. And that was all that mattered. I didn't notice when the other two left.

"You know what would be great?" Chase breathed.

"I've got a few ideas…"

Her ideas were very different. Ignoring my response, she said "If you'd bring your novel to Sam & Eddies tonight."

The fact that the novel in question didn't actually exist was overshadowed by the fact that she thought so much of me. "No problem. I was thinking just you and me, but if you're more comfortable at your friends' place, that's fine." She looked confused, so I said, "Are Sam and Eddie guys, or is that short for Samantha and Edna?" Chase didn't look like the type to have a friend named Edna, but it was the best I could do. A wild evening with three co-eds was intriguing, but only if I was in the minority.

"I have no idea," Chase said, frowning now.

I echoed the frown. "If you don't know them, why go see them? Especially to share a private manuscript?"

The elfin face cleared. "It's not people, it's a book shop. You can read your stuff and have it discussed by the group."

"How about the Trail Tavern instead?"

"Do they do readings there?"

We just weren't communicating. I decided to spell it out. "With enough beer they'd probably let me do anything I wanted."

Chase stood up, frowning. She'd barely touched her food. If she didn't start eating, she'd waste away to… I pushed the mother figure back into her special place in my head and refocused.

"I'll be at Sam & Eddies at ten," the girl said. "There's nothing more exciting—sexier—to me than a man strong enough to expose his inner most creativity."

She strode away, leaving me to shriveled up pizza crusts and three and a half hours to come up with a novel. Reading it before a group wasn't nearly as exciting as reading it before a trio of lovely damsels, but I'd take what I could get. At least Chase would be there. Before I could form a battle plan, visitors in the form of the Culbreaths and a man I didn't know descended upon me. I recognized him as the ancient one that was talking to Dallas the night of the reception.

"Rex," Rose screeched, "how have you been? Where have you been? Isn't this just the most inspirational time you've ever spent? Are you meeting a ton of people? Have you met Mr. Sharpe?"

Having lost track of which answer went with which question, I decided to go with the last. "No," I said and took the elderly gentleman's hand in my own. His bones felt dry and fragile. A quick squeeze and they would be so much dust. The image was unsettling—extremely—so I disentangled myself. "Are you guys having a good time?"

Roger and Rose, on either side of Mr. Sharpe, nodded in unison, resembling bizarre bookends. "Oh yes," they cried, then looked at each other and exploded into laughter. At least they'd ditched the tweeds, trading them in for matching khaki shorts that exposed plump legs etched with a roadwork of varicose veins. That was one gene pool that needed draining.

"What about you, Mr. Sharpe? Are you finding the workshop inspirational?" Preoccupied with how to deliver an epic worthy of the lovely Chase' favors—in a rapidly diminishing time frame—I didn't care if he'd found a new religion, but it was workshop etiquette. I masked my impatience with what I hoped was an interested expression.

"I'm not a writer," the old man insisted.

His eyes became bright and he gave a loud sniff. It wasn't that big a deal; technically I wasn't a writer either, but I didn't cry about it. "Then why…"

Roger broke in with uncharacteristic seriousness and saved the moment. "Mr. Sharpe's wife wrote a novel before she—went away. He's here to have it reviewed by an expert."

"Oh." It was the best I could dredge up.

"Yes," Mr. Sharpe said. His eyes were still bright but the threat of tears had passed. "A Mr. McGuire is going to critique

Peg's manuscript."

"I'm sorry," I said. And I was. Not just for Mr. Sharpe's past agony, but because it wasn't over. "What kind of book is it?"

"A romance."

Worser and worser. "Well, remember Dallas McGuire is just one person. If he doesn't like it…"

"How could he not like it? It's wonderful, a masterpiece," Mr. Sharpe said, his voice rising and cracking.

Rose patted his shoulder. "Of course it is. Rex means well, but he's not the professional that Dallas McGuire is. Let's get some coffee, okay?" Mr. Sharpe nodded and the couple led him away. Rose' eyes shot daggers at me over her shoulder as the group moved towards the exit. I hardly noticed their departure. The only hope I had to get laid was to come up with a novel before ten and now there were only three hours left.

Angelica stares. I feel like a cockroach strolling about on the Formica table. "What did you read?"

"Do you want some more coffee?"

"In a minute. What did you present?"

"Well, ummm, it's kind of hard to explain…"

The look of exasperation returns. I'm not sure if it ever completely left. "How hard can it be? You either came up with something to read or you didn't."

"Ummm, I kind of didn't."

"Okay, then what did you do?"

An itchy tingle of embarrassment crawls up my neck. "I went back to my room to take a shower. While I was waiting for my hair to dry, I sort of fell asleep."

"And when did you wake up?"

"The next morning. Around nine-thirty."

It's not that funny. Her hysterical laughter has to be from lack of sleep.

7

The job that was supposed to make my writing career possible was sabotaging my current efforts. Years of bartending had turned me into a creature of the night. And late, late mornings. That would've been okay, except that on my nights off I tended to frequent the place that paid my bills. So when I should have been writing, I was either serving, partaking or sleeping. The only thing that had changed since arriving in Yellow Springs was that I was no longer earning a living.

At least I didn't have a hangover.

That was the most positive aspect I came up with as I zipped through a record-breaking shower, nearly ripped my face off shaving at Mach 10 and threw on whatever clothes were closest to the door. The morning sessions were out, but if I hurried, there was a chance I'd still make my appointment with McGuire. Optimism born from an uncharacteristic lack of a headache led me to believe he would see my state of disarray as that of a creative genius; too distracted by contemplating future works of indescribable literary beauty to be concerned with mundane trivialities such as fashion.

"You didn't really believe that junk, did you?"

"It was the sun. I'm not used to it. I think it boiled my

brain."

Fifteen minutes late for a half-hour session wasn't a great beginning, but the voices droning behind the door were reassuring. The last appointment must be running over. I plopped down on an extremely uncomfortable chair and waited. Half an hour later, just as I began to worry about the lack of feeling in my lower extremities, the door flew open. McGuire and a buxom blonde emerged. I hoped their intimate proximity was not indicative of how McGuire treated all his students. There's only so much I'm willing to do for my art. The young woman—not sure of her name, but I recognized her as the tasty blonde from class; a head for math and a body for sin—didn't notice me as she flitted her lashes and swayed off. McGuire and I were silent as we watched her move down the hall. Once she was out of sight, McGuire blinked and looked around, seeing me for the first time.

"Ah. Mr. Barker."

"Don't worry," I said with an understanding smile while I shook his hand. "It's not a problem."

He countered with a sardonic smile and a cocked eyebrow. "What's that?"

"That young lady. Running over her time."

"She didn't," he said in a voice dry enough to evaporate Niagara Falls. "Unlike you, she can read a clock. As a matter of fact, since Miss Elmira was early I let her take your slot. Now you have fifteen minutes instead of thirty."

While he'd been whittling me down, the white-haired de Sade had led me into his inner sanctum. His chair enveloped him in an upholstered hug; mine was the evil twin of the horror I'd sat on in the outer sanctum. This didn't bode well. It was time to turn the conversation.

"Just between you and me, does she have any talents beyond the obvious ones? Or did you not waste time discussing her writing potential?"

Angelica stares again, and then shakes her head as she sits

back in her chair. "Smooth, Rex, smooth…"

"I thought so; Dallas McGuire did not."

"Since there are now ten minutes instead of fifteen," Dallas snapped, "I'll cut to the chase. Your synopsis is so much drivel; I've seen better plots on *General Hospital*. And this," he tapped my manuscript with a finger that had a better manicure than most women I know, "this is embarrassing. The weak plot you've concocted gets lost in a plethora of tedious details." His eyes blazed as he warmed to his subject. "The worst thing about this mess is that it adds to the morass of substandard writing that keeps editors from having the time to consider authors who actually know how to write."

"And that would be you?" My catalogue of witty repartees came up blank. It was the best comeback I could dredge up and Dallas blew by it.

"The best thing is—actually there is no best thing. Honestly, Mr. Barker, don't quit your day job."

Ah-hah. I had him. "Not an option. I work at night."

Dallas lied. Once he got into the swing of things, he kept me longer than ten minutes. Much, much longer. It was late by the time he wearied of torturing me and I escaped to the cafeteria. Late enough that the real food was gone. The only evidence that it had ever existed was a morose-faced person swabbing listlessly at empty stainless steel serving trays. And please don't mistake my use of non-gender specific nouns as PC; there was no way to determine sex. Even the tufts of hair peeking out from the armpits of an amputated tank top didn't offer a clue.

"Where can I get some edible food?"

It was amazing that a youth with blue spiked hair and a skull charm hanging from an eyebrow stared at me as if I was a mutant. I thumped my chest, pantomimed shoveling something into my mouth and grunted, "Me. Food. Where?"

Eyes rolled. Weary sigh. Thumb jabbed over one shoulder. I looked in the indicated direction and said, "No, that's—" but the creature was gone. And I was alone with tofu lasagna and the pathetic remnants of what had once been a proud and plentiful salad bar.

After loading up my plate, I wandered into the main section of the cafeteria. Finding a seat wasn't a problem as there were only a scant number of diners remaining. Of the half dozen or so left, two were familiar and one of the pair was waving. I joined the legal eagles with a disheartened thump.

Judge S. shook her head as she glanced at my tray. "I wish I had your discipline. Tofu is the way to go, but I just can't stomach the stuff."

The bigger part of a sauce drenched meatloaf slice, a pile of au gratin potatoes and a chocolate chip cookie with one bite out of it filled her plate. Not only was she ignoring the feast, but she'd piled napkins and other trash on it. I brushed away a tear before anyone could notice and attacked my vegan lasagna. It met my assault gamely and repulsed the advance. And my taste buds. Beneath the harsh fluorescent lights, the wilted, partially slimy salad looked even less appealing. With a deep sigh, I pushed the plate away and slumped in my chair.

"What's wrong?" John asked with the air of a man who's just eaten an incredibly satisfying meal. I hated him. But not as much as Dallas.

"The Marquis de Sade just trashed my manuscript."

"Who?" Well-fed and ignorant. Was there no justice?

Without the sensitivity she'd shown to John the day before, Sylvia grinned. "I take it McGuire didn't care for your style?"

"He didn't care for my style, my plot line, or my grammar. Hell, even my shirt pissed him off."

This warranted a raised eyebrow. "Well, I haven't read your manuscript, but I have to agree on the shirt," Sylvia said.

I slumped lower. At least John appeared sympathetic.

"God, I'm sorry. What're you going to do?"

"This isn't a setback worthy of hara-kiri," I assured him. "It's not as if I've got much invested in it. Other than my sixty bucks, of course."

"How can you say that? You have your time, your energy,

your—your soul invested in those pages. How can you be so calm?"

"Easy. This isn't *War and Peace*. As a matter of fact, I threw it together about an hour before the deadline for getting it postmarked."

The horror was back. "And you still sent it in?"

"Sure, what'd I have to lose?"

John leaned back in his chair, causing it to creak an ominous warning. I held my breath, but relaxed when it held.

Sylvia studied me as if I was a gang member that had just knocked over a 7-11. "What are you doing here, Rex?"

"I'm beginning to wonder," I admitted. "Being a writer's been my dream since I was old enough to dream, and now that I'm in a writer's world, it's not what I expected."

"What did you expect?" There was amusement in her voice, but it wasn't unkind.

"I don't know."

John's chair came down with a smack. "It's everything that I expected. But then, I've been living in a writer's world for two years. That's the time I've invested in my book. And I have something to show for it." There was a mixture of pride, defiance and desperation in his statement that swept away any temptation to make a smart comment.

"That's quite an achievement." Lame, but he didn't notice. Sylvia flashed me a grateful smile that also went unnoticed by the lawyer.

"That book is the only thing left. I lost my wife, my children, my house, everything."

"Don't do this," Sylvia begged. "There was nothing you could do."

"I could have worked less... Paid more attention, given her the love she wanted—needed..."

"She left you for a woman." Sylvia announced and the words blazed angry neon in the silence.

"It's not as if you have the equipment to compete," I offered.

It was hard to imagine human beings angrier than the two

sitting before me. Until Mr. Sharpe interrupted our cozy little group. The light shooting from his eyes could've sliced steel.

"M-m-monster," he stammered. "Horrible. Idiotic m-m-moron. Blasphemer!" Little flecks of spit sprayed from his mouth and created rainbows in the bright sunshine. Rainbows that dissolved into a fine mist and covered everything within a two-foot radius. This included my lunch. Good thing I'd wanted to lose a few pounds.

"Sit down," Sylvia said and patted the chair beside her. "Tell us what happened." The soothing tone would have convinced King Kong to shinny down the Empire State Building. Mr. Sharpe, definitely not a twenty-foot gorilla, didn't resist. He sat.

"Dallas McGuire is an inhumane, unfeeling c-cretin," the old man said. He took a napkin and wiped the table. When he was satisfied that the already spotless surface was absolutely spotless, he laid a dog-eared manila envelope on the cleared space.

"Did McGuire critique your wife's book?" As soon as the question was out, I realized I deserved the disgusted looks from John and Sylvia. Mr. Sharpe didn't seem to notice, however.

"If you call it that," he said and pulled out the pages. "That man would have panned *Gone With the Wind*. Look at this, he butchered it. It's a bloodied victim!" The choice of words, while melodramatic, was appropriate. The red ink splashed across the pages did resemble a series of razor cuts.

"I thought editors were supposed to use blue ink," John interjected.

"They are," Sylvia murmured, "but from what I'm beginning to know about this McGuire, he probably likes the impact."

Seeing a chance to redeem myself, I offered, "That does look bad, but just print out another copy. Then send it to someone who isn't a literary snob."

Mr. Sharpe shook his head. "This is my only copy. Peg didn't trust computers. Said they were evil. It took her two years to type this on her Corona." He sighed. "This book was what kept her going. Once it was done, she just drifted away."

"Why don't you—" I was about to suggest retyping the marked up pages, but I never had the chance.

"No," Mr. Sharpe screamed. "This is a horrible desecration and the only thing left is vengeance." He tottered to his feet and began cramming the sheets back into the envelope. His withered hands were shaking so hard that I thought the manuscript was going to wind up on the floor, but I didn't dare offer to help. His heaving chest and purplish-red face alarmed more than just me.

"Mr. Sharpe, please sit down," Sylvia pleaded.

Again, the old head shook side to side, this time with a great deal more violence. "Have to go. He has to see reason. He just has to. He can't be that unreasonable. Nobody can. Nobody human, that is." The pages were finally in the envelope, which now had a ragged tear down one side and the old man scuttled off. We sat motionless and watched him go.

Finally, John broke the silence. "It's obvious what happened."

"McGuire's power trip would put Attila the Hun's to shame?"

John rolled his eyes. "No. What's obvious is that Dallas McGuire is a professional. Schlock writing, whether the author is dead or alive, is still schlock writing. Dallas has to be completely objective and not let sentimentality come into play. It's tough, but that's what he's paid to do."

"What about mine?" I protested. "He ripped mine, too."

Sylvia shrugged. "John has a point, Rex. By your own admission, the manuscript McGuire reviewed was substandard. It probably took him longer to read than it took to write."

Even Perry Mason couldn't get an acquittal. "Maybe you're right, but it'll be interesting to see what the great Dallas McGuire has to say about your stuff, John. How are you going to react to the merciless pen of blood?"

A flush began to crawl up the lawyer's cheeks. Sylvia shot me a look then reassured John. "Don't get worked up. It'll be fine."

Acting in unison, the two picked up their trays and left without bothering to say good-bye. Three days into the week and my newfound acquaintances were already treating me as if they'd known me for years.

8

Angelica rubs her temples.

"You okay?" I ask.

"Just thinking I need a better class of friends."

"Ouch. Not fair..."

"Hopefully that was a wakeup call," she says.

"How so?"

"You have a lot of talent, you just never apply yourself. That's what this was supposed to be about. Have you attended any of the sessions you paid good money for or, god forbid, have you gone somewhere and actually tried writing?"

Young's Dairy must shop for furniture at the same place as Antioch. My butt is stuck to a chair that is at least as uncomfortable as the ones at the college. "I meant to..."

"But..."

"Well, I'd enjoyed all the abuse I could stand for one day so the formal sessions were out. Doing some writing had a nice, relaxing feel to it, though."

"But..."

The chair is worse. I shift my left cheek. Then my right. "On the way to get my stuff, I passed the student lounge."

"And..."

"Give me a break," I burst out. "I hadn't watched

television for days. I'm only human."

Angelica relents. "Okay, so you spent the afternoon in front of the boob tube. Then what?"

"When I realized what time it was, it was too late to make the evening sessions." Her lips are very straight and very thin. "I didn't want to walk in late," I explain, my voice rising. "It would've been rude to interrupt." Incredibly, her lips compress even further. "I decided to go to Ye Olde Trail Tavern. You know; pick up some local culture, mingle with my colleagues…"

"Get drunk…"

I swear her lips disappeared.

The Tavern was built in the 1800's when people enjoyed throwing back a few cold ones in dark, claustrophobic warrens designed by M. C. Escher. In other words, my kind of place. That evening every inch was packed with humanity, from the stools at the bar to the outside patio. There were even people loitering on the ramshackle stairs that led to the bathrooms. Buying a six-pack at the corner grocery and sneaking it into the other claustrophobic warren I called home was beginning to look appealing. Before leaving, however, I had to use the facilities. On my way through the crowd, a frantically waving arm caught my attention. Its plumpness and the stridently colored shirt it was poking out of, provided the identity of the owner. I pushed through the crowd and joined Rose, her sibling and a group of boisterous strangers at a dangerously tilting table. At least, dangerous for the half-full pitcher that rested in front of Roger.

"Rex, where've you been? Park your ass and help us finish off this pitcher. I'm afraid we've already imbibed more than our customary lot. It's making me feel a bit frisky…" The gleam in her eye was unnerving, but there was free beer. I parked my ass.

After flagging down a beleaguered waitress and convincing her to deliver a mug, I began to enjoy the evening. The beer was icy and took the edge off the day. "How's the murder research going?" I asked. The two beamed.

"This was an excellent idea," Roger said. "Not only are we honing our craft, this place is brimming with tension."

"Oh yes," Rose gushed. "Can't you just imagine one of these creative types going off the deep end and running amuck with a violent weapon? Like an Uzi or a Berretta or a BAR or—or something."

"Maybe a long bow?" I suggested. The pioneery atmosphere of the Tavern was pressing in on me.

"What a wonderful idea," Rose gushed as she refilled my glass. "The ghost of a murdered Indian possesses a shy, retiring housewife with delusions of being Margaret Mitchell. Suddenly, she's picking off her competitors with the expertise of Hiawatha. Wonderful."

Gooseflesh rose on my arms. It was frightening to think that we were on the same wavelength. But there was at least one more glass left in the pitcher and she and Roger hadn't touched it since I came up. Didn't want good beer to go to waste.

"I still think it's a shame that there aren't more hands-on workshops," Roger commented with a tone that gave my gooseflesh gooseflesh.

"On what?" I couldn't think of a single topic that wasn't being covered.

"On murder, of course. Target practice, knife handling, poisons." Neither sibling was smiling and I noticed an aftertaste that I'd never encountered before. Wasting beer no longer seemed a sin.

"Thanks, but you know what?" The two stared with solemn focus. "I'm going to wander around a little bit. Don't want to monopolize your evening." Before they could protest, I was up and working my way out, heading for the safety of my room and a tamper-proof six pack obtained from a disinterested stranger.

"You didn't honestly think there was poison in the beer, did you?"

"Nobody ever died from being too careful..."

The place was jammed and I was beginning to think I'd never reach the door and freedom. I'd maneuvered through the restaurant area, made excellent time in the hallway that led into the bar, but then got sideswiped by a waitress carrying a tray twice her size and an attitude even bigger.

"Sorry," I said to both the disappearing waitress and the woman sitting at the bar who cushioned my landing. She was dressed in black leather and silver studs with a lace-up corselet that rounded her chest in a way that belied her membership in the five decades club. Looking up I saw deep crow's-feet at the corner of her eyes that confirmed it. Off balance from the fall and the beer, it took me a moment but the combination brassy voice and voluptuous breasts dialed in recognition.

"No problem," replied Kandi with a smile as big as her hair. "Now that we've skipped the formalities, would you like to join us?"

"This is a private party," said a boy that I assumed was her son. And he really should keep his hand off mommy's knee.

"That's all right, I'm on my way home," I explained as I tried to extricate myself.

"Alone?"

"Uh—yeah. Hopefully," I said and succeeded. Over my shoulder, I could see that Kandi and the boy had contrasting expressions of disappointment and relief.

The door was in sight when a familiar voice pulled me up short. "Hey, join me and I'll buy you a drink." Sylvia waved at an empty barstool with a smoldering cigarette. From the overflowing ashtray, I deduced she was making up for lost time.

"You're on, as long as it's not a beer."

"No problem. Beer's for pansies." She took a long swig, which finished off her martini. While I was waiting for the promised Jack on the rocks, I noticed her cancer stick of choice.

"Why Camels?"

The judge snuffed out the cigarette, lighting another with a silver lighter before answering. "Why not?" She peered at me. "Who are you working for, R. J. Reynolds or the Surgeon General?"

"Neither. Bartender. A lot of women smoke, but I can't remember the last time I saw one smoking non-filters." My gut instinct said this was a statement she used repeatedly on the losers she pronounced sentence on. Independent, tough, no-nonsense. My instincts were wrong. Or at least partially.

"Years ago I went to the Cleveland Clinic for a quit smoking seminar," she paused and gave a little laugh at the expression on my face. "It was a long way to go and cost a lot, especially since it was a bust, but I always figure if you're going to do something like that, do it the best you can. Anyway, while I was there, I had a chance to talk to a doctor whose specialty was smoke related problems."

"Busy man…"

"You know it. Anyway, he brought up some interesting points. First, people have been smoking for ages, but serious problems have only started cropping up since the fifties. He blames it on filters. First, a filter has all kinds of toxins in it. Formaldehyde, asbestos, that kind of garbage. It can only absorb so much and the tar builds up ahead of it. If a person smokes the cigarette all the way down, they'll get a concentrated dose of the bad stuff that they wouldn't get otherwise."

I nodded. The woman had a point. Or the Jack was taking effect. Whichever. I'm known for my open mind.

"Especially when a woman has an open wallet."

"Exactly…"

"It's sort of like birth control."

"Pardon?" Maybe it was the alcohol, but the connection was elusive.

"The best way to avoid STD's or unwanted pregnancies is abstention, but there are some people who insist on partaking."

"Amen to that," I cheered and raised my glass.

"Those people should use a condom. If someone insists on smoking—and they will—the second best option is unfiltered. Kind of a reverse condom."

The woman was a genius. "Safe sex. Safe smoking."

"And I practice both," the judge said and pursed her lips to exude a thin stream of white smoke into the hazy air. For an older woman, she'd kept herself up pretty well. A sharp inhale and suddenly guttural coughs racked my body.

"Easy there big fella," John boomed in my ear as he pounded me on the back. I forgot Sylvia when I noticed the woman hanging off John's arm. Chase. An extremely drunk Chase. It was obvious that she was using the lawyer to make me jealous.

"Oh," she breathed to Sylvia, "can I bum a cigarette?"

"No problem," said the judge, "but I'd have pegged you for a Slims kind of woman. Sure you can handle a grown-up smoke?"

Even in the dim lighting, I could see Chase flush, but it only added to her fragile beauty. "Actually," she admitted, taking one from the offered pack, "I do smoke Virginia Slims, but I ran out. Thanks."

I snatched up a pack of matches, but Sylvia was faster. Plus Chase kept herself at an angle to keep from facing me. It was too much. I chugged my drink and, as the fortifying warmth worked its way through my system, said, "Chase, I'm so sorry about last night."

"Don't worry about it," she said, snuggling up closer to John. "If it wasn't important to you, it's not important to me." Her words were brave, but there was a brightness in her eyes that signified tears. Magnified by her glasses, she looked as if she had spotlights shining from her face.

"It's not what you think. I fell asleep."

John and Sylvia laughed with the lawyer drowning out the judge. "This fast-paced life too much for you, Rex old boy?"

"Or maybe it was who he fell asleep with." There was a

nasty edge to Sylvia's comment that didn't sit well. With Chase or me. A tear slid down the girl's cheek.

"I don't know why this keeps happening to me," she said in a voice so low I could barely hear her. John and Sylvia, engrossed in a private conversation, were no longer paying attention.

"There wasn't anyone else. I slept alone," I insisted. My mouth felt stuffed with cotton and I sipped at the magic glass that never drained. Chase' mournful face swayed in and out.

"Don't you get it?" she hissed. "The sex is irrelevant. The betrayal was because you didn't trust me enough to share your novel—your innermost thoughts—your soul—with me."

"But…" then I remembered that there wasn't a novel and my protest faded away.

"See, you can't even deny it. Either you don't trust me or you don't respect me. Just like Dallas." With a sob, she disentangled herself from John and bolted towards the bathrooms, tears streaming down her cheeks.

"What the hell did you do?" John demanded.

"It wasn't me. It was Dallas." I started to explain, but it was unnecessary. I'd said the magic word.

"That son of a bitch," John swore. "Not only does he have the literary taste of Larry Flynt, he's just ruined a sure thing. That bastard is destroying my life."

"I take it you got your critique?"

"If you could call it that. The man wouldn't know good writing if it jumped up and bit him in the ass."

Sylvia's laugh had a surprisingly bitter edge to it. "It's a good thing I didn't have the esteemed McGuire read something of mine." She drained her martini and started on the waiting drink. Professional envy twinged. Damn, the bartender was good. To test him, I drained mine. Another magically appeared. Damn.

John, oblivious to all else, raged on. "His exact words were 'pedantic and plodding, full of tedious detail that only a feeble-minded paralegal with delusions of grandeur would find interesting'." Both Sylvia and I burst into laughter. John glared at us and screamed at the bartender. "Scotch straight up. And don't give me any of that watered-down swill. I can sue. Sylvia, let me have one of those Camels."

Sylvia frowned and then handed him one. She hesitated, and then lit it. He puffed like a steam engine.

"I didn't know you smoked," I said.

Jaws clenched, Sylvia said, "And I thought you gave it up."

John continued to puff. "I save my nastiest habits for special occasions," he said, just as his drink arrived. It must have been okay, because he immediately ordered another one. And another. The judge and I exchanged glances.

"Don't you think that's a little much?" Sylvia asked. Her tone was once more gentle, the nasty edge gone.

"Who cares? My future's gone. Not only am I alone and broke, I have no talent. Nothing to fall back on, nothing to hope for, nothing to dream about," he said and reached for another cigarette.

"That's not true," Silvia protested. "Just because one pompous idiot—" As if on cue, the door opened and the pompous idiot himself strode into the bar with the voluptuous Elmira draped across his arm. There was a small explosion and glass shards were spinning to a halt all around John's chair where his drink hit the floor. And that was good, because the way he was clenching his fists indicated he could have squeezed the glass to powder. Or at least tried. Then there would have been blood and the emergency room and stitches and who knew what else... John was right; Dallas was ruining our lives.

9

"Did he break the glass on purpose?" Angelica asks.

"I don't know. But the look in his eyes—"

"What?"

"Nothing specific, more a feeling." I'm careful since it's obvious that Angelica is looking for suspects. But she also deserves the whole story. Plus it helps me remember the truth. "He was barely under control."

"Angry?"

"Very."

"Could have killed someone? Dallas?" Angelica narrows her eyes and scrutinizes me as if to see through me to the truth.

Slowly I nod. "As if he wanted to break something more than the glass. Sylvia acted weird."

Now Angelica really perks up. "How so?"

"She's always completely in control; unflappable. When the glass broke she looked scared."

"So the iron lady flapped. And in public. Interesting," Angelica says, almost to herself. She taps her teeth – an old habit she does when she's deep in thought. There is a pause and then she looks up. Refocuses. "Sorry. Go on."

"Hard to say what caused the following chain of events. I

personally blame it on the evil kid behind the bar. If he hadn't been so damned efficient, I wouldn't have had so much to drink. That made what happened next difficult to describe because it's all kind of blurred and jumbled together. But this is what I remember."

McGuire strolled through the tables like a patriarch, stopping here and there to chat a bit before moving on to the next group. Elmira never took her adoring eyes off his face. A gasp sounded in my ear, making me spin around and almost knock down Chase. Her well-endowed chest heaved with emotion.

"How could he?" she sobbed. "That slut is nothing but a walking proposition. Can't he see that all Elmira has to offer is sex?"

Chase had a point, but I think Dallas was well aware of Elmira's talents. And happy to be a recipient. "You deserve better," I said and patted her shoulder.

She shrugged off my hand and sobbed. "I don't want better. I want Dallas." Before I could respond, Dallas reached the bar.

"Ah, the gruesome twosome," he said. I assumed he meant John and I. "Butchered any prose lately? Really, Chase, I thought you had better taste." With a strangled cry, the girl ran out the front door and disappeared. Dallas grinned at Elmira who laughed and rubbed up against him.

"Who the hell do you think you are?" John snarled.

"A professional. An artiste. Unlike the majority of this assemblage," Dallas said with a cool assurance that made my jaw clench. "If you can't take criticism, you've picked the wrong business, my friend."

Splintered dreams flashed through my head. John, Chase, Mr. Sharpe, myself. Happy, excited, hopeful and, above all, trusting. Only to be squashed like insignificant roaches. The answer is yes. Roaches do dream. And squash back. An inky red haze blinded me and my right fist swung out, connecting solidly with the perma-smirk on Dallas' face. Drops of blood rained as a kaleidoscope of images played in slow motion. Elmira, hands to her cheeks, eyes wide, mouth wider and screaming. John and Sylvia staring at me; mouths also wide, but silent. Dallas falling over backward, arms pin wheeling and chairs flying in every direction. Face after nameless face staring at me, then at Dallas, then back at me. It took forever but was over in an instant as time caught up and began careening forward at breakneck speed.

"You son of a bitch," I yelled and leapt onto the prone man. His arms came up to protect his face, but otherwise he did nothing to protect himself as I pounded blow after blow upon him. There was nothing I wanted more than to wipe the arrogance off that patrician brow. Suddenly, he was gone, replaced by a ceiling and I was flailing away at nothing. John had me around the chest and was holding me away from my target. "Put me down, you bastard," I screamed.

"Not until you calm down," John said, his voice coming fast and shallow. I continued to swing, but this time with another target.

"Get that asshole out of here!" the creepy little bartender yelled. "Or I'll call the cops!"

I could feel John nod as he struggled to the door, dragging me along. Somebody opened it and fresh, cool air slapped me in the face. John threw me down the steps and I landed on my hands and knees. I jumped to my feet and began to swing again. A meaty fist stopped mine in mid-air and began to squeeze. The bones grinding together in my hand brought me to my senses.

"I'm okay," I grumbled.

"You sure?"

"Yeah." The toes of my shoes became extremely interesting.

"Let me drive you home."

"I'm fine, I tell you," I said with the righteous indignation that only the deeply inebriated can produce.

"All right. But how're you going to get back?"

The suspicion in his voice grated, but arguing didn't seem

to be the best course of action. I set my jaw and tried to act sober. "It's not that far; I could use the walk."

"That's not a bad idea," John said, but the hesitancy in his voice belied his words. "I'll go with you. Just let me check on Sylvia and I'll be right back."

As soon as he disappeared, I took off down the sidewalk. I passed Ha-Ha Pizza and lost some time in a giggling fit. On the back wall of the dining room, there was a painted mural. Bright with color, it featured a dog leaping over the moon. But it wasn't a moon. It was a pizza. A pizza! I pressed my face against the glass, celebrating with the canine. Celebrating until the glaring patrons killed my merriment and encouraged me to stagger away. There was a drive-thru next door. Its neon sign winked and cackled with me—a fellow merry-maker. It was a lot closer than my room, which might as well have been on Jupiter. Walk, my ass...

The Jack Daniels without ice was a little harsh at first, but went down easier and easier as the night rolled on. It's hard to say where I wandered, but given that it was Yellow Springs, I wasn't worried about muggers. Or the police. Or even being noticed. Just one more eccentric loner. The more I wandered, however, the more I thought. And the more I thought, the more outraged I became. It became imperative that I return and face the object of my rage. Halfway through the bottle, I decided to confront Dallas McGuire.

It took a moment to get my bearings, but when I did, I realized I was on Walnut, which would take me behind the Tavern. A few blocks sped by and I was at a path, not quite an alley, that ran between a coffee shop and the bar. The village's obsessive attention to historical detail carried onto the walkway, which was lit only by the waning moon and paved with uneven stones from the local quarry. I staggered down a series of three steps plopped in the middle of nowhere and caught my toe on one particularly wicked stone. The bottle of Jack flew one way and I flew another, the sound of breaking glass obscured by the furious oaths spewing from my mouth.

After a few minutes—hard to tell how long; I think I passed out—I struggled to my feet. There was something sticky all over my hands and a weird smell, kind of metallic, but sweet. Spoiled. Of course, that wasn't strange given that I was behind a bar. Spilt alcohol, vomit, spoiled food; it'd never been in my best interests to catalogue the myriad smells surrounding a drinking establishment. The only thought in my clearing head was to locate John and see if the offer of a ride home was still valid. I staggered to the front of the Tavern and pushed open the door. My entrance met silence and then someone began to scream. Then a bunch of someones began to scream. In slow motion, I looked at my hands. Even in the dim lighting my alcohol fogged brain recognized blood. There wasn't anything to do but join in. I think my screams outdid everyone's.

Angelica shivers. "And then the police came?"

I nod. "I guess somebody called them immediately, because they were there in seconds. They handcuffed me and led me out to a squad car parked on the street. The siren was off but the lights were still on. Red and blue. Everywhere. There was an ambulance behind the tavern—I could see its lights as well, but that was about it—and I could see a bunch of people gathered in the walkway. It was surreal; the flashing red and blue lights made it look like a scene from the 'Masque of the Red Death.' If Kubrick had directed it. The cops hauled me to the station, asked a bunch of questions, took a lot of pictures and let me make my phone call."

"When did you find out it was Dallas?"

"As soon as the police grabbed me. The first question they asked was 'Why did you kill Mr. McGuire?' not even 'Did you kill him?' Jeez, I feel as if I'm already convicted."

"It does seem fairly damning," Angelica agrees, concern darkening her already deep brown eyes.

Fear tickles my spine. "You believe I'm innocent, don't you?" I plead.

She relaxes and forces her mouth into a smile. It's a very

sad smile, but I love her for it.

"Of course I do. Now we just have to make sure everyone else believes it. Come on," she says as she stands up. "You need sleep. I'm assuming the police told you to stay put and not go anywhere, not even Dayton?"

I nod, standing up with her.

"Okay, then, it's back to your room. After you've had some sleep, we'll get back together and develop a plan of action."

Getting in the car. The drive to the room. Climbing into bed. I don't remember anything. The only thing that stands out is that I'm not alone. Angelica believes in me. Everything will be all right.

10

After being awake for more than twenty-four hours, the normal, sensible thing to do is sleep. But I can't. One reason is that the room could fire pottery. The other is that sunshine is prancing about outside. And that is not right.

What would be right is if a vicious storm had rolled in, complete with thunder, lightning and maybe even a few dollops of hail. Or, if that is too much to ask for, maybe some dense, creeping ground fog. Something that Jack the Ripper can hide in. But no, this is Ohio. The only time the weather turns nasty is when the Girl Scouts have an Easter egg hunt planned. Or maybe when the Elderly Kite Flyers Association leaves the home for its annual kite-flying extravaganza.

I spend a few wretched moments lying in bed sweating and despising the Midwest before accepting the inevitable. Sleep is out. I gather my toiletries with much grumbling and shove them into a wad with a towel and semi-clean clothes. Reminiscent of camp, I stagger down the hall to the communal bathroom. In a rare stroke of luck, the water is as hot as my room and it steams the ache out of my body.

Within the hour, I'm strolling down the sidewalk enjoying the sultry August day. This is the silver lining to the cloud that is my room. It makes everything else seem balmy. When I finally reach the building that houses "The Writing Life", I'm even humming a little.

This is the first opportunity I've had to participate in one of these sessions. There is a large, buzzing crowd pushing their way through two sets of double doors, so I pick the least frenetic side and join the melee. Once inside, the masses split again and spill down four aisles, rushing to fill the front rows. Not wanting to seem over eager, I select a desk on the aisle and about a third of the way from the back. The classroom is auditorium style, sloping to a stage at the base, which ensures there are no bad views. On the stage are a podium and a long table with chairs. I consult my schedule and see that the speaker is a reporter from the New York Times. The topic is ethics. Seems like an oxymoron, but that's what I'm here for. Enlightenment. I settle in and wait for the fun to begin.

Picking the aisle seat is a mistake. The rest of the workshop participants don't have the same trouble with sleeping in that I do and show up en masse. And make a beeline for my row. After the umpteenth insensitive clod tromps on my feet and sticks their butt in my face while climbing over me, I quit smiling. And still they come. I am so frustrated that I don't notice the woman at the podium pleading for attention. Everybody else does because the room becomes deathly silent as they await her announcement. Which turns out to be an incredibly poor choice of words.

"As some of you are aware, a tragedy has struck our happy group," the woman proclaims. Then her voice catches and I notice that her makeup barely covers red, swollen eyes. I hunch down in my seat. "A beloved colleague has been brought down at the apex of his career. I don't know how to soften this news, so I'll just say it." With a loud sniff she says, "Dallas McGuire was brutally murdered last night."

A motherly type helps the sobbing woman off the stage amidst a chorus of gasps, whispers and even a few nervous giggles. I slide down even further and try to become invisible. I have no idea what is ethical about newspaper reporting because I don't hear another word for the entire session. "Brutally murdered" chants in my brain and blocks out everything else. Except for the feeling that accusing eyes are burning into my skull. *How did they know? What do they know?* I feel sick.

Eventually the lecture drones to an end. Lacking the courage to creep out early, I stay until the last speaker leaves the stage. It is easy to slip out of my desk and into the crush of aromatic bodies, pretending to be just one of the gang. Freedom is in sight and I convince myself that my earlier paranoia is just that, when a voice curls my stomach into an icy pretzel.

"Rex, yoo-hoo, Rex," yodels a hefty woman.

She grins at me with a familiarity that makes me hope last night's blackout only masks the answer to a murder and not some sordid animalistic hijinks. A tangy odor emanates from her perspiring body and makes my head swim. I need an alibi, but not that badly, I hope.

"Wasn't that the most inspiring discussion you've ever heard?" she gushes.

Memories slam into my brain. "Where's Roger?"

Rose gives a lascivious smile that curls my toes. And my nostril hairs. "Can't a girl have some time on her own without big brother watching? This isn't 1984…"

"Uh, no, no, it certainly isn't," I mumble and back away to safety and my workshop. It doesn't work. Rose falls in step beside me.

"Isn't it just too exciting?" she says as she links her arm in mine and presses her sweaty body up against me. Together, we stumble across the commons. "Such a tidy little murder. On the other hand, maybe it's a touch too neat. That nasty character was so lacking as a human being that his removal was predictable to say the least. You'd have thought, given the venue, that the murder would have been more creative. Even a little more savage. More James Patterson and less Agatha Christie, don't you think? Of course, that may have been the intention, a cozy, not a psychological. What are your thoughts?" Her eyes gleam as she digs her pointy chin into my shoulder.

The suffocating heat, Rose and the lack of sleep give the journey a Dali-like edge. When my classroom swims into view, I almost cry.

"Great talking to you Rose," I say as I disentangle from her squidly grasp, slip into the room and close the door on her gaping face. Apologies will come later. Maybe. Now, the only thing I want is to ease into a chair and relax.

"Glad you could make it," says the woman at the front of the table. My eyes narrow in suspicion. Her face is guileless; pleasant with the bronze cast that comes from countless hours spent weeding peonies and mulching roses. She smiles. "It's been a crazy day for all of us. I'm just amazed that any of you kept to your schedules in the face of such an immense tragedy. It shows a discipline that makes me proud."

Everything about her is warm, from her chestnut hair sprinkled with gray to brown eyes sparkling with dancing green lights. I relax. And smile for the first time since leaving Angelica.

"I'm sorry for the interruption, Mrs.?" I ask, hoping that the query doesn't sound as transparent to her as it does to me. Her answering grin assures me it is.

"That would be Miss or Ms. Franks. But you can call me Stephanie." Our eyes lock for a brief moment and then she adds with a briskness that I'm sure is covering up other emotions, "I prefer given names to surnames. It releases creativity."

"Ms. Franks, do you honestly believe you are a suitable replacement for a man of Dallas' stature?" Elmira sits tall and straight, regal in her defense of the late, not-so-great McGuire.

Her frigid composure is revolting. To be so cool, so poised this soon after the brutal death of her mentor, most likely even her lover, is the act of a soulless creature. Then she blinks and a single, sparkling tear creeps out of the corner of one eye. For an instant, the mask drops and Elmira's perfect features twist with fury and pain. Then the ice queen returns and the fluorescence highlights what I missed before. Makeup that coats inky circles under her eyes can't do anything for the veins that shoot across the whites. Pain twists through me. *Will anyone grieve like that if I kick off?* I drag my attention from the younger woman and focus on the older. Stephanie flushes and my heart goes out to her.

"I'm not trying to replace him," she says, "but I'll do my best to give you what you came for."

Elmira's sniff, echoed by the rest of McGuire's groupies, leaves no doubt that this is a noble, yet impossible task.

"You've already given me more than I wanted—or got—from Dallas." Enter Sir Galahad.

There is a moment of confused silence, then sprinkles of laughter and a hearty poke from John. I didn't realize he was in the room, much less at my side. "Didn't know you swung that way, buddy. Good to know that now before you and I get too much closer," he roars. Even Stephanie joins in, but her comments take the edge off.

"Thank you. I think. I'll try to live up to first impressions. Now, let's get down to the business of writing."

"Don't you think that's, like, the wrong perspective?" Elmira drawls.

"Excuse me?"

"Equating writing with business. Shouldn't it be like, you know, art?"

Stephanie smiles. And the smile is a smidgen Cleopatra, a touch Mona Lisa and a lot Helen of Troy. "Actually, it has elements of both. The foremost constituent in writing a successful novel is creativity. I won't argue that point. But to achieve the ultimate goal—getting published—one has to have discipline, structure and an understanding of the business aspects."

All the color leaches from Elmira's skin. Her model-thin face takes on a skeletal cast. "You believe that writers should aspire to be published above fulfilling their creative muse?" Her husky voice vibrates with emotion. Stephanie blunders on; an elephant in a Ming vase consortium. The tinkling sound of shattering porcelain is deafening.

"Of course. That's assuming that you want to make a living at writing. If not, then you can ignore my advice and follow your own dreams. Otherwise, there are certain tricks you can employ to make that dream a reality."

"Such as?" I prompt. Support is imperative. She's dying. Damn it. There it is again…

"Well, I like to set a goal of at least a thousand words a day. That's about four pages. At that rate I can crank out a novel in about three months."

I wince. That innocent, benevolent creature has no idea what vicious characters lurk in the Pandora's box she's just pried open. My cowardly instincts take over and I sink into my chair and watch the slaughter commence.

Although there is an admitted bias on my part, I say that the ensuing battle is a draw, leaning only slightly in favor of the intriguing Stephanie. Maturity and wisdom maintain a narrow technical advantage over Elmira who meets the challenge with the unshakeable enthusiasm and confidence of youth and the strength of a wounded lover. It doesn't actually deteriorate to the level of "Oh, yeah?" "Yeah…" or "So's your mother…", but it comes close. Eyes shining bright with tears, Elmira and company clear out immediately and Stephanie fields questions with the aplomb of a weary general. I shake my head to clear the cobwebs that were festooning my brain cavity and start towards the instructor lady. My goal is to fawn relentlessly until she agrees to join me for a drink. Or dinner. Or matrimony. A familiar leer interrupts my progress.

"Not too bad for an old gal, eh?"

"She's not old…" I retort and appraise her from John's perspective. Probably about my age, forty-ish, maybe a little thick in the hips. Tanned arms clad in a brightly flowered cotton top, khaki shorts and sensible white socks and sneakers. No sex kitten, sure, but that smile. It flashes and a glow settles on me, igniting one of my own. "Youth isn't everything."

John shrugs. "Didn't say it was. Excuse me, buddy boy,"

and he is chatting up a fluffy little blonde so quickly my head spins. At the same moment, I notice the crowd has dispersed around Stephanie and I grab my opportunity.

"Ms. Franks, I'd like to apologize…"

"Stephanie, please. And what would you have to be sorry about?"

"The Attack of the Living Bimbos. I should have helped you out."

Stephanie laughs and her eyes don't just dance, they waltz and tango. "Don't worry. I can handle child-women like Elmira on my own. And it's easier if I'm not encumbered by amateurs." There is no petty hurtfulness in her tone, so I don't take exception.

"Regardless, I feel as if I owe you something. How about joining me in a drink?"

"I'm not sure we'll fit, Mr.?"

"Yes, but think how fun it will be to try." Beauty, brains and a delightful sense of humor. And I'll bet she even knows who the Little Rascals are. "It's Barker, but you can…" The sentence is never finished due to the explosive entry of Hurricane Chase.

"Rex, there you are. I've been looking for you everywhere." She looks awful in a winsome, orphan-ish kind of way. Above a small, pale face, her hair floats in Medusa tentacles, while owlish glasses magnify the dark bruises under her eyes. She looks like a terrified twelve year old. Her chest heaves in short, sporadic bursts.

"You're Rex Barker?" The Ginsu-like tone could slice a can. It takes me a second to realize it came from Stephanie. My stomach tumbles in a slow, nauseating somersault.

"Yeeeessss…" My imitation of a trapped python is admirable. Stephanie doesn't share my opinion.

"On second thought, I'm busy Mr. Barker. At least too busy to consort with murderers. There's no telling how I might slip up and offend you. Critique a poem written by your mother? Reject your clumsy advances? Who knows what your retribution could be." And she is gone.

I sigh. "What's up?" I ask Chase. It seems impossible, but her eyes are bigger.

"I need to talk to you," she whispers.

"Look, I'm really sorry about the other night…"

Scowling, the girl twitches and jerks her head over each shoulder, then back at me. "Why? You weren't there…"

"Yes. Yes. I know I wasn't there. I overslept, remember?"

Her face stays still but her eyes flit back and forth. "Oh. You mean the Sam & Eddies night."

"Of course. What are you talking…"

"You're looking particularly lovely this morning."

John's timing is usually bad, but this time it's also frustrating.

"Gotta go," Chase mumbles.

Before I can blink, she vanishes. I really need to figure out how women do that. I tune John back in, which is becoming harder by the second. Need for sleep is bearing down like a freight train.

"…amazing, really. I didn't think one human being could drink that much and still be breathing. And look at you. Attending to the noble pursuit of bettering yourself and looking only slightly like something the cat drug in. You are a monument to resiliency."

While he natters on, we work our way out of the building. John doesn't seem set on any particular path, which is fine with me. My overwhelming goal is to reach my room and indulge in a three or four day nap.

"My reputation seems to be cooling most people's attitudes towards me." Overlaying the memory of Stephanie's distaste is an equally vivid image of Rose cozying up to me. I shudder. "Why aren't you afraid of keeping company with a murderer?"

John's ear splitting bray of laughter slams me at the exact moment he throws open the outside door, resulting in a dual whammy of din and laser-level sunshine. Nausea roils through my body and I almost puke. My companion doesn't notice. "Like Sylvia told the police, buddy boy, even sober you're too much of a screw-up to pull off a murder successfully."

"The judge stuck up for me?"

"If you can call it that. She said you were too drunk to stand up straight, let alone hit a target as small as McGuire's pea head."

My corroded brain isn't following the intense flow of data. "That's how he died? From a blow on the head?"

"Yeah. With a Heineken bottle. Remnants of a whiskey bottle—Jack Black, I think—was found a couple of feet from the body. Had your fingerprints on it, but no blood or hair or anything."

Bile rises in my throat and then subsides. I can feel sweat dripping from every pore in my flesh. The boarding house silhouette teases me in the distance; close enough to recognize, but still too far to ensure sanctuary.

"What happened after I left?"

John halts and rubs his chin, frowning from the effort of remembering. Panicked by the lack of forward movement, I bite my lip to keep from screaming.

"Let's see. McGuire had a tiff with his floozy, Elmira, because he was chatting up that speaker lady."

"Ms. Hellstrom?"

"Yeah. And hell hath no fury like an out-bimbo'd bimbo." Now that the memory train is moving, so is John. I sigh in relief and fall in beside him. "She threw a temper-tantrum and McGuire told her to go home until she could act like an adult. There were a lot of yucks at her expense and she ran out. In tears. I don't think Hellstrom was too amused because she followed not long after."

"Leaving McGuire alone?"

John stops again. Note to self: don't ask difficult questions. The boarding house seems to be moving away. An ivy-covered carrot manipulated by a sadistic god. Abruptly progress resumes.

"A cluster of groupies hovered, but they just seemed to irritate McGuire. None were of a caliber to interest him. You know, substandard boobage." Even though I hate myself for it, I have to grin. "He left within, oh, let's say, fifteen minutes and things got pretty dull. Since there weren't any unfolding dramas and no one to talk to, I was about to leave when you showed up. The evening picked up after that, especially since the judge is in pretty tight with the locals."

"Why?"

"Oh, it happens all the time. She's got a lot of big city experience and a way with people. Not to mention a reputation for a hard line approach to justice. The combination is irresistible to the Barney Fife's you find in most of these little burgs."

"It doesn't make sense. Why is she interested in a crime that doesn't involve her?"

John's manner flashes to somber respect. "Sylvia ran—and got elected—on a platform of no tolerance. Not for criminals and not for police who make mistakes or don't follow procedure. In her eyes, they're equally guilty."

"Wow," I say with a matching somberness.

"Yeah. As far as she's concerned, a cop that allows a criminal to get away on a technicality is an accessory. The same goes for lousy detective work. There's no way the good judge would stand by and let the local yokels railroad you."

"Seems obsessive," I say, laughing to take the edge off. John doesn't laugh back.

"To a certain level, we all have obsessions."

I'm reminded of Norman Bates. I have to do something fast. "Sylvia's done so much for me and I barely know her. I wish there were something I could do in return. She's not a bad looking woman and she's been away from her husband for a while; do you think she'd appreciate some thank you sex? I'll let her be on top."

John stops on the sidewalk, allowing me to enter my temporary abode alone. He is not amused. His stony red face is the last vision imprinted on my consciousness before I drift into slumber.

11

I'm sweltering in a volcanic mineshaft, desperate for the miners to finish their rock breaking, take their coal and leave. Out of the blackness, vague forms coalesce, gradually taking on familiar shapes. The mineshaft is my room, but the miners continue, their blows echoing in my pounding head. I sit up, grab the headboard to stop the spinning and concentrate.

At first, the blows are multi-directional, attacking me from all sides. Then they localize. They come from a point to the right of the bed. I scrub my fists into my eyes and focus on a door outline, back lit from a hall light. The pounding fades into knocking. I stagger to the door and throw it open, nearly falling onto the banty hen that runs the place.

"You have a visitor," Mrs. Winthrop screeches, disapproval pouring from her tiny body. "A lady visitor." This female seems to be the cause of the disapproval, but whether it is because the unknown woman makes a habit of visiting men or because she makes a habit of visiting me, I can't tell.

"Does she have a name?"

The fact that there could be more than one has not occurred to my landlady and it throws her into shock. Her gaping mouth and round, glassy eyes make me itch to toss her into a goldfish bowl. Or, since there isn't one handy, the nearest toilet. Before I succumb to the urge, she comes to. Her jaws shut with an audible click.

"I didn't ask." And she is gone.

Closing the door, I switch on the light and rummage through my clothes for something presentable. Judging from the darkness, it has to be late evening or early, early morning. I am shocked when I glance at the clock.

"Six o'clock... P.M.?" The revelation drives me to squeeze behind the armoire and peer out at the world. During my nap of less than two hours, assuming it is the same day, the world has transformed. The sunny August sky twisted into a menacing caricature of its previous self. Storm clouds boil and rumble, gravid with the promise of thunder and lightning. Lots of thunder and lightning.

"Friggin' Ohio," I grumble as I drag a comb through matted hair. "At least the stage is now properly set for a murder." The thought sends chills rippling through my spine as I clump down the stairs to greet my lady friend. I pray that it isn't Rose. With or without Roger.

Not only is Roger absent, so is his amorous sister. Angelica has looked better—lack of sleep is beginning to wear on her—but to me she is gorgeous.

"Hello, beautiful," I whoop and give her a spine cracking hug. She presses up against me for a moment, her shining head resting on my shoulder. A loud sniff emanates from one of the countless doorways that feed the parlor. Along with her cluster of cats, Mrs. Winthrop is getting an eyeful. Good. She'll have something to yammer about at the next meeting of the Yellow Springs Old Bats' Association. It will go well with her Eye of Newt Stew. I hug Angelica tighter. "It's great to see you, but you look like hell," I murmur into her hair.

A reciprocal hug, then Angelica pulls away with a wan smile. "Good. I hate to look better than I feel. It's dishonest."

"Have you slept at all?"

"No, Derek was waiting when I got home. He grilled me

pretty good. Afterwards, I was too wired to sleep."

"I'm sorry."

Angelica runs her fingers across her face and through her hair, wiping away the sickly smile in the process. "Don't be. If it weren't this mess, there'd be something else to fight about."

"But I…"

"Look, let's go somewhere and get some coffee before I pass out. Much as your landlady would love that, I don't feel like giving her the satisfaction."

I look over my shoulder in the direction she is staring. There is a flash of chintz and sensible shoes, then nothing. Raising my voice a few decibels, I announce, "If we hurry, the free clinic will still be open. Besides, I'm sure it's just prickly heat." The loud gasp that follows us into the street is better than a symphony.

Neither one of us want to return to Young's. Extensive as their menu is, we'd fairly well exhausted its offerings in our marathon breakfast session. Besides, it is only right that we bless the other culinary establishments of the village with our discriminating taste. The Sunrise Café draws the short straw.

The tiny restaurant is crowded, but the bubbly hostess, festooned with the familiar eyebrow, nose, lips, ears and belly button hoops, leads us to a booth right away. A waitress that has to be her clone delivers rich, fragrant coffee and richer, more fragrant pie with the finesse and speed of a sorceress. A few minutes pass before either of us come up for air.

"For a health food place, this pie is sinfully good," Angelica says.

A hint of animation sparkles from her eyes. This along with the food and caffeine makes me feel better. I glance around the room, bright with primitive art that glows with a vitality lacking in the amateurish creations littering the boarding house. Antique matchboxes, bobbins and oilcans complete the décor, which intrigues rather than insults. Typical Yellow Springs. The only place I know where antiques and kitsch, vegan and bar-b-cue ribs, middle-aged conservatives and teen-aged liberals coexist without cultural implosion. I nod in approval and crunch a forkful of sugar-encrusted pie between my teeth. In spite of all that has transpired this burg is growing on me.

"What did Ron say?" Angelica asks as she sips her coffee.

"Who?"

"My lawyer," she answers with just a tinge of exasperation. Not too bad considering everything she's been through in the last two days.

"Sorry. He slipped my mind. He wasn't the one who got me out of jail anyway," I add before she has a chance to yell at me. "Judge S. did."

"Who?"

Now it's my turn to be exasperated. "Sylvia. The judge from Columbus. She stood up for me in front of the locals."

"I don't get it. Why would she help you?" she asks, frowning.

"Jealous?"

She doesn't have to laugh so quickly. Or so loudly. "Don't flatter yourself. In all honesty, I'd love to see you hooked up with someone. Especially a female with a steady job and a halfway decent standing in the community. But, this doesn't smell right. Why would a judge you barely know go out of her way to protect you?"

"John explained it to me this afternoon. Sylvia's a stickler for justice, to the point of obsession. He didn't say it exactly like that, but that's the implication. She's hard core."

"Okay, but why doesn't she think you did it?"

My face burns as I admit the truth. "The lady judge told the police I was too much of a screw-up to get even a crime of passion right."

"Hey, it if keeps you out of jail, take it as a compliment," Angelica says, smiling now. "What else did John tell you? If the judge is talking to the police, she's probably also talking to John about what the police are doing."

"Nothing much. He did fill me in on what happened after I left," I say and repeat John's oration. In condensed form, it doesn't take long.

"The cause of death was a blow to the head?"

"Blows," I correct. "With a Heineken bottle. That gives us two clues."

"Two?"

"Uh-huh. We need to pinpoint the Heineken drinkers and then find out which one hated McGuire."

The answer is a vigorous shake of her platinum head. "The bottle type is incidental. For two reasons. Let's take the most unlikely first. This is a pre-meditated murder, committed by a coldly rational, thinking individual. They're not going to use their poison of choice; they're going to pick something farthest from their own taste. To throw suspicion elsewhere. I mean, think about it. If McGuire had been bonked with an MD 20/20 bottle, would you be picking on homeless winos?"

That makes sense, even though I like my scenario better. It's easier and gives us a sleuthing direction. "Maybe you've hit on something. McGuire had a knack for bringing out people's insanity. Since he'd used up his other targets, he could have been chatting up a wino and—BAM—the world's a better place."

A tiny smile twitches at the corner of Angelica's mouth. "All right. It's a possibility. But let's put that one at the bottom of the list until we've exhausted the other scenarios."

"Okay. What's the other one?"

"A crime of passion. A rational human being reduced to a brutal non-thinking animal. You're in a rage, the object of your rage appears, you grab whatever's handy and whale away."

"Before you continue with this train of thought, clarify one thing. 'You' is being used in a generic, non-specific manner, right? I mean, you don't think I did it, do you?"

Angelica reaches across the table and squeezes my hand. "No. I agree with Sylvia on two points. You're too much of a screw-up. And the locals are out of their league. It's more important to us to find out who really did it. Sylvia's holding off the police for the moment, but if their leads get cold, you'll look better and better. It's in your best interests for us to figure out who did do it."

Emotions duke it out inside. Am I insulted or grateful? In a second, gratitude wins by a knockout. My feelings may be bruised, but I'm not stupid. Regardless of current public sentiment. Angelica is the only person I trust completely and now isn't the time to get sensitive about her choice of words. Or her opinion of me, which is no different from how she normally feels. Plus it doesn't help that we're both exhausted. Once this mess is over, if I'm still hurt, we can talk about it. Right now, we need to be strong, united, focused. God, I sound like a Bengals coach. Murder is a hideous crime. I tune Angelica back in.

"My vote is for an unplanned moment of opportunity. Who hated Dallas enough to pummel him to death?"

"It'd be easier to figure out who didn't," I grumble. The thought gives me chills and I glance around the eatery. Booths are crammed into every available inch of real estate and each one is packed with enthusiastic diners; none paying attention to our conversation. Potentially, any one could have murdered McGuire. And feel happier for it. I shiver.

"You okay?" Angelica asks, looking up from scribbling on a napkin.

"Yeah. What's that?"

"A list of suspects. I've got Chase, Elmira, John Townsend, and Mr. Sharpe so far."

"Why Chase? She's a sweet kid."

"She's a scorned woman. So is Elmira. John and Mr. Sharpe had their dreams crushed. I see both groups as dangerous people."

Depression settles over me in a gray cloud. "There could be an endless number of suspects that fall in those two categories. Those are just the ones we know about."

"That's true, but let's stick to what we know," Angelica says with a reassuring briskness. "These people were also on the scene and become more likely than some unknown faction. Anybody I've missed?"

"The Culbreaths."

"You can't be serious."

I certainly am. The woman especially. "You haven't seen the maniacal gleams darting from their creepy little eyes. In their twisted dimension, it would be perfectly logical to take the workshop to the necessary level. After all, they're paying good money to become better writers. First hand knowledge would do it."

With obvious reluctance, Angelica writes their names on the napkins. She'll thank me for it later. It's a shame prison stripes are horizontal. Those two could use some slimming. Maybe I'll suggest that at their indictment. Dragging myself back from the pleasing courtroom image, I return to the napkin. One of the names brings a memory to light.

"Chase wants to talk to me about something," I blurt.

One artistically plucked eyebrow arches. "Confession?"

I want to protest, but can't. "Don't know. She was about to tell me something when John blundered up. Before I could stop her, she scuttled away."

"Why would she run off?"

"Probably scared for her virtue. He's been panting after her like a buck in rut. The poor girl's obviously terrified."

The skeptical frown is definitely unwarranted. "Townsend's just a horny old man, not a rapist. She can handle him."

"How can you be so sure? You haven't actually met any of these people."

"Good point," Angelica accedes, without having the grace to be humbled. "My opinions have been based on your observations. It's time to meet this cast for myself. And find out what Chase has to tell you. Where's the best place to find these characters?"

"All of them?"

"All of them."

"I don't think that's a good idea. You're exhausted and they won't be..."

Before I finish, Angelica cuts in; her voice like tempered steel. "Don't patronize me," she snaps. "I'm a little tired, but

E. SABBAG

if I can handle a board of directors, I can take care of a bunch of Hemingway wannabes."

Her face takes on a granite cast, but I persist. "I'm not patronizing you. It's just that they're hard enough to take one at a time. Meeting the whole gang at once will be like drinking from a fire hose. You've already done enough for me; my conscience can't handle this as well. It could demagnetize my moral compass."

"Don't you mean finish demagnetizing it? I can't believe it has that far to go," she adds. One corner of her mouth rises in what might be a semi-smile. Her eyes twinkle.

"Maybe so. But it certainly doesn't need a push," I grumble. From a distance, I hear a voice whine. I cringe until I realize it's me and then I cringe harder. "What's the hurry, anyway? Why can't we just sleep on it and start fresh tomorrow?"

The granite face melts a little, but not enough to give. "At the end of the week, the prime suspects are going to scatter. If the police haven't figured out who done it by then, my guess is that you'll be getting writing inspiration from your new love interest, a convicted felon named Bubba TuffLuv."

My stomach pitches and I swallow the bile that rises in my throat. Along with the protest. There is no other choice. "The Tavern," I force out. "That's where they congregate after the sun goes down and they feel safe enough to leave their coffins."

"Let's do it then," Angelica declares and drags me out of the cozy security of the Café and into the abyss.

12

Even though the blood is long gone, as I step through the Tavern doors my skin prickles in anticipation of the shrieks. The gentle hubbub typical of late evening in a neighborhood bar neither decreases nor increases at our entrance. Other than a few casual glances, lingering on Angelica and dismissing me as inconsequential, the clientele remains focused on their own business. After the excitement of the previous evening, the anti-climax is disappointing. Even insulting. Then I remember Stephanie's reaction that afternoon and am grateful for the anonymity. Face averted, I creep behind Angelica as the bored hostess shows us to a table snugged right up against the bar. I squeeze into a chair wedged between the table and the bar, facing the window overlooking Xenia Avenue. In any other small town in America, it would be Main Street, since it is the main drag. But this is Yellow Springs and Xenia is so much harder to spell than Main. Angelica sits directly across from me, her back to the half dozen tables accommodating sardine packed patrons.

"What can I getcha?" bubbles our waitress. Since the Tavern serves alcohol, she has to be at least eighteen, but on the street, I'd have taken her for twelve. Pigtails, puck-ish grin, tomboy build and symmetrical tattoos of Piglet and Pooh, one on each arm, proclaim tween. She's dressed in the uniform of her species, hip-hugging jeans, skin-tight, reptilian tank top and three-inch wedge sandals. It's a nice touch that the chartreuse gum she alternately snaps and blows into little bubbles matches her hair color perfectly. Kids these days really know how to accessorize. Right down to the bejeweled skull decorating her nametag, which proclaims Hannah.

"I don't know," Angelica murmurs, still poring over the six-by eight-inch menu. "The pie took the edge off, but I want something to nibble on." Her lower lip is caught between her teeth, a study in concentration as she weighs the merits of each selection. With her spiky blond 'do and eyes enormous by lack of sleep, Angelica looks only slightly older than the waif who stands with infinite patience, anesthetized to—and tolerant of—the indecision of the elderly. Contrasting the two, it's amazing that I ever thought Angelica's new look was anything other than ordinary. Even boring on a certain level.

"Are the nachos any good?"

A perfect bubble snaps between perfect white teeth. "My favorite. Especially if you want to share." A dimpled grin is tossed my direction. Diet Coke for Angelica, fat Coke for me and Hannah clumps off.

"I'll bet those shoes weigh more than she does."

"What?" Angelica asks in a blurred voice. She's rubbing her right temple and her eyes are heavy and lidded, on the verge of coma.

"Are you okay? Maybe you should go home and sleep. It's been a long day."

She shakes her head. "I'll be fine once I get some caffeine in me. Besides, I'd rather wait for the storm to die down a little."

In my own zombie state, I hadn't noticed that the leaden clouds were giving up their harvest. Rain splats an angry tattoo and lightning backlights the serpentine branches of a maple. The windowpanes' antique glass magnifies and distorts the erratic flashes of light, while heavy, pre-plasterboard walls mute the accompanying thunder. The ghastly light illuminates nineteenth century photographs of our country's forefathers and foremothers and even some forechildren, causing their eyes to glow with demonic accusation. While the hackneyed landscapes adorning my room will never be considered lovely, at least they are more comforting. Just as I am about to suggest moving to a less judgmental table, our drinks arrive. Along with John.

"Man, this place is packed. Mind if pull up a chair?" he asks as he pulls up a chair.

Since our intention was to have Angelica meet the gang and ferret out clues, I should be glad to see him. And I would be, if he wasn't quite so close to Angelica. From the flush on her cheeks, I gather that she isn't any more thrilled than I am, but now isn't the time to antagonize the best information source we have.

"Angelica, John Townsend. John, my friend, Angelica."

John never takes his eyes off his prey. "I have to revise my opinion of you, buddy boy. You're not a complete screw-up. At least not in the friend department." Using his mahogany beer bottle as a pointer, he gestures towards Angelica and splashes Samuel Adams' down the front of her shirt. "Need some help with that?" he leers as she dabs at her soaked chest with a napkin. I wonder if she's revising her earlier assessment of him.

"No. Right now, I just have a little beer on me. I don't need to be diseased as well." She bats her lashes as she tosses a smile in his direction. The smile could freeze fire.

That answers my question.

"You know what your problem is?"

Angelica's eyes gleam. "No, but I'm sure you're going to help me out."

"Absolutely. Too much caffeine." Another jab. And another splash of beer, but this time into her diet Coke. He grins. "That'll help, but not enough. Hey, pretty lady." This directed at Hannah, who approaches the table with a plate of nachos wider than she is. "Bring a pitcher of whatever dark stuff you have on tap and three mugs. My friends need a little loosening up."

Before protests are voiced, Hannah is gone. And John is digging into the food. "God, I'm starved," he proclaims around a mouthful of cheese, shredded beef and sour cream.

Angelica rolls her eyes and helps herself. I follow suit and marvel at the enchanted plate. There isn't even a dent in the mound of food. The way John's shoveling it in; that's a good thing.

In spite of the crowd clamoring for attention, Hannah is back with the pitcher in less time than it should have taken to pour it. The picture of efficient hospitality, she fills three mugs and whisks away John's empty bottle even faster.

I'm surprised that Angelica doesn't protest the beer, but it's probably to get John talking. Nothing shuts down a drunken suspect faster than refusing to socialize with him. Watching Angelica hoist her glass, I appreciate what Joan of Arc must have looked like as they led her to the pyre. Martyrs must stick together, so I clink my glass to my companions' in a mock toast and take a swig. My stomach lurches. For a moment, whether or not the ale will stay down is questionable; then it eases into place. The second swallow is almost tolerable and, by the time I've downed half the mug, I've settled into a familiar, easy rhythm. Either Angelica is putting on a great show or she is as tough as she claims. She matches me drop for malty drop.

Malty Drops. What a great idea. If kids can have malted milk balls, why can't adults have beer flavored "Malty Drops?" The preferred candy of lushes everywhere...

In slow motion, the Tavern shimmers back into focus. Two pairs of eyes analyze me much like Al Fleming and his wife, the Lady Ethel, viewed moldy bread.

Desperate for a witty retort to cover my lapse into the world of demented treats, I cleverly blurt, "What?" To my horror, Angelica and John exchange an understanding look and roll their eyes. In unison.

"Please," Angelica purrs to an enraptured John, "go on. What happens after the admin steals the experimental drug?"

John's head is in danger of splitting from the grin that spreads from sideburn to sideburn. The only thing he enjoys more than the possibility of sex is talking about his novel. With Angelica, he has both.

"No, no," he corrects, a wise old sage nurturing an enthusiastic protégé. "She doesn't steal it. That's an important plot point. It's late and all the pharmacies are closed. Janet— that's the administrative assistant—hasn't been sleeping well and she figures one or two won't be missed."

"Janet," Angelica says, rolling the name around on her tongue. "I don't know…"

"It doesn't sing, does it?" John jumps in. "I was actually thinking of changing it. To something more romantic. Like Angel or Angelica. If you don't mind, of course."

Angelica's smile makes my earlier nausea return. Complete with bile.

"That's so flattering," she murmurs.

John is wriggling like a puppy. "She's a major plot point. It's almost a shame she dies as soon as she takes the stuff. Pretty gruesome too. Chokes on her own vomit."

The nausea seems to be contagious. "What a lovely vision," Angelica forces through clenched jaws.

John is a smoothie. It's obvious why his ex-wife went lesbian. Strange that it hadn't happened sooner.

"This must be the place," announces Sylvia. Angelica and John both jump and almost knock over their mugs. In unison. They are becoming downright creepy. The judge pulls up a chair and waves Hannah over with one motion. "Get me a Martini and take away the kiddie drink," she says with a wave at the pitcher. "Name your poisons. As long as they're adult poisons."

"I really don't think…" Angelica demurs, but Judge S. cuts her off.

"Don't be a candy ass, sweetie."

Nostrils flare and then relax. "All right. Are you buying?"

"If it's worth paying for," Sylvia replies. I'd missed something, but I don't obsess over it. It's obviously a woman

89

thing.

"Fine. I'll have a Chivas Regal. A double."

Sylvia smiles. "You intrigue me. A glimmer of taste. Of course, you talk the talk, but you have yet to drink the drink."

Angelica returns the smile. "Don't worry your pretty little head. I will."

The women remind me of two cats squaring off in an alley. Just before the scratching and spitting starts, our party expands. Damn.

"Look, Mr. Sharpe, a covey of composers." Rose should have been named Pelee. She gushes more than a volcano.

Three more bodies pack in around our table. Not only does Rose squeeze up against me; the resulting crush forces Angelica and John up against each other. Nobody except Rose and John look happy.

"What's your pleasure?" Angelica asks, the perfect hostess as she passes drinks around from Hannah's tray. When the newcomers hesitate, she adds, "The good judge is buying. And she insists on the very best."

Always the public figure, Sylvia smiles at each one of us, saving the most radiant for Angelica. It's nice to see their friendship blossoming.

"Oh, my. How kind," Rose says, her tiny black eyes glinting like raisins in a bran muffin. "Let's see—oh—how about something fun. Nothing quick; maybe one of those slow drinks. They remind me of the tropics. Especially if there's a little umbrella."

Roger, his corpulent body wedged between the table and the wall, laughs and the resulting seismic wave almost overturns the table. "That's not 'slow' like speed, sis. That's 'sloe' like gin."

"That's what I said. Slow gin, because it sneaks up on you." She glances from face to face, a bewildered smile plastered on her face. I almost feel sorry for the poor silly woman. But not quite. She is pressing so hard against my thigh that the circulation is going. And the pain is coming. Angelica comes to the rescue.

"Sloe is a type of plum. That's why the drinks are pink."

Rose giggles and presses harder. If gangrene sets in, I am demanding half their next royalty check for undue pain and suffering. And emotional duress.

"Whatever," the Culbreath sister says and rolls her eyes. "I still want a sloe gin fizz, but make it fast."

Hannah scribbles and arches an eyebrow at Roger.

"Make mine the same."

"That's what I like to see," John raises his mug in a salute. "A man who's not afraid to flaunt his feminine side."

Roger frowns and stares at the concentric dew rings glittering on the varnished wooden tabletop. Hannah pauses for a second and then points her eyebrow at Mr. Sharpe.

"Coffee," he barks.

"Want anything in that?" the girl asks around her wad of gum.

"Bailey's."

Hannah grins. "Good choice, pops," she says, snaps a tiny bubble and is gone before Mr. Sharpe can choke out his indignation.

"Did you hear what she called me?" he sputters.

Sylvia reaches across the table and pats his hand. He snatches it back as if he'd been stuck with a branding iron. She ignores the rebuff and says smoothly, "Don't take it personally. At her age, anyone above thirty is older than Methuselah's great grandfather."

Only slightly pacified, the old man cheers up immensely when Hannah reappears. Clutching the coffee with both hands, he drinks deeply then sits the cup on the table, his eyes closed for a second in contentment. Rose's outcry snaps him back into his normal agitated state.

"My, that's almost as good as sex," she announces with a lewd wink thrown my direction. The pink froth nestled in her mustache hairs offsets her fuchsia lipstick nicely.

A dozen snappy comebacks spring to mind, but, afraid they'll be taken as mating banter, I down a large swig of Jack instead. I spit it out in a coughing fit at her next comment.

"I think this whole murder thing is just wonderful. Are you all right dear?" she asks and whaps me on the back.

To save my spine I choke out, "Fine. Just fine. What did you say?"

Roger leans forward, his own pink mustache not complemented by anything. "The murder, of course. Although you'd have thought such a creative group of people could have come up with something a little more original."

"Original?" I sound like a stoned parrot, but at least I can form words. The other four at the table just sit and gape, their eyes wide and unblinking. A school of shocked guppies.

"That's what I said," Roger confirms with an edge of exasperation. "Look at the 'victim'." He makes virtual quotes around the word with his index and middle fingers. "Could they have picked anyone more unsympathetic? I mean, really. Arrogant, rude, promiscuous."

"That's right," Rose breaks in. "The poor man had no redeeming virtues. Why, the critics would have laughed us off the Times list if we'd have come up with a character that two-dimensional." She slurps at her drink in noisy punctuation.

"This wasn't staged," John blurts out. His exclamation breaks the spell and everyone clamors at once.

"McGuire is dead."

"It's real."

"Rex is the number one suspect."

For no discernible reason, the last statement rises above the alcoholic din. Scores of accusing faces stare in my direction. I start to sweat. Unbelievably, the pressure on my leg increases and Rose positively sparkles with excitement. Just when I think the situation can't get any worse, laughter rips through the silence.

"Unbelievable," Sylvia gasps, barely able to choke out the word. "Next to a Star Trek convention this has to be the largest collection of uncommitted lunatics on the planet. What did you do to get accepted? Check your grasp on reality at the door along with your pride?"

"What do you mean by that?"

John's tone isn't just cold; it's sub-arctic. And while out of his normal jocular character to talk to anyone like this, it is exceptionally strange since it's directed at Sylvia.

"What I mean is that this place is the Mecca of the Ungrounded. It's bad enough that you pay obscene amounts to have your dreams ground into dust; do you really think that even these arrogant jerks would stage a fake murder?" she yells, glaring around the table. She takes a deep breath and, with a calmer voice and a pensive frown on her forehead, she adds, "Although you are right about him being two-dimensional. He was evil personified. Drugs, sex, arrogance. No redeeming qualities whatsoever. In fiction, justice is not typically played out so neatly. There are twists and turns and hidden clues. In life, bad guys kill bad guys and that's that. The hard part is figuring out who became a bad guy and picked up a weapon."

Mr. Sharpe, in the process of draining the last bit of coffee, brings his cup down with a slap. "Who do you think you are?" he sputters. "All you judges are the same."

"What?"

"You heard me," he rages, shaking a bony finger in Sylvia's general direction. "No respect for life or dreams and even less respect for death. This is divine retribution, not a joke. But you don't understand that anymore do you?"

Sylvia stares, bewilderment clouding her face. The little man narrows his eyes, the bushy white eyebrows shadowing all but a maniacal gleam. Pinpoint stars in black holes. He points an accusing finger in her direction and quavers, "I thought so. You're so far above us common folk. God complex. That's your problem. God complex."

Before Sylvia can recover, Hannah appears. "Another round?" she chirps.

The judge nods. "Put it on my tab."

"You're the boss," Hannah says and clumps away.

No one speaks while she is gone; everyone seems too interested in their empty glasses or condensation rings on the table. Rose shreds a napkin and looks to be on the brink of tears. When Hannah returns with a full tray, everybody grabs their drinks. Angelica ignores hers.

"I've really enjoyed meeting you all, but I've got to go," she announces and rises from her chair.

"Perfectly understandable. Can't get enough of that beauty sleep," Sylvia purrs; her previous discomfort nonexistent. I shake my head, wondering if I'd just suffered a hallucination. Or a shift in the space/time continuum. Angelica rolls her eyes and strolls away.

John and I jump up in a dead heat, but I beat him to the winner's circle. "I'll walk you to your car." Angelica nods, too tired to do more than waggle her fingers at John, and follows me out of the bar.

Fresh-scrubbed air tickles our faces as we walk to her car, skirting the worst of the puddles and splashing through the smaller. A few are deceptive, their mirror-like surfaces concealing fathom deep potholes that suck at my feet and fill my shoes. Angelica has an innate ability that enables her to avoid the watery traps. As a result, she is still elegant and poised when we reach her car; I squish and flop. I assume what I hope is a posture of cool indifference while she digs out her keys. She curses under her breath as the slippery devils elude her. Her intense concentration worries me.

"Are you okay?"

"Yes," she snaps, then her face clears and she laughed as she squeezes my arm. "Don't worry. I'll stop by McDonald's and get some coffee."

"Biggie size it?"

"That's Wendy's"

"Ok, clown it up?"

"I think theirs is Super-size it."

"I scares me that you know so much about fast food," I say and smile when an exhausted smile flits across her mouth. "That'll get you home, but what about once you're there?"

The answering hug squeezes out most of my fears. "I'll be fine. Derek should be asleep. That'll give me until tomorrow to come up with an explanation."

I return the hug, and then wait until she gets in and pulls

away. A weak drizzle is all that is left of the earlier tempest, but it's enough to chill me to the core by the time I reach the Tavern.

13

Inside the Tavern's main door, I pause, allowing my shivering body to soak in the smoky warmth. A vision of a turtle crawling onto asphalt still warm from the afternoon sun flashes through my brain. A young linebacker, probably from a local high school since Antioch doesn't boast a football team, jostles me as he makes his drunken exit. Another turtle vision splashes into my head, but this time a semi has turned him into a reptilian Frisbee. I decide it's time to move out of the main thoroughfare and onto a side avenue. A plump arm beckons and I wander back to the gang. I ignore the chair that Rose is patting and take Angelica's place. John pokes me in the ribs.

"She's quite the dish, isn't she?"

"Who?"

John heehaws loud enough to expose his cavity-laden molars. "Don't play dense; it's not your style. Angelica. What an appropriate handle."

"She's married," I huff. Angelica is like my baby sister and she's going through a tough time. I know she can handle John but she shouldn't have to, especially not now. But, true to form, the oaf doesn't take the hint.

"That's the way I like them."

"Like what?"

"Married. Especially the lifers. All those years with one flavor makes a person hungry for sprinkles, if you know what I mean…" The leering wink brings all the wrong emotions bubbling to the surface.

"You hardly pass for sprinkles if you know what I mean," I counter. Rose and Roger glance in our direction, identical frowns etched on their faces. Sylvia blows a perfect smoke ring and raises an eyebrow. The only one that doesn't sense the rising tension is Mr. Sharpe. He is engrossed in mumbling something into his laced coffee.

John looks at me and then at the group and then back at me. With a grin he says, "I think your little friend felt something for me. And I think you know it."

"She has more taste than that." Now the neighboring tables are staring, but I don't care.

"Oh, I don't know. Angelica has you for a friend; she can't have that much taste."

"You asshole," I hiss between clenched teeth.

A laugh explodes from John. "Nice comeback, big fella."

Everyone laughs, but there is a strained, uncomfortable tinge. The group at the table watch me as if I might start flinging Heineken bottles at any moment. I should laugh along with them, defuse the situation, but I can't reach through my rage. It's building, breath by laboring breath, until it is something tangible—a living beast inside me. I look down, expecting the fingers clutching my tepid glass of Jack to sprout wiry black hair. The Wolfman of Antioch. But that's ridiculous. The moon isn't even full. Or did it have to be? The Hulk doesn't need a natural phenomenon to appear. Neither did Frankenstein's Monster.

The thoughts dampen all effects of the alcohol. Blind sober, I contemplate this new side of me. How deep can my rage go? A few off-color jokes and I'm ready to rip a lawyer's lungs out through his throat. Okay, it is a lawyer, but it's still beyond the norms of polite society. What am I capable of when somebody really trashes me? Is murder that far-fetched?

The thoughts tumble through my head in an eternal instant.

I snap to and realize I've lost my audience. Patrons at neighboring tables are chatting and sipping drinks; music I hadn't noticed before is providing a backdrop to the din. John is leaning over Sylvia and moving his lips by her ear. I am forgotten. Almost. Every so often Rose or Roger sneak a sideways peek and then jerk away when we make eye contact. I wonder if this is how Lizzie Borden felt at the Fall River Spring Cotillion. Sylvia's laugh, low and husky, breaks through my musings.

"We've worked up quite an appetite," Sylvia declares. "And we're in search of a cure." John leans close to her ear once more and whispers. Even in the semi-darkness her flush is obvious. "Would anyone like to join us?"

It's a strain to hear over the bar noise. I assume she's talking about food, but I don't like the weird vibes flowing from the couple. I decide not to risk it. "No thanks. I'm not really hungry."

"Count me in. I could eat a horse," Roger says, quickly followed by "Ow. What'd you do that for?" to his sister.

"We can get something on the way to our room. Good night all," Rose says as she hauls him to his feet. His protests echo all the way to the door and halfway out to the street.

"Sure you're going to be okay alone?" John asks.

"I'll be fine," I assure him, ignoring the fact that his hand is resting intimately on Sylvia's thigh. Especially since I'd catch a glimpse of someone who interests me a lot more than a middle-aged couple engaging in a potential game of Hide the Salami. Sylvia follows my line of sight and her mouth twitches in a wise smirk.

"My guess is that he won't be alone for long…"

"What—" John starts but is interrupted by the tug on his arm.

The two wave and are gone, but so is Chase. I blink and look back to where I had just seen her. For a second there is nothing and then Chase steps out from behind a post and scans the room, her head jerking left and right. Her terrified look stifles any laugh that might have erupted. When her eyes sweep my direction, I wave her over. She scuttles to the table and plops down beside me.

"What are you drinking?" she asks in a low, conspiratorial tone.

"Jack on the rocks," I whisper back, mimicking her paranoia by glancing over my shoulder.

She ignores me and pleads, "Buy me a drink?"

"Sure."

Within seconds, Hannah appears and snaps her gum. "What's your poison?"

"Jack. Straight up. With a Bud Light chaser."

We sit in silence until the drinks come. Chase slams back her whiskey and then gulps her beer. Not to be a wimp, I drink half my double shot in one swig. When the coughing fit passes and my eyes quit watering, I attempt to draw Chase out.

"So, what's up with you these days?"

"Too much."

"Still bummed about Dallas, I guess."

"I guess. Can you get me another shot and him another drink?" she says to Hannah. Hannah raises one eyebrow and nods, returning way too quickly with the requested round. I gulp the remainder of my first drink and tackle the next. Chase' shot is already gone.

"Shouldn't you slow down?"

"Why? I don't have to drive anywhere. Do you?" Before I can answer, she asks, "Got a cigarette?"

"I don't smoke."

"Oh. Right. I forgot. I lost my pack and I could kill for a smoke. Hey, kid," she says to a passing wall of flesh. The neckless bullet head proclaims this is another lineman. Or should be. I decide the local high school is dispensing steroids with its Gatorade. "Can you spare a ciggy?"

"Sure," says the gorilla and produces a battered pack of Chesterfield Kings. Chase grimaces, takes one and lets the young man light it for her. When she begins to hack, he grins and ambles away.

"Is that really worth it?" I ask.

"No," she says and stubs it out. "I'm not that desperate. Hannah..."

The next round blurs into the next into the next into the next. Time passes, but I don't know how much. All I know is that when Chase stands up and falls over, I'm not much help.

"Let's get out of here," she says as she stumbles to the door. Disentangling from the chair is harder than I anticipate and Chase is out the door and turning the corner before I get my feet working.

"Chase, wait up," I try to yell, but what comes out is a cross between a burp and a gurgle. Regardless, it has the desired effect and she stops. I catch up to her and lean against a tree, gasping. "Where are you going?"

"Home."

"Want some company?"

She contemplates me from behind the thick lens that magnify her eyes into saucers. The wariness bites deep. "What for?"

"You seem like you need someone to talk to. And so do I."

"Just talk?"

"Just talk," I assure her.

"All right," she says and wheels around so fast that I spin from the backlash. I steady myself in time to follow her into the drive-through I'd visited that fateful night.

Just like the Tavern after the fight with McGuire, I steel myself to walk into the drive-through. And it doesn't stop once I make it through the door. The other customers don't seem to notice anything menacing about the fluorescent washed bottles that line the shelves, but I sense evil everywhere. It has to be this atmosphere that caused me to do what I did that night; whatever that was. My head throbs and I sway, sure that the malevolence of this place will overwhelm me. Instead of the robust, vital man that I had once been, there will be nothing but a soulless husk, prey to the whim of any stray breeze or...

"In or out, Pops. You're blocking paying customers."

The door swings open and a unisex couple jostle me aside as the world jerks back into focus. I blink and look at the kid behind the register. His words aren't harsh, just bored and the expression on his pierced, pimply face confirm the observation. It isn't anything personal; I'm just another geezer interrupting his perusal of the literary rag that he clutches in tattooed fingers. I twist my head to make out the title, "The Roach's Dream..." D. McGuire. I groan and hope Chase doesn't see it.

"You okay?" the youth asks with what appears to be sincere concern. Maybe geezers have a habit of wandering in, swaying, groaning and then passing out. I understand his paranoia.

"I'm fine. It's just that it's so bright in here," I explain and move away from the door.

The kid nods in sympathy. "I know what you mean. It's like floodlights in here. A lot of people complain, but the owner won't listen. Says it's to discourage shoplifters. But you know what I tell him?"

I wait, but then I realize he's waiting for an answer. "What?"

"People are—like—good, you know? Suspect them of bad things and they'll do—like—bad things. You know?"

Now understanding the drill, I nod. What a mistake. I'm exhausted, coming off a drunk and the blaring fluorescence is making my head throb. Nodding my head churns the little gray cells into seething oatmeal. I swallow hard and tune the conversation back in.

"Expect them to be good and they'll be—like—good, you know?"

I nod again—carefully this time, thinking the owner probably has a better handle on his clientele than the trusting cashier. "Do you go to Antioch?"

His turn to nod.

"Sociology or philosophy?"

The boredom is gone and he grins; his face shining with the waxy pallor of a toadstool. "How'd you guess? I'm—like—

double majoring. I figure I'll be able to help the less fortunate gain a better place in life and mind."

I nod. I've always felt that the best audience for philosophers is a captive one. With a double major like that, he'll probably be able to take his pick of prison jobs. The inmates will be extremely open to socialization and Socrates. Or fellowship and Freud. Before I can point out what lay in store for the young scholar, Chase approaches the counter and plops down a bottle of Jack Daniels. My stomach protests with a slow somersault.

"I have to see some ID."

"I'm not buying," Chase tells the once-again bored cashier. With a jerk in my direction she says, "He is. And I'm sure you don't need any ID from him. Oh, and throw in a pack of Virginia Slims."

"Funny," the boy says, eyeing me head to toe. "I'd have picked you for a Marlboro man."

The interest in his eyes bothers me almost as much as the slam from Chase. "I'm not either. I'll pay for the booze, but not the cigarettes; put them back." He shrugs and removes the offending pack. Chase isn't that easy.

"I need them," she wails, voice rising with each decibel.

"I thought they're for him," the boy interjects.

"Oh shut up," Chase snaps and then whirls on me. "Please!"

"Absolutely not. As drunk as you are, you'll pass out and set the place on fire. Besides, I won't be responsible for poisoning you."

"Oh, I see. Alcohol is okay, but cigarettes aren't? Why? Because one makes me easy? Seducible?"

"No..." It's hard to tell what makes my head pound worse – the whisky, the lights or her voice. "It's just that you need something to calm you down; nicotine's a stimulant."

"Hey, you should have said something, Pops. I can hook you up with some smokes that'll calm the lady down, if you know what I mean," the boy says with a wink that's older than the Tavern.

Chase' expression is hungry; she quiets at once.

"Nah, let's stick with the legal toxins," I say, disappointing both children at once.

"Suit yourself, but I'm telling you, it fits your needs." The kid has a great future in the penal system; creating the felons he will later rehabilitate. Talk about job security.

"Just the booze."

"Creep," Chase cries and runs out the door. I throw a twenty at the kid and grab the bottle as I trot after her.

"Your change," calls the socio-philosopher.

"Keep it and buy a real degree..."

"Cool," he says as I push into the uncool night.

14

Chase has covered half a block by the time I enter the sauna that is the night. I take a deep humid breath and trot after the vanishing girl.

"Hey," I say as I catch up with Chase and grab her shoulder. She shakes me off walks away. I catch her again, this time spinning her around before she can get away. "Wait up. I'm sorry."

She pushes her lower lip out in a fetching Shirley Temple imitation. "You're not my mother…"

"No and I'm not even your father. Nor—" I stop her comeback with a raised index finger, "am I old enough." This warrants a tiny smile, which fades as quickly as it appeared.

"Maybe not, but you sure act like it. I can take care of myself; I don't need your lectures."

"I'm not lecturing. It's just that you have this great life ahead of you and I don't want to contribute to it being cut short."

"Fair 'nough," she grumbles. "But I could really use a smoke. I'm all twitchy."

"All right. I'll get you a pack. But just one. No more."

Chase shakes her head and looks resigned to a fate just one level above living hell. "No, I get it. I get what you're trying to do. It's misguided and irritating, but I get it. Besides, I probably have a pack squirreled away upstairs. Come on." The girl links her arm in mine and heads down an alley lit by nothing more than starlight. I hope she isn't counting on me to protect her from whatever evil lurks in the dark.

The alley crosses a main thoroughfare and leads into another alley even darker than the first. On my own, I would have missed the narrow flight of stairs that led into the next level of blackness. Feeling like Alice down the rabbit hole, I follow my guide into nothing.

Despite my misgivings, the efficiency apartment at the top of the stairs is cheerful in a dark, melancholy way. Before Chase flips on the light switch, I stop her and stare at the ceiling. I thought the whisky had worn off, but the stars twinkling down from a pitch-black night tell me otherwise.

"What's wrong?" Chase asks in her best grumble.

"Your ceiling's gone," I say with awe and a little fear. What had happened? Why was she living in an apartment with no roof? The giggle shocks me more than the celestial room. Chase can laugh? There's a click and light splashes into the room. The stars remain, but now they're muted. And a ceiling is revealed. "What the—"

Chase shrugs and enters an area blocked off by a Japanese room divider, the scant traces of happiness evaporating as she relaxes into her normal demeanor. "It's the southern hemisphere. There's the Southern Cross," she points to a cluster of glow-in-the-dark dots that look just like the other thousand glow-in-the-dark dots that cover the black ceiling. Remnants of a careless brush, streaks of black paint ooze down electric white walls; ebony blood dripping from a monochromatic wound. Various oils ala "The Scream" pop up here and there, completing the hopeless aura. I no longer wonder why Chase is perpetually depressed; now I wonder why she hasn't thrown herself off a grain silo.

From behind the screen, I hear the sounds of ice dropping into glasses. I examine the pictures on the walls. The subjects are primitive with stark colors. The overall affect has a great deal more depth than the insipid watercolors I've seen everywhere else.

"Who did the paintings?" I yell.

"A friend."

I continue my stroll around the tiny apartment and wind up at a black plastic futon with white plastic cushions. Since it's the only thing to sit on except for the floor, I plop down but lose my balance and almost wind up on the carpet anyway. What stops my backwards progress is my feet hooking underneath a faux wood coffee table. Luckily, the only item on the table, a wad of shapeless clay, bounces but doesn't break. The same tortured soul that did the paintings probably created it, which means it must mean a lot to Chase. Why else would she keep something that ugly? It does complement the tackiness of the furniture, but somehow I doubt that was her intention.

I sit and critique her furnishings, ignoring the fact that it is at least ten times better than the milk crates that adorn my apartment. Looking around, I realize her abode differs from mine in another aspect as well. Doesn't the girl realize that living alone means she can be as messy as she likes? The obsessive cleanliness scares me more than the alien influenced paintings. There's a lot I can teach this little one...

"Here," the subject under scrutiny announces and slams a glass down in front of me. She has a similar drink that she upends and drains to the halfway mark in one gulp.

"Did your artist friend do that?" I ask, pointing to the wad.

Always the conversationalist, she nods.

"What's it saying?" I ask.

"Put your ashes here."

"What?"

"It's an ashtray."

"Oh."

Chase drains her glass. "Want another?"

I gulp at my drink, hack when it sears my throat and hand it over. She leaves and is back in an instant with two more drinks. My voice rough, I ask, "What did you want to tell me?"

This time she drains her glass in one swallow. I refuse to give mine up, so she leaves without it. When she comes back this time, she brings the bottle and a bowl of ice. Even though I've barely touched my drink, she tops it off.

"Chase, what is going on?"

"Wish I had a cigarette," she mutters.

"Don't you have a pack hidden somewhere?"

"I thought I did. But I've looked everywhere and I can't find it."

There aren't a lot of places to look, so if she thinks she's looked everywhere I have to agree with her. "Do you want me to go get you some?"

"No. It's okay. I'll live," she says with a smile that makes my heart ache. "Just drink with me, okay? I need to talk and I need the alcohol to give me the courage."

The last thing I want is more alcohol; I can barely keep my eyes open as it is. But the hand clutching the tumbler of Jack Daniels is shaking and the eyes are pleading through unshed tears. And besides, she doesn't have any cigarettes because of me. I owe her. "Okay, but bring me some Coke. Straight whiskey isn't going to do either of us any good."

Chase wrinkles her nose. "Sorry. The hard stuff isn't in my budget any more... Maybe you should have dealt with the kid at the drive-through."

"Wha—no. That's not what I mean. Coca Cola. Pepsi. RC. You know, soda. With caffeine."

"Oh." Her face clears and she bounces off the futon making it undulate. I brace myself and keep from sliding onto the floor. Before the movement settles down, she is back with a half-empty can of Diet Pepsi. "Here. It's all I have left. You can have it all."

"Thanks." I pour some into my glass. It's as tired as I feel. Not even one bubble comes to the top. I hope the caffeine isn't as flat as the carbonation.

"All right. Enough stalling," I order. "What is going on?"

Chase ignores me, mesmerized by the ice floating in her

drink. Round and round she twirls the glass, watching the cubes grow smaller and smaller. Her wounded waif act is irritating me.

"Is it about Dallas' death?"

Nothing.

"Did you kill him?"

She drops her glass onto the table and bursts into sobs. I put my arm around her heaving shoulders and wait until the outburst fades into soft hiccups.

"Chase. If you don't talk to me I can't help you."

"Nobody can help me."

"Maybe not, but I can try. Now just calm down and tell me what happened." I hold her close and use my free hand to smooth the hair back from her forehead. She feels so small and hot. A curious mixture of protective desire washes over me. I want to hold her and kiss her and then beat myself to a pulp for taking advantage of her despair. A quick swallow of my disgusting drink brings me back to my senses. Chase takes a sip from hers and relaxes against me.

"I feel safe with you. For the first time since that night."

Guilt stabs through me, but I ignore it. "And you know you're safe with me. And so are your secrets."

"Mmmm," she says. Then becomes very quiet. Just as I am about to prod her, she murmurs, "I was there."

"Where?"

"In the alley. At the murder."

Now it is my turn to go quiet. My vision is blurring, but I'm sure I heard what I thought I'd heard. I wait.

"I couldn't believe he didn't want me anymore. It had to be a mistake, a misunderstanding. Maybe even a test."

"So you didn't leave after you ran out of the Tavern."

"No. I stopped when I reached the alley. And waited."

"For him." Instead of seeing the nod, I feel it.

"If I could get him alone, I knew we could talk things out. Make everything the way it used to be."

The desperate purity of her unrequited love is depressing. I can't say anything. Instead, I sip my drink and enjoy the feel of her soft breasts pushing against my chest. It's hard to believe that this beautiful child can be telling me a story of murder and mayhem. Hard to believe that a world that created her created Dallas. Dallas. The victim. I give her a squeeze. "Go on. You waited in the alley. Did anyone see you?"

"No…"

"What do you mean? Either someone saw you or they didn't."

Chase sighs. "While I waited I smoked. The police found the butts and my pack and put two and two together."

"What pack?" I push away and sit upright. The room is getting blurry and so is her story. Tears are running down her cheeks and fogging her glasses. Her eyes, normally distorted by the Coke bottle lenses she wore, are completely obscured.

"When—when I saw him come out, I was pulling out a cigarette and I-I started to shake. I dropped the pack and cigarettes went everywhere. I knelt down to p-pick them up and heard voices."

In an eerie recreation of that night, she begins to shake. I know this is very important and I have to be supportive, but the evening is wearing me down. "Who was it?"

"Dallas and-and the k-killer," she sobs.

"Chase, honey, this isn't helping. Who was it? Who is it?"

"I looked through the bushes and he was lying on his face. I was so s-scared. I should have helped him, but I didn't. I loved him, but I didn't help him. I killed him just as surely as the beast that crushed his head," she wails.

Now it's my turn to shake. This is completely out of my league. "You've got to tell the police."

"No," she cries and this shriek nearly crushes my head.

"Why not?"

"I just can't." Her panic is growing by the second.

"Okay. How about John? He's a lawyer. Or, better yet, how about the judge? We'll go together and talk to her. She's got connections and—"

"No. No. No. I knew it was a mistake. You don't understand. I never should have trusted you."

I try to put my arm back around her shoulders, but the girl pushes it away as if it were a python. Her eyes widen and she claps her hand over her mouth.

"Are you all right?"

"Going to be sick," she mutters between clenched teeth.

It has been a while since I'd affected a woman like this, but I still remember protocol. "Are you going to throw up?"

Chase gulps and nods.

"Do you want me to hold your hair?"

Her eyes bug out either in alarm or because she is transforming into a tree frog. She jumps to her feet and hops away. Within seconds, I hear retching emanating from the bathroom.

I struggle to my feet and test the bathroom door. Locked. "I guess she'd rather do it herself," I explain to the blue and pink aliens staring down from the canvasses on the walls. I stand for a minute and the room slowly spins. I try to concentrate on Chase' story. What did she mean? Was she afraid of being blamed? Just because she was there? Or did she see something? What is frightening her? The murderer or the police?

A sigh escapes as I settle onto the futon, carefully, and reach for my glass. The evening was so promising and is now just another disappointment. Like my drink. It is tepid, nauseating and just what I expect. I finish it off and lean back on the cushions. Slippery from condensation, the glass pops out of my fingers and behind the couch. Rolling on my stomach, I reach for the glass. It's just beyond my grasp. Stretching as far as I can, my fingertips brush the curved surface and it rolls away. Positioning my body on the edge of the futon, I reach for the elusive glass just as the couch slides away from the wall. In one motion, the tumbler dances away and I tumble onto the floor. Dizzy from the fall, I rest on the carpet in semi-darkness. The cushion settles back into place, creating a cozy canopy. Lulled by my clever alliteration and the rhythmic sounds of vomiting still seeping from the bathroom, I settle into my nest. The last thought I have before fading away is that Chase certainly doesn't have to worry about me taking advantage of her that night. A monk would have had more desire.

15

Polychromatic aliens with almond shaped eyes and O shaped mouths chase me through a night lit only by stars. The fact that my body is transforming into a frog is hindering my escape. With each leap, my amphibian shape becomes more distinct. A svelte tree frog would be okay, but it was more a bullfrog. An obese, out of shape bullfrog. I croak and leap and the aliens get closer and closer, their feet beating a tattoo into my brain. One last, superhuman—superfrog—effort and I leap into the night.

A clang followed by agony yanks me out of my dream. The aliens disappear, but not the pounding. That's inside my head. My skull connecting with some kind of overhang does not improve the hangover that is making my limbs react like so much linguini. At least I'm not a bullfrog anymore.

Lying quietly so as not to resurrect the aliens, I take stock of my surroundings. There's a wall to my left, a plastic frame to my right, and what has to be a cushion drooping overhead. Memories slowly march through my consciousness. The Tavern, the drive-through, the kid, Chase. Chase' apartment. Drinking with Chase at the tavern; drinking with her at her apartment. Chase throwing up. Me passing out. Another stellar performance. Jeez. No wonder I'm still single. And overwhelmed by a desire to pee.

Struggling against my hangover, limbs stiff from sleeping on a carpeted floor and the close confines, I have to shove the futon away from the wall before I can get out. This accomplished, I grab the edge to pull myself to my feet. Instead of couch cushions, there is something cold and rubbery. I jerk my hands back and slide to a sitting position. I peek over the side of the couch. The air is thick; difficult to move through and almost impossible to breathe. I close my eyes. Suck in a ragged breath. Force my eyes open. And look again. The rubbery thing is an arm, its light blue cast complementing the white couch. Chase' blank eyes stare into mine. I crumple down to the safety of the floor.

Once again, books fail me when faced with reality. An appropriate reaction would be a scream, fading into sobbing, maybe even beating on my chest and wailing "Oh the humanity…" Instead, my throat constricts, choked by the emotions crowding to escape. Terror, pain, sorrow, guilt. Guilt because a beautiful human being is dead and my main thought is that the need to pee is reaching catastrophic proportions. I am a monster; cold, cruel, unfeeling. But alive. The guilt escalates. Why am I still alive and the girl, with her entire life ahead of her, is dead? If I hadn't passed out, could I have prevented this? Is this my fault?

My brain shuts down. The only thing left is animal instinct. My tongue is plastered to the roof of my mouth and my bladder is rapidly approaching critical mass. Flipping onto my belly, I wriggle snakelike from behind the futon. Once clear, I consider standing but don't trust my quivering muscles. Evolving from reptile to crustacean, I rise from my stomach to my hands and knees and sidle across the floor. Once I reach the bathroom, my vocal cords loosen and a whimpering "ohgodohgodohgodohgod" escapes as I stagger towards the toilet.

Relief brings realization. I am ninety-nine percent sure this is a murder scene and I shouldn't have touched anything. Not only had I failed Chase in life, I am now failing her in death. A sob rises in my throat, but I gulp it down. There is no way I could have waited for the police in my previous condition. And I don't think the neighbors would have been sympathetic, even if I could have explained either my story or my plight in time. I say a quick prayer to Chase, asking for forgiveness, and concentrate on what to do next.

The trip from the bathroom back to the couch and its gruesome burden take a small eternity. I execute each step with delicate care, but I manage to hit every creaking board in the place. I don't remember the floor being this noisy when I was crawling across it, but I also don't remember paying much attention at the time. Eventually I'm standing over Chase. There's no question. She's stumbled off her mortal coil. And I've stumbled onto another dead body.

My first impulse is to run for it but luckily, reason takes over. First, half the town saw Chase and me tossing back whiskey at the Tavern. The other half witnessed our stop at the drive-through followed by the stumble to her apartment. But, most importantly, there is no way I can wipe down every surface that I've touched in the past twelve hours. And, thanks to the efficiency of the Yellow Springs police force, I am now a fingerprinted suspect. It would take no time at all to figure who had been in this apartment. No, the best course of action is to call the police and hope they believe my latest story. At least I hadn't fought with her while we were drinking at the Tavern. This thought has amazing restorative powers and I decide to call the authorities instead of cowering in fear. Best to use a neighbor's phone. Resolve strengthens my backbone and I stride towards the door. And stop, sweat beading up on my forehead.

Chase' apartment resides at the back of a house occupied by a group of Antioch students who raise pocket money by selling incense outside local establishments. And I'm pretty sure that isn't the only fragrant substance they sell. They probably won't be excited about lending me a phone to call the cops. That means the closest phone is at least a house away if not two. Or three or four. That means I have to leave the house in search of aid. And leave the body. A body that I don't believe died of natural causes. And a body I was fairly sure didn't commit suicide. That leaves murder. Potentially a double murder. As this logic worked its way through my hangover dulled head, my legs turn traitorous and buckle underneath me. I plop onto the floor. So what does all this mean?

Even though I'd never been accused of being the sharpest knife in the drawer, there are some things that even I can figure out. For instance, if there is a killer, he/she is probably lurking around outside to keep an eye on traffic in and out of the apartment. If they see me come out without having seen me go in, they'll assume I'm a witness. Which I am, but an extremely poor one. But they don't know that.

"God," I moan and bury my face in my hands. The convoluted thoughts are making my head hurt even worse. If I leave and the murderer sees me, what's one more murder? There's only one thing to do. Call on Chase' phone and then sit tight. There's only one more problem to add to the growing list. No phone. I moan again.

There's a slight possibility that Chase had stowed the phone in a closet to avoid disrupting her apartment's artistic décor with crass practicality, but I doubt it. Mainly because there's a phone jack beside me on a baseboard and it's staring back at me just as blankly as Chase had earlier.

Sanity leaves me for a while. I sit on the floor and hum, lost in a swirling fog. Human voices drag me out of it.

It takes me a moment to figure out where I am. And in that moment, the voices are gone. Panic-stricken I scuttle across the floor to the open window. Thank god Chase can't afford air conditioning, either. Clutching at the sill for support, I hang out of the window and try to locate the source of the voices. For one wild instant, I can't see anyone. The fifteen-foot drop, the trauma and the dregs of my hangover convince my stomach to show off by performing somersaults. Swallowing hard, I dig my fingernails into the wood and scan the horizon again. A couple is just about to turn the corner.

"Hey," I call out. The couple is almost out of sight. Terror gives me voice. "Hey!" This time they stop. I collapse in a grateful heap and then—they start walking again. "Are you deaf? Can't you hear me? Do you think I'm yelling for my health? There's a dead woman in here. Get the police. Get an ambulance. Are you brain dead? Too many drugs? Too much booze? How'd you get into college? Pay somebody to take your SAT's?"

One minute there is only the solitary couple. The next there is an ocean of faces staring up at the ranting lunatic in the sultry August morning. "Can somebody call the police?" I ask.

From the number of phones whipped out and the people scattering, I assume somebody called 911. Probably brought down the switchboard. While I wait, I pace. While I pace, I think. Down the length of the living room and then back again. As I make the circuit, I study the scene. Chase' obsession with cleanliness will both help and hurt me. Help because any evidence a killer left will be obvious. Hurt because any evidence I left will also be obvious. Hopefully the police will realize that even I am not so stupid as to kill the girl and then stay around. Unfortunately, the truth will throw doubt on that assumption. If only I hadn't drunk so much…

The memory brings me to a halt. Where are the glasses? I go into the kitchen and look around. Nothing. Back to the living area. Nothing. Except, of course, for the body on the couch. I stare at the girl and try to process the information. In the past forty years, there have only been a couple of grandparents tucked neatly into coffins—impossible to reconcile with the vibrant human beings I had played catch with and coerced into giving me one more cookie. In the past forty hours, two lives have been snuffed out right under my nose and I can't reconcile that either. It just isn't right. Death never is, but this goes beyond the peaceful and inevitable passing on of the elderly. Someone has deliberately stopped two beating hearts. It is unthinkable. I inhale deeply and try to jumpstart my brain.

Something else is wrong. Not just the dead girl. Not just the missing glasses. Something is out of place. I study the room, but I can't see it. Without consciously willing it, my feet move again as if they can force oxygen into my brain. One lap, two laps, faster and faster. The paint dripping from the ceiling oozes towards the oil paintings as if to engulf the shrieking aliens. The room spins and I know that if I don't stop on my own, my body will do it for me. I stand in front of the coffee table and breathe, slowing my pounding heart. Outside, sirens scream in the distance, their wail steadily rising as the police draw near. It hits me.

The ashtray is full. In that sanitized apartment where dust bunnies show nary a whisker, the wad of clay on the coffee table boasts a clutch of snaky ashes. And then the door bursts open and a child in a police uniform is pointing a gun at me and shrieking "Freeze!"

16

I talk as fast as I can, but the officers still frisk and handcuff me before I can spit out the entire story. The kid that'd had me in his sights only minutes before is now scrutinizing me like a bug under a microscope. He makes no attempt to uncuff me as his fellow officer, a young lady that looks at me as if I was Ted Bundy, stands close by, her pistol pointing down but itching to be pointed at me. The fact that I am probably the only person in the apartment old enough to drink doesn't give me warm fuzzies. Especially since the couple looks familiar. Details of the night Dallas was murdered are sketchy, but I remember thinking that Big Bird was probably the graduation speaker for the Yellow Springs' police department. May have even commented to that affect. That might be why the atmosphere is decidedly hostile in the apartment. Oh, and the dead body of course. Mustn't forget the dead body.

"Let's see what I have here," male baby cop says as he flips through his notes. "After getting drunk at the Tavern you bought some whiskey and came here to continue drinking."

That's the essence of last evening, but I dislike hearing it read back in that cold, matter of fact tone. Sounds tawdry. I nod.

"And you came here to tell the deceased that you saw who

killed Dallas McGuire."

"No, the deceased wanted to tell me."

"Why would the deceased want to tell you that you saw who killed Mr. McGuire?"

"She didn't." My protest's decibel level acts like a magnet. The girl cop's pistol whips up and looks me in the eye. The boy waves impatiently and, with way too much hesitation, his partner lowers her gun.

"There's no reason to get belligerent Mr. Barker."

"I'm not being belligerent. I'm being irritated." My head hurts, my back hurts, my wrists are hurting where the handcuffs are biting and the eyes boring into mine are narrowing to little slits. Not to mention the fact that the body draped across the cushions is being given as much respect as an afghan crocheted by a dotty old aunt. The last is creeping me out. I sigh. "Look. I didn't sleep very well and I'm too old to be drinking as much as I did last night. Plus, I'm not used to waking up next to a dead person."

The eyes relax slightly, probably in deference to my age. A curt nod and he says, "But you are making a habit of stumbling across them, aren't you Mr. Barker?"

Another tawdry reality I can't refute. Again, I nod.

"What did you come here for?"

I take a deep breath and try to dispel the innuendo packed into the simple question. "Chase was extremely agitated and wanted someone to talk to. The whiskey was to help her relax. She said she was in the alley the night Dallas was killed, was about to tell me what she saw and then she got sick and ran into the bathroom."

"And you fell off the couch and passed out."

"Right."

"Just as she was about to reveal a murderer."

"Right."

The woman child snickers and Deputy Fife grins. "Figured you weren't going to get any so it was a good time to catch forty winks?" The two don't even try to keep their hilarity a secret. They are still laughing when the ident technician shows up to gather evidence. Since he carries a digital camera in addition to his other paraphernalia, I gather he is also the photographer.

"That the body?" he asks and jerks his head towards Chase. I wait for a clever retort from the Keystone Kops, but they just nod gravely.

"That's her."

"That the perp?" This time the head is jerked towards me. My arms are cramping up.

"Mr. Barker is innocent until proven guilty." I want to hug the astute officer. "Although he looks guilty as sin." Spoke too soon. I want to smack the sanctimonious little twerp.

The photographer/technician nods and snaps pictures of every inch of the tiny apartment. The scene takes on a dreamlike air as the cop restarts his line of questioning to the cadence of snapping clicks and strobe-like flashes. The aliens looking down from the canvasses are no longer threatening, merely pitying.

"All right. You were on the floor. Passed out. Did you see anyone come in?"

"No. Even if I hadn't been passed out, which I was, I couldn't have seen anyone because the cushion obscured my vision."

Barney writes furiously, his little pink tongue poking out from clenched teeth. "Cushion obscured vision. Okay, did you hear anyone?"

"I was passed out." I think this is a clever plot to make me admit I hadn't passed out. If I had been awake, I'd admit it immediately as it would be a lot less embarrassing.

"That means no," the young lady explains, looking over her partner's shoulder. He nods and scratches this note onto the pad. The photographer lays his camera down and takes out a pad.

"What's that for?" I ask, dreading another interrogator.

"Gotta sketch the crime scene." I watch as he produces a tape measure and jots down the room's dimensions and relative positions of the furniture.

"Mr. Barker…"

"Sorry," If this lasts much longer, my legs will give out. My brain already has.

"You didn't see anything, you didn't hear anything, you woke up and your girlfriend was dead."

"She's not my girlfriend."

"I'm ready to gather evidence. Where do I start?" The technician asks his question with a look that implies he doesn't care if he starts in Alaska as long as he can get this over with. He punctuates the question by snapping latex gloves up to his wrists.

Barney shrugs. "The bathroom is as good a place as any."

"Are you going to take fingerprints?" Three pairs of eyes imply I'm not just an amateur, I'm a stupid amateur.

"Yeah. What's it to you?"

"I used the bathroom after I woke up. My prints are probably on—let's see—the door knob, the seat and—oh yeah—the handle."

Three pairs of eyes roll in unison. In disgust.

"Hey, when ya gotta go, ya gotta go."

The tech walks away shaking his head. A Dust Buster rumbles from the bathroom and then is silent. "Looks like our girl wasn't just into liquid entertainment," the tech proclaims as he comes back into the room holding up a bag of yellow tablets.

"What's that?" the lady cop asks.

"Don't know, but they're scattered all over the john. Not anything I recognize."

Deputy Fife looks at me. "Did you obtain these for the deceased?"

"No. I don't do drugs. Or obtain them," I say with what I hope is the right touch of earnest sincerity.

"Just alcohol," the kid cop sneers.

"Last I heard whiskey is legal."

A muscle jumps in his cheek. "Put the pills with the rest of the evidence," Barney snaps at the tech.

The guy shrugs and carries the bag back to the bathroom.

The two kids stare at me as we wait in the living room; the questioning over for now. I shift my weight from foot to foot, hoping that when this is over I'll still have full use of my limbs. I'm just about to plead with my captors to have pity and let me sit down when the door flies open. A florid man in a crumpled suit breezes into the apartment, filling the tiny space.

"Well, Harry, Lisa, how's it going?" the big man says as he claps the two officers on the back, nearly knocking them over.

"Everything is under control, Mr. Levin. Would you like to see my notes?" The flush on Barney's—sorry, Harry's—face tells volumes.

"Nah. I'm sure you've got all the detail this case is going to need."

The flush deepens and I feel a little sorry for the boy. He can't tell whether this is a compliment or a slam. I could clear it up for him. It's a slam. The detective glances around and notices my arms.

"For god's sake, Harry, uncuff the poor man. He didn't murder anyone. At least, not in this apartment." His laugh doesn't upset me as much as it should have. Not when it means blood is allowed to circulate through my arms again. Officer Lisa fumbles for the keys and unfastens my arms. I could kiss her. Or him. Or all of them. With tongue.

"Thanks," I say, rubbing my wrists and trying to ignore the tingling that shoots up my arms. "Since you know I didn't do it, do you know who did?"

"Nobody. It's obvious. This is suicide."

"How do you know that?"

Detective Levin hesitates and then, "I'm not in the habit of discussing cases with civilians, but since you found the body I guess you deserve a little something. First, the girl had a reputation for being depressed. Even tried to do away with herself before."

I can't argue the first point and I didn't know her well enough to argue the second. But I have a few observations of my own. "Chase wasn't the most cheerful girl in the world, but that doesn't mean she was ready to pack it in. Besides, doesn't it seem a little convenient that she saw a murder and then killed herself before she could tell what she saw?"

Levin considers this for a moment and then asks, "Did she tell you that?"

"Yes. Well. Sort of. She was there. And she was scared."

"That fits the pattern. She was looking for attention. A girl like that is a lot more interesting if she knows something nobody else does. When you didn't bite, she got depressed and—" He clicks his tongue against his teeth as he draws his finger across his throat in a slashing motion. Harry and Lisa nod in worldly-wise affirmation.

"That doesn't make sense. I was interested; I just passed out before she finished throwing up." This warrants a raised eyebrow, but I plow on. "And there are some suspicious things that need to be explained." Out of the corner of my eye I see the lab guy approaching the window. "Hey, I was leaning against that when I called for help. My prints will be all over it."

With a disgusted look, he shakes his head and sprinkles dust over the sill. Harry breaks in. "Is there anything you didn't touch, Mr. Barker?"

"The girl." There's a snort from the window and powder blows up in a cloud, transforming the tech's laughter into sneezes. Serves him right. "Look, I didn't know I'd have to account for my fingerprints or I'd have been more careful. Maybe even worn some gloves," I add.

"Isn't that taking safe sex a little too far?" Lisa says, nearly choking on her own wit. The only sounds less attractive than her giggles are Harry's.

A warm tingling crawls up my neck and I take one step towards the giggling pair, my hands clenched and rising. Levin lays a meaty paw on my forearm. He's not laughing; not even smiling. "What suspicious things?"

Deep breath. Count to five. "First, the very fact that she was depressed. She wanted to talk but she killed herself before she said anything." An encouraging nod and another deep breath. "We had drinks, but the glasses are gone."

The detective raises his eyebrows at Harry. Harry shrugs. "There's not a single dirty dish anywhere. Nothing drying in the drain."

"How about the dish towel? Is it wet?" I ask. Harry shrugs again. "See. It's obvious. There were at least two glasses, mine and Chase'. When the killer shows up, Chase fixes him a drink. Once he gets her to take the pills, he washes the glasses and puts them away to remove any fingerprints or traces of saliva."

"He?" Levin asks.

"Or she. I was using a neutral pronoun."

"Ah. What pills?" The tech scurries over with the bag. Levin looks them over and hands them back. "Were these hers?"

"I don't know," I admit. "I don't think so. But I can't be sure."

"Let's assume the killer brought them. Why would she take them?"

"I don't know," I pause. "Maybe the killer said they were anti-depressants or sleeping pills. They would help her."

"And she took these from a stranger? Someone she suspected of murder?"

"I don't have all the answers!" I start to yell, then lower my voice at Detective Levin's stern look.

"But you are a writer; a creative type used to filling in the gaps of a story."

"How do you know that?" I squirm at his encouraging tone. Creative maybe, but writer? Not doing very well in that department.

"All strangers in town are here for the workshop." He offers a slight smile. "And I interrogated you after the McGuire incident. Or did you forget?"

I squirm harder but let my pride take over. I ignore the question. "Maybe she knew the person, but didn't know they were involved in the killing."

"Hmmm… Interesting." The apartment is silent as the big man contemplates my scenario. "What else?"

"Chase was out of cigarettes, but there are ashes in the ashtray. The killer must have smoked with her. Or gave her some and she smoked them by herself."

"Maybe she had a stash and pulled them out after you fell asleep."

I shake my head. "She thought she had some hidden away, but couldn't find them."

"When she was so drunk she could barely make it up the stairs?" Officer Lisa's eyes are wide and innocent and totally unbelieving.

"Okay, she might have found them later, but she was obsessively neat; she wouldn't leave a full ashtray."

"You mean she was the kind of person who couldn't stand to let dirty dishes sit?" The eyes are even wider and more guileless.

"Is that all?" Levin breaks in. His tone is sincere, warm, encouraging but the steeliness in his eyes belies every bit of it.

I exhale slowly and say, "Look, if Chase had the pills, why was she interested in getting pot from the drive-though guy?"

"Did she buy pot from the drive-through guy?" Levin's steely eyes hardened even more. "Did you buy pot from the drive-through guy?"

"No. And she got mad at me. That's why I bought the whiskey."

Levin smiles again. Actually grins. "Well, Mr. Barker, this story—and your suspicions—will be checked out. But I'm curious. What do you write?"

The apartment is deadly quiet again. Everyone waits.

"Detective stories. Mysteries."

"Ahhh…"

"But not like this one!"

Levin's smile is now shark-like. His hand is once again on my arm. Light, but threatening. "Not like a juicy little murder full of sex and drugs and shadowy figures?"

"That's not what this is about," I insist. The hand tightens on my arm.

"Calm down. Mr. Barker. Calm down. This is real life, not

125

some Raymond Chandler scenario. Reality is usually just what it seems; boring. You've had a rough couple of days. Why don't you run along to your room and rest up? We'll do our job and you can do yours."

"I'm a bartender." This elicits the guffaws that were rumbling below the surface.

Harry snorts. "Even a bad detective wouldn't have fallen asleep just as a murderer was about to be revealed."

"Or before he got laid," adds Lisa. "The judge does have you pegged. You are a screw-up."

My memories clear like clouds before the sun. I remember where I'd seen the Keystone Kids. They were at my first murder. With the pistol and the handcuffs.

17

The quartet at the apartment has cop stuff to finish, so nobody offers me a ride. That's okay because the walk pumps oxygen to my brain and clears out the cobwebs. Sweat pours out of my skin either from the rising temperature and matching humidity, the last vestiges of the alcohol working its way through my veins or the scalding beverage I balance in one hand. I grabbed some coffee at a convenience store and it smells like paint thinner. It's probably having the same effect on my system. But it is also caffeine in a cheap, ingestible form. So here I am, just before noon, sweating, sipping and grimacing my way back to campus.

My plan was to get to my room and take a power nap. Once there, however, I alter the plan to include a shower before sleep. The rush of steamy water finishes clearing my brain; I must have slept more than I thought. The prospect of staying in the sauna masquerading as a room with visions of a pale blue Chase lying cold and still in my head is not appealing. Glancing at the clock, I realize that if I hustle I can just make the intensive. Being with people—breathing people—lifts my spirits and I head downstairs.

"Mr. Barker."

The high-pitched screech is easy to ignore, so I do, picking up my pace as I scoot through the living area. My hand is on the doorknob when the screech echoes.

"Mr. Barker."

A sigh escapes. "Yes, Mrs. Winthrop. What is it?"

"You didn't come home last night."

I am tempted to ignore the implied question, but tolerance for me in Yellow Springs is running thin. Antagonizing my landlady more than I already have isn't wise. "No, I didn't. I stayed...with a friend."

"Humph." Her lips are thin and white underneath her fuchsia lipstick. "And I can just imagine what kind of friend it was."

A dead one... A giggle created from hysteria and horror threatens. I choke it back and shrug.

"Well let me tell you one thing young man. This is a respectable house and I don't put up with shenanigans. You do what you want in whatever den of iniquity you've uncovered, but in my house you act like a gentleman. Don't you be bringing any friends back here and having wild parties or orgies or satanic rituals or anything like that."

Another giggle raises its ugly head and I know I have to get away from the self-righteous piece of pink and white fluff that bars my exit. "Wouldn't think of it. Sorry, but class. You know. Can't be late."

Her chest heaves and I know she is gearing up for another tirade, but I'm faster. I dart around her and through the door with the dexterity of Barry Sanders. The Lions would be proud. Touchdown and game.

The tiny victory over the dragon lady gives a bounce to my step as I head towards class. Thinking about something besides death and murder will do me good. After some cerebral exercise and a quick lunch, I'll give Angelica a call. By that time I'll be ready to Sherlock Holmes it again. Game plan firmly in place, I walk into the already full classroom. My exchange with Mrs. Winthrop has thrown my schedule off just a hair. I'm late, but not terribly. As soon as I locate a chair, the interruption will be over and we can all get down to the business of writing.

"Well, well, well. If it isn't the Grim Reaper. Late, but that's what we've come to expect. Looking for a chair, Mr. Barker or just picking out your next victim?"

As I stumble down the hall, Stephanie's nastiness and the slamming door still echoing in my head, I almost miss John's cheery hail.

"Rex, hey Rex. Wait up. If you can't give me my weight at least pity me my age."

At first I keep going, my earlier desire for human companionship burnt away. But John won't be ignored. The footsteps pick up and then he is on me, his breath gasping hot in my ear.

"Didn't you hear me? Hang on; let me catch my breath."

Unwilling to be accused of yet another death even if the real cause is being overweight and underexercised, I pause. John holds up one hand to keep me quiet while he uses the other to support himself against the wall. I wait. What else do I have to do?

"Man," John wheezes. He straightens up and his vast bulk kicks up a breeze in the stuffy hall; a breeze tainted with Obsession and sweat. My eyes are watering, but he is my friend. Maybe one of two.

"You okay?" I ask.

"Yeah, let's get out of here and into some fresh air."

I nod and follow him out into the sunshine.

John senses that I don't want to chat because he keeps quiet until we reach the sidewalk. And even then, he doesn't talk to me, but to a straw-hatted woman sitting on a bench. I groan when I read the title. "The Roach's Dream…"

"Have you gone native?" John bellows.

The woman, eyes hidden by huge black sunglasses and body swathed in neon-bright scarves that pass for a dress, doesn't laugh back. Instead, she snaps the book shut and throws it into a shrub that is nestled against the bench. She stands on be-sandled feet and pulls a Camel out of a pack. She lights it, blows a smoke ring and gestures at the bush. Ashes flick onto the leaves. "I can't believe anyone buys this garbage."

"The cigarettes or the literature?" I ask.

Judge Sylvia snorts as she inhales again. "You're being generous."

"I'm being sarcastic. And I'm with John. Are you becoming a Yellow Springer?"

"I thought I'd enjoy myself more if I blended. Since I'm not having much luck writing my memoirs, I figure I can be a literary groupie."

"And you think Stevie Nicks on acid is representative?"

Sylvia laughs and twirls. The scarves and the smoke tumbling around her body look as if a genie is about to appear. "Around here? Are you serious? I blend..." Still laughing, she flicks her cigarette into the grass.

I hold my breath, waiting for the dry weeds to burst into flames. But the weak tendril of smoke curls up and out. I exhale and a gasp escapes from my lungs. "Don't you know that only you can prevent forest fires?"

Sylvia links one arm in mine and one in John's. The look that passes between them makes me wince. For a brief moment, I wonder how Angelica is doing and then we are heading towards lunch.

"The butt was out before it even hit the ground," Sylvia says.

"Okay, but you're a judge for god's sake. A law enforcer. Not only is littering illegal, think of the wildlife. Millions of seagulls choke to death every year on cigarette butts."

"Seagulls," John snorts. "This is Ohio. There isn't a beach within a thousand miles."

"It doesn't have to be a seagull. It could be a—a that thing," I gesture with my free arm at a bright yellow something or other that flies past us and lights on a clump of pink topped weeds. "That beautiful bird could be flying along, see the butt, think 'My, a fat tasty caterpillar' and wham! He's choking to death. I'll bet none of his feathered friends know the Heimlich maneuver, either."

"Sorry to disappoint you, nature boy," Sylvia says, "but that's a goldfinch and he's a seed eater. He wouldn't be the eensyest bit tempted by a caterpillar. Even a fat one."

"Humph," I grumble in a perfect imitation of the landlady from hell.

"What are you so grumpy about?" Sylvia asks as she squeezes my arm.

"He's been like that since he strolled in late and Stephanie gave him hell," John explains.

"Who's Stephanie?"

"The instructor. And you'd be grumpy too if you'd spent your night with a corpse," I add. Neither seems shocked by my brutal comment. My grumpiness gets grumpier.

"Small town," John says. "News travels fast. Especially bad news."

"That seems to be the only kind floating around these days," I say, sinking into a depression. Again, the squeeze on my arm. It's nice.

"At least the police don't think you did this one," Sylvia adds.

"Who's the prime suspect?"

John shakes his head. "No one. The girl had a history of moodiness and substance abuse. Scuttlebutt is that it was only a matter of time. And that came from her friends."

"Maybe, but I feel responsible. I kept pouring alcohol down her and then I passed out when she wanted to talk. What kind of human being am I?"

John stops walking. "Let me have one of those Camels," he asks Sylvia. She frowns and then hands him one. He lights up and a blissful look flows over his face as he inhales. As he exhales, he flicks the ash off the glowing end and his shoulders slump. "You're not the only one feeling guilty. You know those pills they found?" he asks.

I nod. It's one of a string of memories burned into my brain. At least I hadn't 'obtained' those for her. We start moving again as John talks.

"The damndest thing. It's an experimental drug—Activex. Used to fight depression."

"Why's that odd? If Chase was depressed, it's not surprising that she took an anti-depressant."

"That's not the point," John wheezes. It's the pace we're setting and the thick, murky air we're trying to suck into our lungs. None of us is enjoying this forced march. Sylvia isn't sweating the way John and I are, but she's a lot quieter than normal. John, however, is on a roll. "I shouldn't be talking about this but—"

"Then don't," Sylvia snaps.

"But." John glares at her. Then he turns back to me. "My law firm is representing a client who was taking that drug and had a psychotic episode."

"A junkie?"

"No. A captain over at Wright Patterson Air Force Base. A doctor. He'd volunteered to be a human guinea pig and started thinking about taking out his family. Attacked a nurse's station at the hospital. Cost him his career and almost his marriage. I'm doing everything I can to keep him out of jail."

We've reached the cafeteria but there's a reluctance to go inside—a need to remain in the sunshine where girls don't kill themselves and doctors don't attack nurses. Of course, there are a few nurses I wouldn't mind taking a swing at... Still...

"And?" I prompt. John is gazing at a weathered poster that proclaims "George Bush is a serial killer!" and Sylvia is gazing at him with pain and concern and deeper emotions I can't fathom.

"If we'd worked faster, then the drug would be off the streets. Then Chase—and who knows how many others— would still be alive. The tragedy is that it gave them hope. Horrible, false hope that actually fed the disease."

There's a poignant silence and then Sylvia clears her throat with an impatient cough. "And if we all drank our Ovaltine and ate our oatmeal the world would be a rosy place. And girls like Chase would be teaching kindergartners to recycle cans instead of smoking and drinking and taking drugs and pining away over men who write literary trash."

John gives an embarrassed laugh, but I refuse to be diverted. "If it's experimental, how did she wind up with it?"

This time the laugh isn't embarrassed; it's pure John. Patronizing and smug. "How'd you get here? Turnip truck? Next time ask them to slow down and let you off so you don't fall on your head. College students want drugs. Drug dealers come to colleges. Antioch's a college. Got it?"

"Actually," Sylvia says with a crocodilian grin, "the police thought you'd gotten them for her. Especially after that kid in the drive-through offered to get you guys some pot."

"How'd you find out about that?" I ask, anger percolating just below the surface. Crawling like ants down my spine.

"Small town…"

"All right, all right. What changed their minds?"

"Let's just say the late, not-so-great Dallas had a reputation that went beyond just the ladies," John smirks.

"He dealt drugs?"

"He did have a certain entrepreneurial spirit that wasn't satisfied by selling literary tomes," Sylvia offers.

Ideas swim around in the mush that's left of my brain. "Maybe," I say, forming the words as carefully as the visions forming in my head. "Maybe Chase wasn't just afraid because she saw a murder. Maybe it was a drug deal that went bad."

"Now you're thinking," Sylvia says in an encouraging voice.

"But why didn't she go to the police? That would have solved everything."

"Unless," John says and then stops. He tosses the spent butt into the grass, his eyes darting side to side. He even glances over his shoulder as he gives a harsh cough. Still coughing, he croaks in a low rumble, "It's been my experience that cops have the best drugs."

Perspiration prickles on my forehead as a goose marches across my grave.

18

The last thing I want in my stomach is tofu. I beg off John and Sylvia and head back to my room. They stand and watch me go; a portly, sweating lawyer and a slender judge that rivals a bird of paradise. In spite of her finery and the brightness of the day, their stance has a somber aura that chills me. The walk back to my room is hotter than an oven and I welcome every second.

In spite of the blessed heat, dread builds as I approach the house. Being with the work shoppers is gruesome; being alone is worse. By the time I make it up the stairs and into the foyer, my pace matches that of an elderly tortoise. And, thinking of elderly reptiles, the thing I dread the most is my landlady. She hasn't sensed my presence, but I know it's only a matter of time. There's movement in the parlor and I brace for the shrill greeting.

"Hey sailor, got time for a lady?"

"Show me a lady and I'll show her the time," I whoop and wrap my arms around Angelica in a sweaty bear hug. "God are you a sight for a sore heart…"

"What?" Angelica laughs as she returns the hug, briefly, and then pulls away. "I think your brain melted down your back."

"I've had a pretty rough night."

"And that's different from every other night, how?" she teases. "Did your new girlfriend, Chase, wear you down? Or did she just leave you high and dry again?"

There's no way she could have known, but her grin stirs up the fury that's becoming an old friend. I slap her with the latest and watch her merriment dissolve.

"Chase killed herself?" Angelica whispers; face gray with shock. She trembles and I feel as guilty as I deserve. I put my arm around her shoulders and this time she doesn't pull away.

"That's the official story, but I have my doubts," I admit. "Let's get something to eat. Something cheap, fatty and totally un-Yellow Springish."

"You're on," she says and follows me out of warm Americana in search of cool modern day.

The thoroughly modern Burger King is worth disobeying the "Don't Leave Town" edict. The closest thing to fast food that Yellow Springs offers is a Kentucky Fried Chicken and it's too close to healthy for the mood I'm in. In order to get the grease craving satisfied, Angelica and I sneak out of town to the neighboring community of Xenia. The only thing we have to fear from this burg is a stray tornado or two.

The Whopper, fries and Coke are ambrosia, set in a paradise of air conditioning and plastic furniture. With the exception of her drink, which is diet, Angelica's meal matches mine. And so does her appetite. In the past week, I've learned that nothing whets a person's zest for eating like somebody else's death. We wolf down our sandwiches in silence and talk only when we start on the french fries.

"There's a lot of sense in what the police believe, Rex," Angelica says. "Chase wasn't the happiest of people and killing herself isn't hard to believe."

"In a vacuum that's true, but you can't discount everything else."

"Like the glasses?"

"Yeah. Would you wash, dry and put away dishes if you were planning suicide?"

Angelica chews on a fry much longer than the potato deserves and then washes it down with a slurp of Diet Coke. "No. *I* wouldn't. But you said Chase was obsessively neat. Most suicide victims tidy up their affairs. It would be in character for her to clean up this world before tackling the next."

"Okay, but that contradicts the ashtray."

"You've never smoked, have you?" The smirk is back, but this time it doesn't bother me.

"No. What's that got to do with anything?"

"You don't empty an ashtray as soon as you finish a cigarette. That's a good way to burn down a place. And while the late Chase may have been intent on doing away with herself, she most likely didn't want to go out ala Joan of Arc."

Instead of commenting, I munch a fry of my own. The girl is making sense and it's even more irritating than her smug attitude.

"Plus, she may have been smoking when the drugs took affect. Probably didn't have the chance to clean even if she'd wanted to."

More irritating every moment.

"The good thing about the cigarettes is that if there was a visitor, the butts can be used for identification. Especially if that's where Chase got the cigarettes. A person isn't going to bring along a pack just for someone to mooch. They'd smoke together."

"That's weird," I think back. I picture the apartment and everything I saw. "There weren't any butts. Just ashes."

The silence and the furrow in her pretty brow tell me I hit home. Finally, Angelica shakes her head. "Did the killer take away the butts?"

"Why wouldn't they clean the ashtray, then?"

"Well, you said she couldn't find her stash, maybe she found a different kind of stash."

"Like pot?"

Angelica nods. "Uh-huh. That would explain why she didn't tell you. You made it clear you don't approve of drugs.

When she came back into the living room she probably thought you'd left and began smoking as an escape. She smoked her joint down to the nub or didn't put it out and it burned away completely…"

"How do you know so much about smoking joints?"

"Don't interrupt. Anyway, the girl smoked in order to feel better, but it had the opposite affect and then she saw no reason to go on."

"Maybe…" More and more sensical. The woman is downright infuriating. "It doesn't matter."

Angelica stares in mid-chomp. With extreme effort, she finishes chewing her fry and gulps it down. "The death of someone you knew intimately doesn't matter?"

"That's not what I meant. And we weren't intimate. Never had the chance. I felt something for her and I'm sorry that she's no longer around, but I'm talking about the first murder."

"What about it?"

From the obsidian cast of her chocolate eyes, I know I have to talk fast to get Angelica back on my team. "There are two possibilities for Chase' death: suicide or murder, right?"

A nod, stiff and unrelenting.

"If it's suicide, it's only indirectly related to Dallas' murder if at all."

Another nod.

"If it's murder, the reason she was singled out is because she was a witness. Without knowing what Chase witnessed, I'm not sure how to figure out who killed her."

The third nod and, at last, the granite lady softens. "I think what you're saying is that there isn't anything to gain by pondering Chase' death. We need to concentrate on Dallas' murder and the rest will fall into place."

Relief manifests itself in a deep sigh, which is unfortunate because I'm drinking my Coke. Liquid flows out of the glass and onto the table. There's a delay while we clean up this mess and then we return to the real mess.

Angelica pulls out her phone and starts tapping.

"Calling someone?" I ask with the wonderment of a child

pressing their nose up against a candy store window. I really need to get one of those things.

"No," Angelica says, distracted with her typing. "Just organizing our notes. Ah, here it is. A list of motives. Unfortunately, even Mother Theresa would have rationalized wiping out Mr. McGuire."

"I've got anger, jealousy and drug deal."

"Drug deal?"

"This is a college; drugs are a way of life." I try to emulate John's patronizing tone and I must have succeeded because Angelica doesn't look happy.

"No kidding, Einstein, but what does that have to do with McGuire?"

"Oh. The police think he was a dealer. Turns out his animalistic charm wasn't the only reason the bimbos clustered around him like flies on a rib roast."

Angelica flinches at the simile. The buzzing from the trash receptacle doesn't help. I consider explaining that it's a quote, but decide to let it go.

"Where'd you hear that?"

"Flies on a rump roast?"

"No, and let's drop the flies, okay? About McGuire being a dealer."

"Sorry. Judge Sylvia."

"Ah. Our legal periscope. I still think it's weird that she's so friendly towards you. I would have thought as a judge she'd want to keep details of the investigation close to her chest."

I spread my hands and shrug. "Maybe she's just a decent person and doesn't want me to worry. The fact that she cares is probably an aspect of her persona that keeps getting her re-elected."

"All right," Angelica concedes and bends over her phone. A few taps and scrapes and she looks up. "Drug dealer duly noted. Next list. Possible suspects."

Ticking them off on my fingers I say, "Anger: John, Mr. Sharpe and anybody else that might have been stupid enough to ask him to critique their manuscript."

"Which would include you."

"But I didn't do it." I don't like the look in her eyes, so I move on. "Jealousy: Chase, Elmira and any other female he's dallied with in the past month."

"The memory in this thing isn't big enough for a complete list of potential suspects in this category," Angelica says, grinning wickedly.

I laugh and nod. "Same for anger. I say we stick with our original approach to only include the people we know."

"All right. You saw Dallas in action; was there anybody other than the obvious that should be included?"

A memory tickles and then flits away. My brain is turning into mush again. I shake my head. "No. And I think the drug angle only includes the college students. The writing suspects would bring their own joy potions, not rely on the local suppliers to help them out."

"Good point. Chase and Elmira."

I sigh, but this time I ensure my Coke is out of reach. "It's been three days and a death later and we haven't made much progress at all. I'm not going to have to worry about paying rent for twenty to life."

"At least you'll be able to concentrate on your writing." The mocha gaze is too innocent not to laugh. Angelica joins in. "Look, you're exhausted. Again. Try to relax and I'll see what I can dredge up on each of our suspects. Maybe there's something in their past that will identify who's capable of this level of violence."

"Or who's on the edge and only needed a nudge to drop off."

"Exactly," Angelica agrees and we gather our trays. We leave the modern sanctuary and, in way too short a time, pull up in front of the boarding house.

"Do you really have time for this?" I ask, concerned, but also reluctant to leave. Bad things happen to me left on my own.

"I've taken a few days off," she admits without looking in my direction.

"What does Derek think of all this?"

"I have no idea. Look, there's a lot to do and I'd better get to it."

Still reluctant I oblige and exit the car. She doesn't wave as her car pulls away and disappears down the oak lined street. I turn to enter my abode, then keep turning and head down the sidewalk. My exhaustion isn't physical; it's soulful.

In spite of my aversion to exercise or anything healthy, a walk is usually what clears my head. And right now, it definitely needs clearing. Luckily, Yellow Springs is perfect for people looking to exercise their mind through their legs. Within minutes, I am at the entrance to Glen Helen and its promise of soothing forest peace. The glen is cool and welcoming, unlike a few days (years?) ago when I had just come to the village and was full of hope and innocence and fear of tree huggers. I head down some limestone steps and turn right onto a leaf strewn trail. In the shady glen, the temperature has dropped along with the elevation and I feel relaxation flowing over me. A bend in the trail and a bench with a lone occupant comes into view.

Mr. Sharpe huddles on the wooden seat, his elbows propped on his knees and supporting his balding head in blue-veined hands. He is muttering to himself. My first inclination is to back away, leaving the old man to whatever contemplation he is lost in, but I need information. And I am fast deciding that my needs supersede anyone else's desire for privacy.

"Mind if I join you?" I ask in my jauntiest 'I want to be your friend' voice. The old man starts and peers at me as if trying to place where he might have seen me before. Without waiting for an answer, I sit down.

"Uh—yes, certainly—I mean no, I don't. Oh my," Mr. Sharpe stammers and is quiet. His hands are trembling and he twists them in and out. If I wait for him to start the conversation, I'll be convicted before he gets past the stammering stage. Time for a bold move.

"Is there something you need to talk about?" I ask in a gentle but firm voice.

He jumps again and scrutinizes me with eyes that remind me of a furtive rodent. His twitching nose completes the vision and I bite my tongue to keep from laughing.

"Why would you think that?"

"Because we've all been through a terrible ordeal in the past few days. Even though I know I didn't do it, I still feel kind of guilty because I was so pissed about what McGuire said about my manuscript. Makes me an accessory of sorts. I figured others might feel the same way."

Mr. Sharpe does the last thing I expect. He begins to cry. Not loudly or with abandon, just a snuffling kind of cry with tears running down his lined cheeks. He fishes around in his pants pocket and produces a handkerchief. Blowing loudly into it quiets the snuffling, but doesn't do much for the tears. "I should go to the police," he says. I notice his hands aren't trembling any more. "They're going to find out soon enough. It wasn't Peg's fault, you know."

His eyes are no longer furtive, only desperate for understanding. I nod.

"She came here with hopes and dreams and her lovely manuscript. It was the mirror to her soul—deep and good. Beautiful. But she met him." He spits the words out and his eyes harden. "She was different when she came back; literary and cynical, her goodness destroyed. Before I knew it, she'd passed on to another plane of existence."

"Did she take her life? Like Chase?"

"Are you comparing that little trollop to my beloved wife?" he demands, a rodent again. A nasty, biting little rat.

"No, not at all. I'm just trying to get a pattern; put the pieces together." Again a fleeting memory, but it's too ethereal. I focus on the now ranting dialogue.

"I came to confront him. I brought the manuscript as a last chance for redemption. But he didn't recognize it! Or at least, he claimed he didn't. Claimed he didn't remember Peg. Not even when I showed him her picture. He just laughed. He laughed at me!" Mr. Sharpe jumps to his feet and is pacing back and forth.

"You said it was five years ago. There have probably been a lot of women since then."

Mr. Sharpe freezes, his hands twisted into claws. "Are you saying my Peg was just one in a line of floozies? Someone to be dallied with and cast aside?"

Mouth gaping, I move my head side to side.

The old man clenches his hands into shriveled fists and starts towards me. Then he stops and says, "You're as stupid as everyone claims." He swivels around and trots off down the trail. "You know nothing, nothing…" The last word disappearing along with him.

For a few seconds I sit on the bench and shake, letting the venom work its way out. Not for the first time that week, I regret my aversion to modern gadgets. A cell phone would be very comforting right now…

This time the boarding house is a welcome sanctuary, especially since Mrs. Winthrop is nowhere around. I use the parlor phone to call Angelica, but get her voice mail. I leave a message so she knows it's me and not her big chance to win a cruise to Jamaica and hang up the phone. I only wait a few minutes before the phone rings. The jingling brings my landlady front and center, but I beat her to the phone.

"It's for me," I assure her. Mrs. Winthrop turns on one heel and bustles away, but most likely not very far.

"What's up?" asks a tinny Angelica.

"Just had an interesting discussion with Mr. Sharpe."

"Oh?"

"Uh-huh. His wife was here five years ago and it sounds as if she fell under the spell of the infamous Dallas McGuire."

A pause, then, "Why wait so long?"

"Don't know. Could be interesting. Maybe she committed suicide. There might be another Chase lurking in the past."

"Did he actually say she was dead or did he use euphemisms?"

I think back and attempt to recall the exact wording. "Something about departing and going on to another plane…"

"Sometimes people cover up the humiliation of being deserted by claiming the departee has passed on. More dignity. My bet is that Peg's higher plane was United."

She clicks off and I hang up the receiver.   "Good-bye Mrs. Winthrop," I sing as I tromp up to my room. A loud 'humph' accompanies me.

19

The room holds my attention for about an hour. Just long enough to open every pore in my body. In an effort to lower my body temperature, I take another shower. To be truthful, there's an ulterior motive. The more showers I enjoy the less profit Mrs. Winthrop enjoys. The thought brings a grin to my face and a song in my heart as I dress. I'm still cheerful even though damp patches are spreading under my arms and meeting in the center of my back. I decide not to melt alone and head downstairs to the relative coolness of the parlor.

The professor is showing off his latest coconut-based technological device to Gilligan when a strange idea hits me. Alcohol holds no temptation and neither does the opposite sex but I can't sit here amidst the gloomy dust and let my cerebral hemispheres melt into each other. I'd paid for a wealth of creative opportunities and had only availed myself of a fraction of them, now is the time to get my money's worth. And maybe some air conditioning. A quick stop by my room to brush the cobwebs off my manuscript, grab a notebook and rescue a pencil from under the bed—surprise, more cobwebs—and I'm off.

While workshop days are devoted to listening to those who had made it explain how they made it, night sessions are set aside for the other half. Actually more like the other ninety-nine/one hundredths. In addition to more lectures on "How I Sold My First Book / Short Story / Poem / Song / Screenplay / Greeting Card" and panel discussions of why the other person's first book / short story / poem / song / screenplay / greeting card aren't worthy of being bought, there are a series of writing groups. These sessions are comprised of writers at various levels of development who are eager to critique and be critiqued. This is what I've been missing. To have my manuscript discussed by a collection of my peers, without malice or humiliation, is just what I need to get my creative wheels turning. My enthusiasm swells when I select the long fiction group and realize I'm early. It's an omen.

Scanning the room is quick since there are only a few chairs occupied. And there isn't a single familiar face. The evening is getting better and better. I select a chair beside a wispy looking woman and plop down.

"What's that?" I ask and point to a manila envelope she clutches to her chest.

Her eyes slide left to right and then stop dead center and bore into mine.

"Why?"

"Just curious." I wave mine. "I have one too. See?"

Again, the sideways look and then she relaxes. A little.

"What do you write?"

"Horror." The intensity with which she whispers the word—and still grips the envelope—give me a chill. I check out the room's other occupants, but two are engrossed in a conversation and the others scattered about the room are busy ignoring everyone else in the room. I'm on my own.

"Like Stephen King?"

The intensity deepens and a toothy grin splits her face. Before that moment, I hadn't realized how much her gray streaked hair resembles Medusa. Or one of her sisters. "Interesting comparison," she says. "My daughter says I'm better than King. And she should know since she's read everything he's ever written. Of course, it's not all King."

"No?" I ask as politely as I can. I've heard it's not good to antagonize the deeply disturbed. Or is that sleepwalkers? Either way, it fits.

"No; that would be stealing. I have some Dean Koontz in here as well. Let me give you a visual," she says.

"Please," I waggle my fingers in her general direction, indicating *Proceed.*

The woman relinquishes the envelope and, in a precise, deliberate manner, lays the manuscript on the table in front of her. Once it is perfectly square, she looks at me. Fire burns from her pale green eyes. "Think of King here and Koontz here." She rests her hands on the table, shoulder width apart and palms facing inward. "Got that?"

I nod.

"Now…" With a single chopping motion that would have made Lizzie Borden proud, she brings both hands down on the unsuspecting manuscript. "I'm right here. Dead center."

"Uh-huh," I say in my most profound manner. "And this is what your daughter thinks?"

"And my sister."

"I see. Does anyone not related to you feel this way?"

"What do you mean?" she snaps and snatches up the envelope. Within seconds, it is nestled back in its rightful place against her bosom.

"Have you sent it to a publisher or an agent?"

"I-I couldn't. There's no way. Never."

"Why not?"

"What if they don't like it?" Her panic is building, becoming a tangible entity in the close room. Heads turn our direction. At least we're not being ignored any more.

"What if somebody does? Lots of people like Koontz and even more like King. Think of the fans that would love a combination."

"Oh, I couldn't take that chance." She turns away, her rigid back signaling that our brief relationship is over. More people are drifting in and she studies each one, probably checking to see if they're plagiarists. I feel movement beside me and welcome the new diversion.

"Hi." I say and extend my hand to Ichabod Crane, who had taken the neighboring seat.

"Hi. Oscar," he says and returns the handshake. His smile is warm and friendly, his eyes likewise. In spite of the shiny pate fringed by thinning hair, I put him in his early thirties.

"Rex. What are you writing?" I ask and point to a green folder.

"Novel. First chapter. Thought I'd toss it out and see what everyone thinks."

"Great idea," I say. "How far have you gotten?"

"I told you," Oscar says with a slight frown. "This is the first chapter."

"Oh, sure."

"Don't want to get too far ahead and then find it's all wrong."

I nod. "Good thinking. How long have you been working on it?"

"Ten years."

"Ten years?" This doesn't seem like a good time to mention that I wrote my chapter in an hour. With a hangover.

"Of course, the whole thing is up here," he says as he taps his shiny forehead. "But it's like a fine wine. Don't want to serve up the words before their time."

"Of course," I echo and sit back to re-evaluate my place in this society. The introspection is cut short by a cheerful dumpling in a blue denim jumper.

"Hello, fellow writers. I see we have some new faces. I'm Betsy; I'll be your mentor. Does everybody have their manuscripts?"

Before anyone can answer, a swarm of white tee-shirted students descends. When they pull back, the assorted folders, envelopes and papers that had littered the table are gone. The aspiring writers look as bad as I feel; dazed, scared, robbed.

"Don't worry," Betsy assures us. Her cheery, dimpled face has a predatory cast that makes my stomach tighten. "They'll be right back. With copies. And then we can begin the fun."

Her carnivorous smile gets broader and I feel the group move together. It's us against her. And I have no doubt as to who would win.

Shortly, the novitiates return and pass out scores of pages. A cardinal rule of writers' groups is that everyone has to say something positive. You also have the option of writing comments on the manuscripts, likewise positive. Once a critique is finished, you give them back to the authors so they can review their peers' judgments. I'm sure Lizzie will count each page to ensure no one has absconded with her precious scribblings.

Ichabod/Oscar's chapter isn't too bad so it's easy to be encouraging. Of course, after ten years, it should have made Hemingway weep. In a good way. And Lizzie's story has some merit as well. In spite of her family's opinions, it has neither the character development of King nor the grim intensity of Koontz, but it isn't hateful. She blushes as we praise her work and she even relaxes a little. Two other pieces and I breathe a sigh of relief. It appears that I am going to slide past the time limit without going under the microscope. Or the knife.

"Let's see. The big hand has stabbed the six and the little hand is chasing the ten, so it looks as if we'll only have time for one more," chirps Betsy scanning the room for victims. "Any volunteers? Ah yes, Mr.? You," she says and waves at my pile of copies.

Oscar pokes me in the side and Lizzie beams at me with a toothy grin. Surrounded by sharks. They need a sacrifice and I have to give them one. I split my stack of copies and watch as they pass from hand to hand. Within seconds, the group bends over my masterpiece and I am sweating out their judgment. As the pages turn, a few cheeks turn bright red and here and there giggles break out. I want to make a break for it, but the literary groupies sit by the doors; no doubt to keep the faint of heart from escaping. Finally, the last pages are put aside along with pens and other writing implements. It's hard to believe I'm this worried about what a group of strangers will say. Empathy for Lizzie builds.

"Well," Betsy says, her face beaming. "How interesting, Mr. Barker. I applaud your courage."

"My courage?"

"Yes! It's obvious you are trying your hand at the very difficult genre of farce." She giggles and the group, happy to let go, let out relieved giggles throughout the room. "Yes. Wilde, Shaw, you're not in their league, of course, but bravo. Bravo!" Clapping her hands in mock applause, she turns to her left and indicates the woman should take over.

The group is busily scribbling and the selected woman is no exception. There are variations on "Hilarious." "Surreal" "Warhol in print" "Vivid imagery" Just when I think it can't get more humiliating, a white-haired lady, strongly reminiscent of my Aunt Ethel, takes her turn. With a high, quavery giggle she says, "Dear, your use of profanity makes me all tingly. Makes me wish I was sixty again…" The eighty-year-old eyes batting at me convert the humiliation into nausea. On my way out, careful to avoid my fellow writers, I dump my marked up copies in the trash.

20

The room is stuffy, the maid service leaves a lot to be desired, the television in the common room receives two local channels, barely, the landlady is the modern incarnation of Attila the Hun, but the shower warrants no complaints. It is the perfect beginning to what is sure to be a less than perfect day. Hot, steamy bullets of water assault my body and I luxuriate beneath the attack; not sure how long I've been in here and not sure when I will leave. A sudden pounding at the door makes the decision for me.

"What are you doing in there? Trying to break me? I'm not a rich woman; hot water isn't free. Stay in there much longer and I'll charge you extra…"

With a sigh, I cut off the faucets and step out of the tub. Misty clouds obscure the walls and, for a second, I'm transported to Avalon. I close my eyes and breathe in the damp air, envisioning a sultry moss-covered forest glade far away from the reality of Yellow Springs. Titania and Puck are dancing just around the corner.

"It's about time. Others are waiting you know."

Another sigh escapes as I open my eyes. Where is Oberon when I need him? "Yes, I know, Mrs. Winthrop. I'll be out in a minute," I yell and wait for some indication that this has placated the beldam on the other side of the door. Nothing. No grunt of acceptance, no footsteps tromping down the hall, no whistling intake of air that implies she has imploded from the strength of my voice. Nothing. I dry with slow, careful strokes, dreading what lurks in the hall.

Underwear. Inspected for holes—none. Good. Shaving cream slathered liberally. Gillette Good News razor scraped across my chin, cheeks and under my nose. Skin inspected for pimples and wild hairs. None found. Good. One half-inch Crest Whitening Tartar-control paste positioned in the center of my toothbrush. Night deposited scum eradicated with vigorous strokes. Breath expelled into hand and sniffed. Minty fresh. Good. Liberal deodorant application. Socks, pants, shoes. Comb dragged through damp hair. A few loose strands deposited in trash can, but nothing to be too concerned about. Towel folded neatly. Toiletry items tucked into plastic Wal-Mart bag. One last look in mirror, shoulders back, deep breath and—the opening of the door.

"I thought you said just a minute."

"It was a football minute," I explain and push by the glaring crone.

"Where's your shirt? This is a decent place. I don't allow weirdoes. You don't belong to some kind of outlandish religion, do you?"

"Actually yes. I'm a Rotarian," I snap and shut off the next comment by slamming my door.

My room is a peaceful contrast to the malevolence in the hall. I lean against the door and hold my head in my hands. A slight throbbing signals the return of the headache that had awakened me hours before the alarm clock. Maybe it's a sign. Abstinence is healthy for others, deadly for me. Or it maybe it's the writing environment. Interacting with creative literary types is wearing on me. Luckily, I won't be subjected to the writing life today. All sessions cancelled out of respect for Dallas' funeral. The saddest part of the whole situation is that I feel better equipped to handle death than the company of my fellow artistes.

E. SABBAG

Walking to the funeral service seems like a good idea. My reasoning is that the exercise will clear my head. And it does. The downside is that even wearing a short-sleeved shirt doesn't stave off the sweat my body manufactures to counter the August heat. By the time I reach the amphitheater where loved ones will pay their final respects, every inch of my body is drenched. I choose a seat near the back and settle in to watch the crowd assemble. Since the closest tree is practically in the next state, the concrete benches have been drinking up sunshine for hours and achieved kiln status. Heat pounds me from every angle as I wait for the service to begin.

"Your attention to hygiene is admirable, but aren't you supposed to dry off after you take a shower?"

"Angelica," I cry and whip around to greet the owner of that lovely voice. She holds up her hand palm out to repel my hug.

"Much as I love you, big guy, I'm afraid we'd stick," she laughs. I slide over to give her room. "Anything exciting happen since we talked?" She scans the growing crowd as if expecting to pick out the murderer by divination. I scan her, intrigued by her seductive profile. The sleeveless black dress she wears contrasts elegantly with her blond hair and fresh, simple makeup. Makeup that almost conceals the bruise-like circles under her eyes.

"Did you sleep at all last night?"

Without turning her attention from the masses, Angelica waves me off. "Too much to do. Is that Mr. Sharpe?" she asks, squinting into the glare bouncing off the white concrete. I strain to make out the person in question. It's difficult to be sure about the one, but the two behemoths that flank him are unmistakable.

"Since the Culbreaths are standing guard, it has to be," Angelica nods and I point to more familiar faces entering the arena. "Looks as if legal counsel has arrived." It's comforting to note that John is not only wetter than I am; his face is redder. In the name of public health, I hope the ceremony is

152

short.

"I learned some extremely interesting things about him," Angelica murmurs.

"John?"

"No." This time it's a hiss. "Mr. Sharpe. Our elderly gentleman made the newspapers," she says and taps her purse.

"Let me see," I say and reach for the bag. At that moment, a red-eyed woman steps up to the podium in a swirl of black satin skirts. With her wild red hair, lace up corselet and pointed-toe leather boots, she would have been burned at the stake in old Salem. Maybe even in new Salem. She sniffs and the resulting squeal from the microphone prohibits further conversation. I tear my attention from the bag and its intriguing contents to Dallas' life review.

As glowing tribute follows glowing tribute, I wonder if they're talking about the man I'd met or if I'm attending the wrong service. My mind drifts as accolades for the late great flow around and over me. Accolades delivered by female voices. Glancing around, I notice that the majority of the attendees are of the female persuasion. I relax. Right service; only Dallas commanded the adulation of so many girlie groupies. This is confirmed when Elmira takes the stage. Her eulogy, much like the others, is difficult to follow, mostly because it's broken up by frequent bursts of sobbing. I'm sure she and the others speak from the heart, but even sincere emotion becomes tedious after it's echoed a million times. The final announcement is met with a certain level of relief.

The Stevie Nicks clone that led the service steps back up to the podium. "As per Dallas' wishes, he will not be relegated to the cold ground." I shift on the baker's stone that supports my butt. If he had wanted to be laid to rest in cold ground, where would they have found it? "Instead, his ashes will be released to the cosmos. For various reasons, it will be a private ceremony and I regret that only his closest friends may attend. Thank you all for coming and I know that in whatever form Dallas has taken, he thanks you as well." She sobs and another member of the coven helps her off the platform. Unisex youths clad in funereal black leather guide the mourners out, front rows first. We sit and watch the procession, waiting our turn.

Angela leans over and, close to my ear, whispers, "Since it's against health regulations to scatter ashes anywhere, I can guess why only close friends are invited."

I nod. "That explains no coffin, but why isn't there a minister?"

She shrugs. "My guess is that Mr. McGuire didn't belong to a structured religion. Too much competition."

A giggle escapes and several of the mourners pause long enough to glare at my impropriety. The rest of the laughter is stifled by a cough. This placates them and the crowd moves on without incident.

"Did you see where any of the suspects went?"

Angelica shakes her head. Even she is starting to look a little wilted. "Lost them in the crowd. That's okay; we'll catch up to them later." Within minutes, the stands are clear and we're allowed to make our exit. A white head of hair catches my attention.

"Hey." I nudge Angelica with my elbow. "Looks as if Mr. Sharpe has ditched Humpty and Dumpty." Instead of the Culbreath twins, the old man is engaged in an animated conversation with a statuesque blonde. She's partially obscured by a large bush so I maneuver Angelica to where we can both get a look. "That's strange,"

"What?" asks Angelica, straining to see the couple.

"Remember the woman that was talking to Chase?"

"Bambi or Casey or something like that?"

"No," I say, a little sharply. "Kandi. Remember she made a comment about a fan club?"

Angelica nods. "Must have been the 'I Love Dallas McGuire But He Jilted Me Because I'm Not Good Enough' club."

"That's what I'm thinking,"

Angelica's brow furrows and then it clears. She roots through her bag. "Aha," she proclaims and holds up a sheaf of crumpled papers. She thrusts her purse at me and flips through the pages. They are a collection of web printouts and newspaper copies. About halfway down the pile, Angelica stops, studies a page, studies Kandi and then back to the paper. She shakes her head and asks, "What do you think?" as she holds out the paper.

I trade her purse for the sheet and look at it. It's a copy of a newspaper article from the Columbus Dispatch. A couple is arguing on the steps of the courthouse surrounded by a crowd of spectators, police officers and photographers. The man is definitely Mr. Sharpe, but the woman is a stranger. Chunky, dark-haired, glasses; not unattractive, but not familiar. I shrug. "So?"

"Block out the cosmetics; look at her stance, the set of her mouth, the way she's shaking her finger, the relative height of the two."

The heat is obviously getting to my friend. Not wanting to push her over the edge, I study the picture once more and then study Kandi. The image clicks into focus. "It's Peg; the missing wife," I say and look back at the paper. Now that I'd made the connection, it's hard to believe I'd ever missed it.

Angelica nods. "Family reunions are so touching, don't you think?"

Before I can respond, somebody else does. "Family reunion? Don't tell me there's another angel on earth," John says as he grins at Angelica.

To my astonishment, she grins back. "Not my family," she admits, a pink flush staining her cheeks.

"That's a shame."

"Whose then?" Sylvia says with a sharper tone than is warranted. I don't blame her though; the two are nauseating. Before I can stop her, the judge snatches the paper and scans the article. She looks at the picture then towards the still arguing Sharpes. "Well, well, well," she murmurs. "Isn't it interesting the way people express grief? It's what funerals are all about." Without taking her eyes from the distant couple, Sylvia hands me the sheet. I pass it to Angelica who tucks it back into her purse.

"Were you invited to the scattering?" John asks.

"Not only do I not want to be counted as a close friend," Angelica says, "I doubt there will be air conditioning."

I nod. "Same here. I've enjoyed about all the great out of doors I can stand for one day."

"Then how about a cold one? My treat," John offers.

Not only does Sylvia look as if she'd rather eat nails, I'm eager to see what else Angelica has dug up. Before I can say anything, however, Angelica comes through. "Thanks, but I'm going to take a rain check. Rex and I have some errands to run."

The emotions in the group run the gamut with Sylvia and me sharing the happy end of the scale. Angelica hooks her arm through mine and leads me away.

"I don't mind running errands, but I hope you aren't teasing about the air conditioning," I say as my skin slides against hers.

"You should know me by now; I don't tease about the important things in life. Let's just hope my Arid Extra Dry lives up to its advertising." We climb into her car and drive away, air conditioning on high.

21

Even though the drive back to the boarding house is short, the air conditioning kicks in and brings my core temperature out of the danger zone. When Angelica pulls around back to the parking area, I stall, refusing to get out of the blessed coolness until forced.

"What about the errands you mentioned? Where do you need to go?" I ask.

"Right here. You can help me carry in the suitcases," Angelica says as she turns off the car and hops out. I sit in disbelief, my mind refusing to accept this turn of events. Unfortunately, once the ignition is off, so is the air. It's only a few seconds before I follow her lead.

They aren't actually suitcases. One is a gym bag-type thing, another is what I call an overnight bag and the last is a laptop case leaning against Angelica's leg. "I'm going to be girlie and let you carry those in," she says as she closes the trunk and throws her keys in her purse.

Without a backward look, she picks up the laptop and heads towards the back entrance as if she owns the place. I've been here almost a week and I didn't know the back door existed. Angelica passes through the door and I scramble to follow her in, afraid I'll lose her in the unexplored section of my home away from home. I grab the bags and almost dislocate my shoulder. The gym bag weighs more than I do. With superhuman effort, I heave it over my shoulder and sprint towards the building.

Two things smack me in the face as I come in through the secret entrance. One is that the décor is bright, modern and comfortable. The second is that it's cool. Blessedly cool. Somebody is smuggling modern convenience into warm Americana. And nobody told me about it. I come around a corner just in time to see Angelica darting through a door at the end of the hallway. I sprint to catch up with her; she has a lot to explain. As I pass through this door, the surroundings click back into focus. Old, stodgy, hot. I'm standing in the boarding house lobby watching Angelica and Mrs. Winthrop chat as if they are dear friends catching up on each other's life.

"What is going on and what in the hell do you have in this bag?" I demand, causing the conversation to sputter to a halt.

"Don't swear, dear," Angelica says. "You know, if you'd work out a little more you wouldn't be such a wimp. Then you could handle two little bitty bags without setting yourself up for heart failure." She shrugs and rolls her eyes towards Mrs. Winthrop who smiles and pats Angelica's arm.

"Men. And a writer to boot." The two women laugh and I struggle to rise above my newfound stature.

"I'll bet you've seen it all, Gladys," Angelica says.

"Oh my dear, the stories I could tell. That's why it's lovely to have you stay here. Gives me that sanity break that is critical to survival."

Gladys? Staying here? My world is once more spinning out of control. "What do you mean, staying here?" I ask, taking deep breaths to circumvent the dizziness that is overwhelming me. "I thought there weren't any more rooms. And what about Derek? Is he coming too?"

"Derek has his own business to take care of," Angelica says.

The look on Mrs. Winthrop's face is suddenly mirrored in Angelica's. Neither gives me warm fuzzies. Alarms are clanging at all levels, but I ignore them and push onward.

"He's okay with you coming by yourself, then?" I should have thought that comment through. The temperature plummets to sub-arctic. Who needs air conditioning when I can't keep my mouth shut?

"Contrary to societal beliefs, I do not make decisions solely on the desires of my significant other," Angelica snaps. "I can think on my own, even though I am missing that all important appendage between my legs."

Ouch. Luckily, no one expects me to respond. The two women march away, leaving me to scramble behind with the luggage. I follow them up the left stairway, which I had assumed led to the left wing of the house. I was right, but what I didn't realize is that the left wing isn't just a separate part of the house. It's a separate world. A separate time.

Gone is the paisley wallpaper and dingy woodwork. Bright paint and gleaming oak adorn these halls. Underfoot, thick rugs cover hardwood floors to not only protect the varnish but also cushion the feet. On the other side—my side—four rooms crowd onto a floor and fight over one bathroom. As Mrs. Winthrop throws open the door to Angelica's suite, I guess that this side boasts two rooms per floor, max. Each with their own bathroom. And refrigerator. And—and air conditioning.

"This is too much," I announce as I throw the bags onto the bed. Queen size.

Angelica and Gladys turn with matching expressions of surprise. "I don't think so," Angelica counters. "The rate is extremely reasonable. Especially with so many amenities."

"That's not what I'm talking about," I whine. The volume is creeping up, but I don't care. "Why don't I have air conditioning? And a bed made in the twenty-first century?"

"You're a writer," Mrs. Winthrop says and turns to Angelica. "The data link is right beside the phone line, so it shouldn't be too hard to find. There's Pay Per View, but I think HBO is better for no extra charge. If you need anything at all, don't hesitate to ask. Enjoy dear," and the old bat is gone. I round on Angelica who is putting her clothes away. In a real closet.

"What does she mean, 'You're a writer'?"

"Isn't she classic? I just love her. A real American classic."

"That's great, but what does she mean?"

"Two things, really. First is that the best writers came from the turn of the century. The quality of books has slid down hill this century therefore modernization breeds substandard literature. Also, suffering is an integral part of an artist's life. As a result, she keeps the right wing of the house in its original state and reserves it for writers, artists, basically any creative type."

"Sadistic old biddy." I move the thermostat down a notch. Angelica moves it back.

"Quit grumbling and fix yourself a drink. I brought sodas, Jack Daniels and beer. Take your pick. I'll call in sandwiches and we can start going over the information I've uncovered," she says and picks up the telephone. A real, honest to god telephone. Mrs. Winthrop's maiden name has to be De Sade.

Once Angelica proves that she does indeed have the promised beverages, I forgive her for treating me so shabbily in front of Mrs. Winthrop and for living like royalty while I'm exiled to steerage. It also explains the bag's excessive weight and I feel much better about my athletic prowess. After helping myself to Jack Daniels on the rocks – I can't believe she has rocks!, I flop down in an overstuffed chair. The combination of cool air and alcohol has me in an extremely mellow state by the time the sandwiches arrive. The home-baked bread and thick slices of turkey, pepper jack and spicy mustard complete the transformation.

"When are we going to talk about you and Derek?" I mumble around a mouthful of heaven.

Angelica sighs and lays her sandwich down. I wait while she takes a deep swallow of Diet Coke. It's one of her stalling tactics, but I'm patient. She sighs again. "Derek isn't thrilled about the time I'm devoting to this."

"Ange, I don't want to come between you and your

husband."

"Don't worry, sweetie," Angelica says with a smile. "Derek and I have been having problems for a while. Your little situation just brought it to a head." She bites into her sandwich.

"What kind of problems?"

"If they weren't affecting my life so deeply, they'd be ludicrous. Stereotypical, tedious issues. Career versus family, alpha male meets independent female, who wears the pants; you name it, it's a problem."

"Don't you want to talk about it? Sometimes that helps."

Angelica shakes her head. "Actually, I'm tired of talking. That's all Derek and I have done for weeks, maybe months. We've even been to counseling. And it never gets anywhere. What I really want is to get away for a while and concentrate on someone else's screwed up life."

"Okay," I say, ignoring the slam and imbuing that one word with as much doubt as possible. "But don't let our friendship ruin your marriage. I can figure this out on my own."

The resulting fit is insulting, but at least it's good to hear her laugh, once she gets the coughing out of her system. "Sorry," she says, wiping tears out of her eyes. "But I think you've collected more bodies than clues."

That hurt. It really hurt. Mostly because it's true. I concentrate on my sandwich and collect my thoughts for the upcoming session. A full belly and two Jacks later, I'm ready to start sleuthing.

One thing that has always impressed me about Angelica is her efficiency. Another is her ability to tackle problems with logic and the latest technology. The third is her energy. There are other things, but these three are brought together to address the predicament that I've landed in. While I'm still relaxing and enjoying the soothing effects of lunch, Angelica is starting up her computer and organizing a pile of paper.

"Why do you have all these printouts?" I ask and fan through the pages. "Whatever happened to a paperless office?" Angelica slaps my hand and I draw it away. It smarts a little more than it should.

"Stay away from those. You'll mess them up. I like printouts. You can write notes on them. Plus, if something is a dead end, it's a great stress relief to rip them apart. Or burn them." There are a series of clicks and whirs from the computer, the papers are stacked in neat piles and then Angelica is staring at me with large question marks in her eyes.

"What?"

"Can we get started?"

"Of course," I say and move to the table. "I was waiting for you."

A brief, obligatory smile and then she's all business. She shuffles through the papers and produces some articles from the local rag. Dallas was the topic.

"Mr. McGuire was almost a stereotypical success story. Unknown makes it big, can't handle success, gets involved in drugs, starts a downhill slide, life is cut short." As Angelica narrates, she points to a different article to support each segment of the late great's life.

"You said almost."

Angelica grins. "The part that's a stretch is that this was a success story. His only claim to fame was a literary novel published by a small press. Sold five thousand copies, mostly in the local area."

"Good thing he didn't make it Stephen King big," I say with an answering grin. "He wouldn't have lived this long. What's the drug angle?"

An article is sought and found, then slid across the table to me. The title screams 'Local Celebrity the Target of Harassment.' I scan the story, mostly opinionated ranting, about how police were unfairly picking on Dallas McGuire. The slant is that allegations of him supplying drugs to students were fabricated because of his outspoken attitude towards authoritarian factions. That is, the cops didn't like him because he was a jerk. I agree with the reporter on that count, but just because someone's a jerk doesn't mean they're not dealing drugs. Angelica tosses me another printout, this one from the Dayton Daily News.

"The rest of the story?"

Angelica nods, her face grim. "The reason the police got involved in the first place was because of a death. Overdose."

"Faun Anderson?" I ask, picking the name from the article.

"Uh-huh. She was a freshman at Antioch; got mixed up with drugs and Dallas. The cops decided there was a connection."

To prove the theory, a sting operation swung into action. The team nailed Dallas trying to sell narcotics to an undercover cop. A young, female undercover cop. Unfortunately, the young woman in question got excited—it was her first big operation—and she forgot to follow procedure. Dallas was released on a technicality and probably became extremely careful from there on out.

"So he wasn't innocent, just lucky."

Angelica nods. "If you read through the rest of these," she taps the pile of pages, "you'll see the same trend I did. After his one book was published…"

"The Roach's Dream."

"Yeah. Weird. Anyway, once the book was published, he became erratic. Would show up late, if at all, for class, same for signing engagements. When he was there, he was belligerent or zoned out."

"Drugs," I state the obvious.

"Uh-huh. Doing and dealing."

"When you consider this and knowing him, even for a short time, the question becomes not why was he killed, but why wasn't he killed earlier."

"Exactly," Angelica says. "To answer that question, we have to look at the usual suspects." She turns the computer screen and I see a table. There is a series of headings across the top: 'Name', 'Suspect?', 'Background', 'Motive', 'Opportunity' across the top and a list of names down the side. The first two names are identical—Chase.

"This is a spreadsheet to help us sort out clues, suspects,

etc. Any piece of information, no matter how insignificant it seems, has to go in here. Once we get this compiled, we'll see what falls out."

"Why is Chase in there twice?"

"She's a special entry," Angelica explains. I appreciate the way her voice softens. It's more difficult to talk about Chase than I would have thought. "There are two cases. One is that Chase was a victim. She saw something that night and became a liability. The second case is that in a fit of jealous rage, she killed Dallas and then later killed herself out of remorse. From what you've told me she has a history of drug use and depression; not a nice combination."

I hesitate, and then nod. Right now, it's more important to discover the truth, not protect the dead. "Using the jealous rage motive, there are multiple suspects."

Angelica types in the information. "To keep it manageable, concentrate on his latest conquests. We'll assume anyone before now could have killed him, but chose not to. The fire should have been quenched by now."

"Does that include Kandi/Peg?"

"Noooo…," Angelica says, the syllable stretching out as she considers the subject. "She's still in the picture because of her comment about the fan club. And the fact that she and Chase seemed to be chummy."

"Definitely. While we're on this category, throw in Elmira."

"Elmira?"

"The thin blond juvenile that gave the soppy tribute at the funeral."

Angelica's typing pauses. "You're going to have to give me a little more detail."

"I don't think you've met her yet. I'll point her out the next time we run across her. Just think Chase only blond. No glasses; more boobage."

A nod and the typing resumes. "Who next?" Angelica asks but the phone rings before I can answer.

"Hello?" I ask. The response is dead air. I wait a second or two and am about to hang up when a familiar voice stops me.

"Rex?"

"Derek. Hey. What's happenin', buddy?" I hope the cheerfulness in my voice sounds more sincere across the line than it does up close and personal.

"Is my wife there?"

"Yeah, she sure is. By the way, I can't tell you how much I appreciate her help. Without it, I'd bet my Christmas cards would be postmarked Lucasville."

"May I speak with her?" The frigid tone leaves no doubt that my incarceration in the state pen wouldn't bother Derek one bit.

"Sure. I'll put her on," I say and shove the phone at Angelica, ignoring her frantic attempt to shove it back. I almost feel guilty when I hear the resignation in her voice.

"Hello, Derek. What do you want?"

From where I am, I can hear him yelling. I wave and head for the door, but Angelica shakes her head furiously and points to the chair. I shrug, fix a drink and pull up close to the television. HBO isn't perfect, but Mrs. Winthrop is right. It does fill my movie needs, especially since Angelica's voice is rising and it doesn't look as if she'll get back to the spreadsheet any time soon.

22

Trying to seem interested in "BioDome" and the immeasurable acting skills of Pauly Shore while Angelica and Derek reenact "Who's Afraid of Virginia Wolf" isn't the hardest thing I've ever done, but it's right up there. I'm close to pulling the phone cord when I hear the receiver slam. I could ask about the swollen red eyes and the runny nose, but Angelica knows she can talk to me. When she's ready, I'll listen.

"Want to get back to something productive?" The defiant tone in her voice confirms my decision. When she's ready...

"Sure. Whadda you have?"

Angelica sits down at the table and swipes at her cheeks, and then starts sorting papers. "Let's go down the list. What order would you put the suspects in?"

"A drug dealer, a junkie, John, the Culbreaths, Elmira, Mr. Sharpe, Kandi, Mrs. Winthrop."

"If it's one or both of the first two, there's not much we can uncover that the police wouldn't. Let's leave them off."

I nod.

"Now, why Gladys?"

"Because she's mean," I say, a petulant tone creeping into my voice. "She'd love to bonk someone over the head."

Angelica shakes her head and clicks her tongue against her

teeth. "We'll leave Gladys off the list. She's a sweet woman with a lot of responsibilities."

"Fine," I grumble.

"Quit pouting. There are plenty of suspects left. As for the Culbreaths, they're exactly what they seem. An eccentric brother and sister team that writes inane travel books. Nothing out of the ordinary; imminently forgettable," she says and holds out a few pages that show reviews, bio's and society columns from their hometown.

"Those are the worst kind. Ordinary and boring on the surface, underneath a festering cauldron of emotions ready to explode. They're dangerous I tell you." I rub my leg as a ghostly hand gropes my inner thigh. Angelica laughs.

"If we exhaust all other possibilities, we'll come back to them, I promise."

"Okay, but just watch your back when they're around."

"I will," she assures me. "What about Judge Sylvia?"

That's a possibility I hadn't considered. "Why? She was there, she had opportunity, but no motive."

Angelica shrugs; her face too neutral. "I think everyone should be considered."

"All right, but put her at the end. I mean, she's a judge for heaven's sake."

There's another shrug, and Angelica busies herself with the papers. She waves a stapled pile at me. "Let's take a look at someone with real potential."

I take the papers and scan them. The Columbus Dispatch again. And a familiar face. The divorce from the lesbian wife is old news, but the lawyer's attack on the lover and the subsequent hospitalization had been omitted from the conversation. "The papers really love John Townsend, don't they?"

"But he doesn't love them," Angelica hands me another page. A rival newspaper had supplied the color photos of the Dispatch reporter clutching a broken nose.

"Our Mr. Grisham has a temper," I offer, aware of the understatement but not sure what else to say. "Of course, it was justified."

Sparks fly from beautiful brown eyes. "Don't give me that. He attacked a woman. A woman much, much smaller than he is. And regardless of gender, nobody deserves a beating for falling in love with someone else. It's not a moral thing to do, but it happens."

I hate defending John, but I understand his situation. I think. "What person wouldn't react irrationally if their dearly beloved hooked up with a same sex partner?"

"Maybe, but he wasn't blameless. Our Mr. Townsend had an eye for the ladies. And a hand and a—well, other body parts come to mind."

"That's not a shock. How'd he stay out of jail?"

"The main papers are silent; strangely silent. But these," Angelica taps another pile, "Underground rags. Mostly Ohio State fare. They scream lawyer hijinks, corporate money buying silence. The usual."

"And?"

Her eyes shining, Angelica seems almost eager. "And judicial favoritism." There is no 'almost' about the triumph in her voice.

"It's hard to imagine the honorable Sylvia playing favorites with anyone. She'd sentence her crippled mother to hard labor for stealing a package of Depends."

"Maybe." It's Angelica's turn to grumble. "There are a lot of articles about how tough she is; a Dirty Harriet-type. The political community holds her in high esteem." Angelica is quiet and then she brightens. "But you think there might be something between her and Big Bad John. Love makes people do crazy things."

"I think they may have had or are having an affair. That doesn't imply criminal tendencies."

"It's breaking one of the ten oldest laws; she is married." Now Angelica sounds out and out peevish.

"All right, all right. She may have helped him."

If there is a way to type smugly, Angelica did it. I notice that she replaces the Culbreaths with Judge Sylvia. "Great.

She's on the list. If not an out and out suspect, at least an accomplice. And let's look at John. He's a dangerous man, he's running loose and Dallas crossed him."

"Good points," I say with a nod. "And don't forget; he's intimately connected with the pills that were found in Chase' apartment."

Eyebrows fly up. "I forgot about that."

I grin. "Good thing I'm here. My brain is still in working order."

Angelica snorts. "You were on the scene. Again."

I cringe. "Don't you need to update that thing?" I ask and point to the computer. I fix us both another drink while Angelica taps at the keyboard. She finishes first and waits for her beer. A quick sip and she sets aside the John papers and brings over another pile.

"Guess who's next?"

"Elmira."

"Annnkkkhhh," she buzzes. "Wrong answer. Mr. Sharpe."

I stare. "That stack is bigger than he is."

"Our Mr. Sharpe has been a busy boy. But he hasn't been alone. Kandi-girl was right in the thick of things. Or Peg. Or whoever she is at the moment."

The difference between these articles and the ones on John are the timing. The majority of these stories are dated about five years ago. Except for the top one. It's from March of this year. About five months ago. I look at Angelica. She's sporting a smug, canary-eating cat expression.

"Mr. Sharpe just exited a funny farm?"

"The correct term is institution."

"Whatever," I say and leaf through the pages. "Wow. Peg had him committed?"

"No. Peg loved him. Or at least, could tolerate him. Kandi is the one who sent him away."

"Is this a Norman Bates thing? Is there a stuffed mother in the basement?"

"Don't be ridiculous." Angelica tries to remain serious, but she isn't having much luck. "Reading between the lines, Peg came to the Workshop five years ago with a manuscript and dreams. She came away with a new name and a new perspective on life."

"She met Dallas."

Angelica nods, scanning a page as she talks. "And Dallas chose her as his latest proselyte."

"And sex toy."

Angelica nods again. "The newspapers don't go into that much detail, but that's a safe bet. When Kandi returned home, her elderly husband didn't hold much attraction for her anymore."

"Except for his earthly belongings."

"Exactly. This story says that Margaret—Kandi—Sharpe showed up at the Delaware police station with a black eye, multiple bruises and a heart-wrenching tale of spousal brutality. The cop who took her statement was skeptical, especially once he met the accused."

"Obviously the police are more astute there than here."

"What swayed the cops and—" a brief shuffling of papers, stopping on one that is quickly scanned "a jury was the testimony of a Mrs. Fiona Ledwalter."

"Who?"

"Mr. Sharpe's only daughter."

"That's what got him put away?"

A nod. "He was determined to be a menace to society and put in a mental institution because of the severity of his violence and in deference to his age."

"But why? What did they have to gain?"

"As soon as he was put away, Kandi was named guardian of his estate. Not much, but it was a savings account and a paid off house. She and Fiona cleaned out his bank account and sold the house."

"Can they do that?" I sputter.

"They did."

"And last spring…"

"Mr. Sharpe was released because the doctors unanimously agreed he was not a danger to himself or society. But his house, his wife and his money are gone. He's been living with his daughter ever since. Probably enough to send anyone over the edge."

"Why would he live with his daughter after she stole from him?"

Angelica shrugs. "Where else could he go? He's penniless. That's the true horror of life; outliving your savings. At least justice was meted out to his daughter."

"How'd you find this out?"

Angelica laughs and speaks in a nasally voice. "Hello, Mrs. Ledwalter? Oh, Fiona? Why thank you. Yes. I'm calling from the Dispatch. Oh, thank you. Yes, we're very proud of our paper. I was following up on a story. A human interest angle. How does it feel to have your father home with you? You must be very brave. Isn't he dangerous?" Angelica smiles. "Or something like that. Anyway, the darling Fiona was thrilled to be back in the limelight and she didn't need much nudging to spill her guts. Her part of the take is gone, by the way. There was something about a family trip to Disney World."

My stomach churns. It might be the whisky, but I doubt it. Alcohol is a lot friendlier than most of the people running loose in the world. "I need air. Buy me dinner?" I ask and stand up. The room spins for a moment and then it's still.

Angelica grabs my arm. "You okay?"

"Just a little closed in. Pizza?"

"Sure." And we venture into the sultry night.

Neither of us talks except to decide where to go. Ha-Ha Pizza is the hands down choice. I order a pepperoni pizza with extra cheese and Angelica goes pure Yellow Springs with a calzone stuffed with tofu, broccoli and mushroom. The only concession I make to health is the whole-wheat crust. As we wait for our food, I soak up the ambiance.

Bob Dylan drifts out of the speakers and fades into Black Sabbath. The lime green walls and vivid murals blend more easily with Ozzie Osborne than with the king of folk music.

An elderly gentleman with a foot long beard and a matching ponytail is at the salad bar. Probably the mayor. For the first time in three days, I feel myself relaxing. Until I see the pictures.

Blue, pink, purple, green. Bulbous distortions of human beings with O's for mouths and almond shaped eyes. For a second, I'm back in Chase' apartment; her corpse lying above me on the couch. The room swims out of focus. A warm touch brings it back.

"Are you okay?" Angelica's eyes are dark with concern.

"Those pictures. Chase had some just like them."

Angelica follows my gaze. "Hmmm. You'd think the manager would be worried about killing appetites."

"You ordered a tofu calzone; if the menu doesn't destroy your appetite, what will?"

Her answering smile is steadying. "You need to broaden your tastes," she says and continues to study the artwork. "Did you know Rod Serling is one of the notable personalities Antioch claims?"

"That makes sense. He didn't make up the Twilight Zone; he lived it." We both stare for a second and then I switch back to reality. "If Chase was killed, John is the obvious suspect. Violent, access to drugs, sex-hungry. She probably rejected him and bye-bye Chase."

Our food interrupts Angelica's reply. The calzone covers a dinner plate and the pizza is even bigger.

"I'll never be able to eat all this," Angelica says. "Help me."

Tofu versus pepperoni. No. "Thanks, but you're on your own." I sip my Coke. Great pizza. No liquor license. No whiskey. Not a bad thing.

"Rex, this isn't a movie. There doesn't have to be a cover-up murder. It was probably suicide like the police said."

A finger placed on my lips silences my protest.

"We're supposed to be relaxing, remember?"

I do and we do. Even so, the alien faces accuse me through the rest of the meal.

23

Friday morning starts out bad and plunges downhill from there. Angelica refused to let me hang out in her air-conditioned paradise claiming that I should be out soaking up the literary culture. And the criminal culture. Since the only alternative was to swelter in my little hell plot, I acquiesced. Which is why I'm suffering through the debate on whether or not Grimm's Fairy Tales are corrupting our nation's children. This segues into a lively discussion on whether or not cartoons such as Wile E. Coyote and the Roadrunner are responsible for the violence in today's society. My thoughts wander to Dallas' bashed skull. Some lively music, a maniacal duck and—voila—tragedy becomes Saturday morning fare. I shiver in spite of the sub-tropical atmosphere.

The next session isn't any better. Creative non-fiction. Or fictionalized true stories. The perky cheerleader-type leading the discussion advocates 'spicing' up dull history. Take a boring case of a wife blowing away an unfaithful husband with a shotgun, add Jodie Foster, an alien abduction, and boom! Best seller. At the end of the hour and a half, I'm not just chilled I'm also nauseated. Exposure to a refined perspective on society is worse than any hangover I'd ever experienced. I head towards the boarding house, willing to embrace the heat

E. SABBAG

rather than the obscenity of the real world. What would Dashiell Hammett have thought of my generation? I shake my head and head for home.

"Hey, Rex. Buddy."

My first instinct is to ignore the hail. But Angelica's frowning countenance swims into view. My first goal is to be a writer—I'd done my best by struggling through the workshop I'd paid good money to attend. The second is to uncover information that will solve what I am convinced are two murders. And the owner of that abrasive voice might possess the necessary clues. I exhale with great effort and face John Townsend.

"Want some chow?" he asks.

"Maybe. That last discussion didn't just kill my appetite; it tortured and maimed it." John laughs and slaps me on the back. Murderer or not, his effusive cheerfulness makes my spirits rise. And my appetite. "Actually, lunch doesn't sound too bad," I admit.

"Good. Let's go to the cafeteria and hook up with the ladies," John says and makes good on his suggestion.

I trot to keep up with him. "Did you say ladies? Plural?"

"Uh-huh. You don't think I'd spend good time palling around with just you, do you?"

"I guess not," I say as I fall in step. The pace makes conversation impossible and arrival at the cafeteria doesn't help. I expected Sylvia; Angelica is a total surprise.

"Rex." She waves me over to the table she and the judge are sharing. The two women seem to be getting along much better than in previous encounters, which frightens me more than their animosity. My precocious appetite disappears again.

"Rex," Angelica bubbles as I sit down. Not beside her, John has already claimed that seat. Instead, I'm relegated to the inferior position beside the judge. At least there I can monitor Angelica and John. "Rex," Angelica repeats, "I thought you said this food was awful. I can't remember the last time I've gotten so much for so little," she says and waves at a plate overflowing with lasagna and breadsticks. The accompanying salad bears no resemblance to the pathetic dredges I've been trying to eat for the last few days. I fumble for an appropriate response and then surrender. The vacuum left by my silence fills rapidly.

"Angelica was just telling me about her room," Sylvia explains. "That's what I love about this town. Quaint, historic, comfortable. Practically paradise."

"Except for that nasty little serpent that's been bonking people on the head," I interject. Three blank expressions fix on me, and then return to their interrupted conversation.

"It is a shame that these distasteful incidents had to happen during the workshop," Angelica says.

"Yes, why couldn't they happen when we're not on vacation? Let the locals deal with this mess," I interject once more. This time, the three don't even acknowledge me. I resolve to keep my mouth shut and soak up the culture.

"You don't know the half of it," John says. "The local bumpkins had the audacity to question me. Me."

Angelica's expression—concerned, sympathetic—makes my empty stomach lurch. She lays her hand on John's forearm and says, "What could they possibly suspect you of?"

"They found some pills in Chase' apartment and my firm is litigating a case involving that same drug. Is that grasping at straws or what?"

The requisite giggle graduates me from slight nausea to the verge of retching. Angelica has no shame. "It's obvious these yokels are completely lost. Taking a suicide and twisting it into murder.

"That's what I said," Sylvia offers. "It's the hint of glory. A place in the lime light. If they turn a simple crime of passion into a serial killer, they'll get this pathetic little burg on the map."

Angelica nods. "Thank goodness there's nothing to link you with the only real murder."

John shakes his head. "I wish that were true. Even though Yellow Springs doesn't have the sophistication of Mayberry, they do have some pretty modern technology. And access to the age of information."

"Whatever do you mean?" This time the wide-eyed innocent routine is a little much. John doesn't notice, but Sylvia's face becomes a stiff, blank mask.

"Seems that somebody ran a background check and uncovered an incident of temper in my past. Blown out of proportion of course," John says.

"Of course," Angelica murmurs.

"Nothing came of it, but it will follow me for the rest of my life. Everybody goes a little crazy sometimes."

Sylvia pushes her chair back from the table and stands up. "John, we shouldn't monopolize our friends. I'm sure they have things they want to do," she says. In an instant, she and her tray are gone. Longing oozes from John's face, but Sylvia's tone doesn't invite discussion. Or rebellion. He mumbles good-bye and then he too disappears.

"What do you think you're doing?" I hiss.

Angelica watches the retreating pair, her brow rippled with concentration. Sylvia is talking; John is listening, his shoulders hunched and his head drooping. Reiteration to self; never commit a crime in Columbus. Ever. The couple moves out of sight and Angelica turns back to me.

"What I'm doing is gathering information. We just found out that the police questioned John in connection with both deaths. What did you find out?"

"That Wile E. Coyote is responsible for the moral decay of our youth?" Angelica's blank stare makes me laugh. "Never mind. Seriously, don't play games with yon Norman Bates clone. If he did kill Dallas, he's dangerous. And judging from the pheromones he's emitting, even if he didn't kill anyone, your honor is at stake."

The bimbo giggle is gone, supplanted by the honest Angelica laugh that I love. "Well, thank you, kind sir, for protecting my reputation. Although I don't have anything to worry about. Not in broad daylight."

"I'm not worried about right now. Predators locate their prey during the sunlit hours and then pounce when darkness shrouds their movements." Melodramatic, true, but it does its job. Angelica sobers and gathers up her tray.

"Come on," she says as she stands up. "Let's blow this joint."

The sunshine seduces us away from the building confines. Angelica and I turn towards the village instead of our rooms. The heat, oppressive earlier, is now welcome; baking away the chills and evils that permeate our existence. We pass the Sunrise Café, the organic grocery and the various coffee houses and tattoo parlors that festoon Xenia Avenue. Along with an animation film festival, an X-rated Cannes Award winner is playing at The Little Art Theater. Angelica pauses and looks over a poster for the 'art' film. The well-endowed actress that touched the critics' frosty hearts smiles back. Any other Midwest town would censure the revealing advertisement; Yellow Springs glorifies it. I'm glad to see that Angelica is appreciating art.

"Wanna catch a flick?" I ask and waggle my eyebrows.

The subtlety is wasted. Without even glancing towards me, Angelica frowns and shakes her head. "No, I won't be able to concentrate. I talked to Elmira this morning," she says and moves down Xenia Avenue again, but this time more slowly.

"And she's thinking about going into the movies?"

"No. We talked about Dallas."

My attempts at humor are not just wasted; they're humiliating. I give up. "Where did you see her?"

"In the Sunrise Café. I invited myself to her table and offered to buy breakfast."

"Didn't she find it creepy that a stranger would buy her breakfast to talk about a dead guy?"

Angelica smiles. "She's a college student."

"Oh."

"Anyway, I used the shock approach and asked her point blank if she knew Dallas was dealing drugs. She shrugged and said everybody knew that. He could get the best stuff. Claimed to have connections."

The roof of Ye Olde Trail Tavern blocks the sun for an instant and the chills are back. Luckily, it's on the other side of the street and we scurry past it. I breathe deeper once we're clear of its evil influence. "It didn't bother her that her mentor was a dealer?"

Angelica shakes her head. "Actually, she said he was performing an entrepreneurial service that was only evil because of the fascist bureaucracy we live in."

"You quote that well. Almost as if you believe it," I observe. "Dallas' influence is reaching beyond the grave."

The answering flush quells any concerns I have along those lines. "I'm quoting a source. It's important to be as detailed as possible. Oh! Bonadies'," she cries and darts across the road.

I follow her, but more sedately, into the stained glass emporium. We devote a few minutes to examining the bejeweled treasures; exquisitely crafted and priced to match. Angelica is standing beside a six-foot floor lamp with a shade comprised of glass peacock feathers. The brass stand is intricately carved into bird feet.

"Look at this lamp," Angelica says, stroking the purple, blue and green glass that out-peacocks the real thing. "Breathtaking, isn't it?"

I glance at the price tag. Thirteen hundred dollars. My lungs constricts. "Definitely. Should you be touching that?"

"Probably not." Her reluctance is heartrending, but I hold firm.

"Let's head back, okay?"

She nods but then stalls. It takes another fifteen minutes before I can guide her back to the safety of the outdoors. Once we're moving in the direction of our lodgings, I bring the Elmira subject back to the forefront.

"Since Elmira knew about the dealing, Chase had to have."

"Definitely. Actually, Chase was his biggest customer."

"How did Elmira know about that?"

"Turns out that Elmira threw a fit about Dallas' continued relationship with Chase." Angelica cuts her eyes at me and grins.

"Her words?"

The grin widens. "Not exactly. Seems that Dallas spent a lot of time at Chase' apartment and Elmira confronted him with it. Threatened to quit stoking his creative fires if it didn't stop. He explained it was just business."

I sigh. I wish I had the man's way with women. Of course, he's dead and I'm not. "What does Elmira think about Chase' death?"

"Suicide."

Retracing our path brings us even with The Little Art Theater. The nubile poster now has a sinister cast to it. I pick up my pace. "You sound fairly certain."

"Elmira was adamant. Chase was a 'mopey, pathetic creature whose suicide was inevitable. At least she did it without taking anyone else down with her'."

"Wow. That's harsh."

Angelica nods. "Where men are concerned, women can be extremely harsh."

I glance at my companion. Granite holds more emotion. "Sounds as if Elmira doesn't think Chase bonked Dallas."

"I asked her about that possibility. In Elmira's opinion, Chase didn't have the backbone."

"Interesting," I say. "Doesn't it take backbone to take one's life?"

"Not in Elmira's book. She thinks it's the ultimate cop-out."

We leave the business section of the village and are back in the residential. The sun is alternately brutal and subdued, shaded by ancient trees. The rhythm soothes my jangled nerves. Drugs and death and obsessive love are miles away. "How truthful do you think our little Elmira is being?"

"Hard to say. Probably the drug angle, maybe some part of the Chase description. All of it is tainted with Dallas obsession, though."

"Do you think she did it?"

Angelica chews at her lower lip for a second before answering. "She could have. There's enough passion. And

179

pain. Chase is still a puzzle, however. Elmira could be setting up the suicide angle to cover her tracks or she could have whacked Dallas without needing to tidy up the Chase loose end."

"So we're back to a lot of questions that need to be answered."

"Oui. Time to focus ze leetle gray cells."

The laugh feels good. "Unfortunately I'm feeling a decided lack of leetle gray cells."

"Too much beer," Angelica says with a grin and a quick arm squeeze. Silence cloaks the rest of the walk.

As soon as we enter the foyer, Mrs. Winthrop scuttles over, clutching a dozen scraps of paper. "Angelica, your husband needs you to call him right away. It sounds like an emergency."

Angelica eyes the scraps of paper in the same way that she would a nest of scorpions. "Did he say what it's about?"

"Just that he's worried about you," the old bat says with a sideways glance in my direction. She thrusts the messages at Angelica and scuttles back to her lair, probably to throw a few more logs on the furnace that I know resides right below my room. I hear her familiars meowing as she rejoins the coven.

At the base of the stairs, Angelica and I part company. "Wanna share some air conditioning?" she pleads. I know my presence will only make the situation worse.

"No thanks, kid. I think I'll stay down here and watch the tube." The hopelessness becomes a tangible entity and I almost cave. Almost. I give her a hug and push her towards the stairs. "You'll be fine. You are woman. Be strong."

A tiny smile brightens her face. "All right. Besides, what will Gladys think?"

"That is one of my primary concerns." I grin back at her. "Now go."

With the tread of a prisoner walking the final mile, Angelica makes her way up the stairs. Tackling my own desperate need to exorcise the death thoughts that are pervading my life, I flop down on the overstuffed couch in the parlor and, being the sole occupant, commandeer the remote. Wile E.'s eternal battle with his feathered nemesis and the Acme corporation escort me into a deep, wild sleep.

24

The first thing I notice is that my mouth is incredibly dry. Sahara dry. The second is that my body isn't. Sweat drips from every pore and puddles in every wrinkle. It's hard to determine how long I've been asleep in the sauna of a room, but the daylight filtering through the brocade curtains lets me know it isn't too late for dinner. Unless I've slept round the clock. The thought fills me with panic. Time is the one thing I don't have. A quick glance at my watch tells me it's six, but doesn't reveal AM or PM. On the television, Tim Allen is berating the gang of "Home Improvement" but that still doesn't solve the puzzle. Groaning from the effort of standing, I stagger into the lobby. For once, I'm sorry Mrs. Winthrop isn't there. Using the ancient black desk telephone, I dial Angelica's number. Panic mounts when she doesn't answer. If she's gone out alone because I fell asleep…

"Hullo?" a drowsy voice asks.

"Angelica?" The name is more a bark than a question, but it produces the desired result.

"Rex? What's wrong?" She has either not been asleep or she comes to her senses a lot quicker than I can.

"Nothing. I fell asleep and got worried when you didn't answer. I was scared you went out without me."

"Worried because you're still concerned about my honor or because you might miss something exciting?" More than her words, the lilt in her voice assures me that everything is okay.

"Worried about your safety. The fun we've been having recently is imminently missable," I growl.

She laughs and then pauses. "Oh my god, do you realize it's after six?" she yelps. "I must have nodded off, too."

"Evening or morning?"

"Boy, you must have been out. Evening of course. Which is great. We're rested, fresh and just in time for dinner."

"Where?" Now the lilt in her voice is scaring me. There is one place in the world—no the universe—that I do not want to go and I have a sick feeling that is where she's dragging me.

"To the Tavern. I'll be right down."

A dozen excuses supporting why we shouldn't—couldn't—go leap to mind, but it's in vain. The phone is dead. Before I can hang up, Angelica is standing by the door waiting for me.

"What'd you do? Twitch your nose and hex yourself down?" The irritation I'm conveying is real, but she ignores it.

"Don't be silly. Now come on. We're already late enough. If we wait any longer we'll never get a table."

"Why do we have to go to the Tavern? There are tons of other places to eat. The Winds, Ha-Ha Pizza, KFC..." The panic, lessened for a moment by knowing she was okay, roars back in full force.

Angelica squeezes my arm. The cool grip eases my desperation. "It'll be all right," she assures me. In spite of a slight redness that betrays the tone of her conversation with Derek, her eyes meet mine with confidence. "The only way we'll figure out who killed Dallas is to worm something out of the prime suspects. That means we have to go where they are."

I fight the urge to scream. "But what if it's somebody else? Somebody we haven't even thought of. This could be a waste of time."

"Maybe," she admits, never loosening her grip. "And if we don't go, what do you suggest we do? Sit around and wait for the police to pick you up?"

There is no clever response to her question. There isn't even a stupid one. Without a word, I follow her out of the building to the car. This time I resemble the condemned prisoner.

The trip to the Tavern takes less than ten minutes and the entire time I hope that no one shows up. Then Angelica and I can have an intimate dinner, a few intimate drinks followed by an evening of brainstorming and solving the world's problems. And mine. Unfortunately, the gang doesn't cooperate. My hopes are shattered when a boppy young thing shows us to the back room and Rose waves us over. The usual crowd smiles in unison—John, Sylvia and Roger—two with enthusiasm, one because she has to.

"Rex, you and your friend must join us," Rose twitters as she bats her eyes. Sylvia quits smiling; John doesn't.

"We'd love to Rose, but there aren't enough chairs," I say and start to follow our server to a booth that looks safe and cozy.

"Nonsense," Angelica beams. "There's always room for a couple of friends, isn't there?"

Rose grins and pats her knee. "Rex, you can sit right here. I don't mind."

"Thanks, Rose, but I don't want to upset Roger. I know how protective big brothers can be." The siblings let out identical belly laughs.

"Don't worry, buddy," Roger says. "The only thing I protect my baby sister from is a bad time. As long as you make her happy, I say go for it."

In a panic, I grab two chairs from a neighboring table and shove one between Sylvia and John and the other between John and Roger. Sylvia hops into the one by John, Angelica wedges in between John and Roger and I wind up beside Rose.

"This evening is getting better all the time," Rose says and squishes her ample thigh against mine.

"Yeah," Sylvia says, speaking for the first time since our

arrival. "The only thing that could make it better is another murder. That would really liven things up." A blanket of silence hovers for a second, and then Rose breaks the tension with another braying belly laugh.

"Oh, I get it. We're all writers; this is a perfect opportunity to exercise our creative muscles. Who should be the next victim?"

If anything, the silence is thicker. Five pairs of eyes stare at Rose, who remains oblivious. "Come on," she insists, her voice sharpening to a grating pitch. "Somebody start. Who's the most likely to get killed? Better yet, make it interesting. Who's the least likely?"

"I don't think our waitress is coming." I push my chair away from the table. "Anybody need anything?" I leave after Angelica nods and before Rose can offer a sexual innuendo. Within seconds, I reach the safety of the bar.

"Bud Light and a Jack on the rocks," I tell the bartender. It's not the young stud from the previous visit. This one is a middle-aged, no nonsense dorm mother-type with 'Mabel' on her chest.

"Hello handsome. Since you're buying, how about a refill for a lady?" The voice emanates from my elbow and belongs to a familiar character cradling an empty wine glass. Kandi tilts it in my direction and waggles her eyebrows. I concentrate on her beaded, glittery hair, which keeps my eyes away from her Spandexed body. As eye catching as her hair is, however, her expansive bosom overshadows it. So much for black being slimming. The cropped top ends just above her pierced belly button and low-slung bellbottoms. An impatient cough drags my attention back to Mabel.

"Well, big spender, you springing for the lady or not?"

"Sorry. Sure. Whatever. Yeah."

Kandi laughs and the bartender goes to the back, probably to open a bottle of Dom Perignon. A scarlet tipped finger traces a jagged trail up my forearm. "Thanks, big guy. Of course, now I'm indebted to you. Whatever can I do to pay you back?" Her lips match her fingernails, the blood red hue made even more vivid by the whiteness of her teeth. Shark's teeth.

I shudder. "Nothing. I don't make women work for their drinks."

"What a shame. You could be quite the entrepreneur." She applies enough pressure to leave a red streak against my skin.

I jerk my arm out of harm's tentacles. "Oh come on," I say with what I hope is a tension-diffusing chuckle from a sophisticated man about town. It comes out more like the hysterical giggle of virgin in a cathouse. "You're worth more than drinks."

A nasty gleam lights her narrowed eyes. "You better believe it. As a matter of fact, I'm worth more than this whole lousy bar."

"Hit the lottery?"

"Sort of. All I have to do is collect."

Before I can delve further into this fascinating conversation, the bar matron is back. Kandi takes the fresh glass of wine and moves towards the rear of the bar.

"That'll be seven fifty," Mabel snaps.

I pull out a ten and try to keep one eye on my change and the other on Kandi. The disappearing black Spandex wins. "Keep it," I say as I grab the two remaining drinks and sprint. I catch up with her just before my table. "Why don't you join us?"

Kandi drops her eyes to my crotch and asks, "You and who else?" Her tongue slides over her lips, leaving behind a slime trail that makes my skin crawl.

"My friends." I wave towards Angelica and the rest of the crowd. John leaps from his chair and holds it out.

"Rex, introduce us to your beautiful lady friend." He gestures to the seat. Kandi simpers at John and wiggles her rear into the cushion. Sylvia, Rose and Roger are not amused. Angelica is.

"Kandi, isn't it?" she asks.

"My reputation must precede me," Kandi says.

"It certainly does," says Rose.

Kandi throws her a nasty grin. "Aren't you my ex-hubby's little playmates?" Rose and Roger glare in stereo. Kandi's grin widens. "You can't believe everything he tells you. Most. But not everything."

"What are you doing here?" As one, the table faces the new arrival. Mr. Sharpe is an unattractive shade of mauve.

"Making new friends," Kandi says and leans back, pressing her head against John's hand resting on her chair. He grins and rubs her shoulder. Scarlet fingernails slither across his skin leaving behind a red snail trail. The streak on my arm burns in sympathy. If the music and the conversations weren't so loud, I'm sure I could have heard her purr. Mr. Sharpe's complexion deepens.

"You—you trollop," the old man sputters. "You're nothing but a cheap floozy."

"Not anymore. I'm about to become wonderfully expensive," the blonde says with another evil grin. "After all, this is the age of information." Ebony lined eyes flit around the table. Mr. Sharpe advances on his ex-wife with fingers bent into claws. Rose and Roger jump to their feet and waddle to his side.

"Now dear," Rose says in a soothing voice, "consider the source."

"That's right," Sylvia adds. "She's just a horrible little nobody fishing for attention."

Roger claps Mr. Sharpe on the shoulder and says, "Let's get out of here and go somewhere that caters to a better class of people." Mr. Sharpe falls in step, his shuffling gait betraying his lack of enthusiasm. Sylvia stands as they disappear.

"John, are you coming?" Her eyes and voice snap crisply.

"No, I think I'll stay and keep the ladies company," he says, mesmerized by the scarlet tips moving across his hand.

Sylvia stares for a second, tapping her fingers on the tabletop. "John, this is ridiculous. You're thinking with the wrong head. Come with me before you do something you'll regret in the morning."

"The only thing that irritates me more than you treating me like a child is your habit of over using clichés," John declares, his eyes fixated on a point below Kandi's chin. Which is a good thing, sort of, because if he made eye-contact with the judge cum Gorgon, he'd turn to stone. Or burst into flame. Kandi's grin blazes with wicked glee.

"Since when did you become a literary critic?" Sylvia spits between clenched teeth. "It certainly doesn't show in your writing." The normally composed lady is tight with anger, her hands opening and closing into white-knuckled fists.

John slams his fist down hard on the table. The mugs dance. Kandi gives a short gasp and then giggles. A glance from Sylvia cuts the giggle short, but doesn't erase the grin or the sparkle in the floozy's eyes. John ignores the interchange and stands, causing his chair to tilt over backwards. Our group now has the attention of everyone in the bar. John is beyond caring and roars.

"At least I have the courage to put something on paper. All you've ever done is trail around behind people who are trying to achieve something and make fun of them. Common, pathetic insecurity. With a healthy dose of jealousy thrown in for good measure!"

Sylvia's eyes narrow to near invisibility. "Jealous? At least I'm still married," she hisses and follows the path of the long-absent trio.

Kandi swirls her wine and stares at the legs. The grin is gone and her expression now mirrors Sylvia's. "Horrible little nobody, am I? We'll just wait and see, won't we?" she mutters.

"What's that?" John croaks as he takes the chair to her left and scoots it practically onto her lap. His voice is thick and rough, his breathing labored. Kandi jerks her eyes away from the dark hallway and back to John.

"Nothing. Just planning for my future."

"Preparation. Good for you. That's how I screwed up. Don't ever let them catch you with your pants down," John advises and gulps his beer. It's obvious she doesn't know who or what he's talking about, but it does get Kandi's attention.

Kandi chuckles. "I don't know. It really depends on who pulls them down. You know, I was just thinking that it's awfully crowded in here. How would you like to go somewhere a little more private?"

John's anger dissolves. "Sure. Your place or mine?" His boy scout-like eagerness is disgusting, but Kandi doesn't seem to mind.

"We can decide that on the way. Shall we?"

And the two are gone. Angelica looks at the empty chairs scattered around the table. Conversations ebbs and flows over and around us. She grimaces. "I think we've been dumped," she says.

I nod. "At least it's not just me this time."

Angelica laughs. "That's some consolation. Unfortunately, we've been humiliated for nothing. We didn't learn anything."

"Yes we did." My companion's arched eyebrows give me a triumphant thrill. "Ms. Kandi is trying to sell information to an interested party."

"And who would that party be?"

I shrug. "Hard to say. Just a lot of hints."

"You didn't find out?"

"Let's say I'm not willing to pay her price."

Angelica taps her front teeth with her forefinger. It's nice to see a sensibly cropped, unpainted nail. "That's okay. We should be able to reason it out. The obvious choice would be her ex. Lots to hide, emotionally vulnerable."

"True, but he's a weak old man. What could he have done? And how much money could he have?"

"I don't know. But it is interesting. What say we blow this dive and head back to more private surroundings?"

"Your place or mine?" I ask, waggling my eyebrows in a caricature of John. Angelica laughs and smacks me on the shoulder.

"Neither. I was thinking more along the lines of a ménage à trois on the back patio of our home away from home."

"Now you're talking," I say but then a thought hits me. "You're not planning on making Gladys the third leg of the triangle, are you?"

This brings out another laugh. "Only if you are."

"My tastes run towards Elmira and her contemporaries, not the wicked witch of the east."

Angelica shakes her head. "Actually I was thinking you, me and Jack."

"Jack?"

"Daniels. And his friends, Mr. Doritos and Ms. Dip."

"That would make it a ménage a five," I say and Angelica smacks me on the shoulder. I stand and offer her my bent arm. She rises and tucks hers into the crook. "You're my kind of lady." Arm in arm, we snake our way out of the Tavern. As we pass the bar, Mabel hails me.

"What happened to your other friend?" she asks.

"She dumped me for somebody else," I explain.

"Man, I can't believe you struck out," Mabel says, shaking her head and clucking her tongue. "That piece of work will put out for anybody. I can't believe you struck out."

"I wouldn't call it striking out," I protest.

"Whatever." She dismisses me and wipes down the bar. Before I can defend my honor, Angelica drags me into the fresh air.

"Why didn't you tell her you'd thrown Kandi-girl over for someone better?" Angelica asks as we wander towards the car.

"I've never thought of you that way..."

"Thanks," she says. "I think."

25

Angelica amazes me with her capacity for both listening to my wild theories and her consumption of alcohol. I tried to keep pace and am now paying for it. The only good thing about our drinking marathon is that it caused me to pass out in spite of the sweltering heat. Strange dreams pervade my sleep and I am almost grateful when a banging on the door wakes me up.

At first, my body refuses to answer; it feels as if I've only been asleep a few hours. I rub the grit out of my eyes and peer at the alarm clock. Six o'clock. This time I know it's morning. And since I crawled into bed at two-thirty, it has only been a few hours. The pounding grows in intensity. Luckily, I passed out in my clothes so I'm able to go straight to the door.

"What?" I grouse as I yank open the door. Harry and Lisa, looking fresh-scrubbed and alert in their spotless uniforms, stand before me. My own wrinkled clothes are an embarrassing contrast.

"Mr. Barker?" says Lisa.

"You know more about me than my mother. How about calling me Rex?" Neither officer cracks a smile.

"Mr. Barker, where were you this morning between the hours of two and four?" asked Harry.

"In bed. Asleep." This doesn't look good.

"Alone?" Lisa's raised eyebrows cast doubts on both my honesty and my manhood, but I can't do much about either.

"Yes. Alone. Look, is this a survey on the sexual habits of the lonely male or do I need an alibi?"

Lisa and Harry exchange a look and then back to me. "What makes you think you need an alibi, Mr. Barker?" Harry asks.

Sweat is dripping down my forehead. "I don't think I need an alibi, it's just that this sounds like an interrogation. Is everything okay?"

Another exchanged glance. Lisa speaks up this time. "We have a report that you were seen with a woman at the Tavern who subsequently," a peek into a notepad, " 'dumped you for another man'. Were you angry, Mr. Barker?"

"Relieved is more like it. If you're referring to Kandi, she scares me." Harry scribbles in his notepad and Lisa's eyes glow bright with interest.

"How scared were you? Did you feel a need to defend yourself?"

"I'm fully capable of handling Kandi and anyone like her." This is the wrong answer.

"Is that why you killed her?" Harry pounces quick enough to thrill Perry Mason. Not to be outdone, Lisa joins in the accusation.

"In the same manner as Dallas McGuire?"

"Kandi was killed? With a beer bottle?" I'm trapped in a bizarre game of Clue. Without a clue.

"How did you know the murder weapon was a beer bottle?" Lisa asks.

"Because you said she was killed the same way Dallas was. And I didn't do it."

Lisa looks unhappy and Harry looks even more unhappy with her. She has obviously revealed their trump card too early.

"Look," I say, impatient to get out of my clothing and into a shower. "I left the Tavern with my friend, Angelica and came back here. The only things I killed were a few hundred brain cells and a bottle of Jack Daniels. If you want to know where Kandi went after leaving the bar, I suggest you talk to John Townsend. And if you want to check up on my story, talk to Angelica. She's staying in the ritzy section of this hotel."

Lisa glares at her shoes and Harry glares at me. "We know how to do our job," he snarls. "Don't leave town." And they are gone, leaving me alone with my thoughts.

I'd like to say that the news racks me with sorrow, or that the death of a fellow human being immobilizes me with rage. Memories of the woman that I had known march through my brain with machine-like precision. In the few encounters we'd shared, she'd exhibited the full gamut of emotions. The night of the reception, she was sociable, chatty, even fun. Screaming at her ex-husband uncovered rage. Drunk on excitement and wine, Kandi had been flirtatious, obvious in her desire and need. But all these faces came across as caricatures, shallow representations of what should have been a vital, exciting woman in the prime of life. When Kandi made her transition from Peg Sharpe to Kandi Sex-kitten, she lost her soul; lost that intangible something that makes a person truly desirable. And maybe that's why Dallas dumped her.

This last thought overloads my mental circuits. There is no way that man could have seen the deeper qualities of a woman and then turned on her when they disappeared. If anything, he was probably the catalyst that caused Peg's premature demise. Mr. Sharpe is right. His ex-wife is dead. Not recently though—she's been dead for five years. Still numb but now wide-awake, I gather my things and head for the shower. I need to talk to Angelica, but I need to wash away the dried sweat first...

Smelling a lot better and thinking a lot clearer, I'm at Angelica's room right on the heels of the baby cops.

"Ange, this is getting serious," I say as I push into her room. She looks as unrested as I'd felt when the kids woke me up.

"What clued you in?" she snips. "The first, second or third body?"

I kiss her on her forehead. "You know you're beautiful when you're grumpy? And smelly," I add and wrinkle my nose. Before she protests, I push her towards the bathroom. "Clean up and I'll make coffee. Then you can tell me what you told the Keystone Kids."

The promise brightens her expression and she trots off as requested. I busy myself with the miniature coffee pot and am sipping a cup when she emerges in a cloud of steam.

"You didn't drink it all, did you?" Angelica asks with near panic.

I assure her I hadn't and soon have her tucked into a chair with her own cup. She is still in her pink bathrobe, her hair damp and face makeup free, but she is looking human again. She sips while I tell my story of the morning. Hers is similar.

"I said you left around two, which was at or before the time of the murder. But I also told them that you were in no shape to handle anything as complicated as tracking down a woman and beaning her with a bottle," Angelica says. "I also told them you've been rejected by women plenty of times and it's never driven you to violence."

"I'm glad you're in my corner. It scares me to think what you'd have told them if you hated me."

"What are friends for?"

The sparkle in her eyes sends mixed emotions spilling through me. Worried that the one I want to give into most, smacking her, will set the police hot on my trail, I give into the most comfortable. I laugh. So does Angelica. She uncurls from her chair and makes a new pot of coffee. Once that's complete and she replenishes our cups, we tackle the latest situation.

"Given the hints that Kandi was dropping at the Tavern, this murder has to be related to Dallas'."

"Especially given the modus operandi. But what's the angle?"

"I've been thinking about that. First, she was a Dallas

groupie. The man had a way of attracting obsession. She could have been following him and saw something."

"Uh-huh. That brings up Chase. Didn't you say she and Kandi were fairly thick?"

"They were talking at the reception."

"What if Chase did actually see the murder go down and told Kandi about it? From the newspaper accounts and what you know about the woman, she wasn't above making money the old fashioned way."

"On her back?"

Angelica smiles. "That goes without saying, but I mean extortion. Did she smoke?"

The conversation switchbacks are making me dizzy. "I don't think so. Why? Her health shouldn't be a concern anymore."

"The ashtray, you moron. Maybe she stopped by the night Chase died."

"Oh." This explains why Angelica is a successful executive and I can't even get an article written. Given her performance with the bottle of whiskey last night, however, it doesn't make sense. If anything, she killed a lot more brain cells than I did. Must be genetic. While I'm considering this new puzzle, a knock sounds at the door. "I'll get it; you're not decent."

Angelica fluffs her hair and pulls aside the hem of her robe, exposing a section of leg that would be carded if it tried to buy a mixed drink. "How can you say that's not decent?" she asks, batting her lashes.

I shake my head and open the door just enough to see who is visiting. I expect Detective Levin. I get Derek. He shoves the door open and pushes me aside in time to see Angelica closing her robe.

"Don't stop on my account," he says, bristling like a porcupine.

Part of my issue with Angelica's husband is my inability to take him seriously. As grim as this situation is, I still can't. Thin and twitchy, intense emotion exaggerates both. Years of stress, caffeine and racquetball has kept his weight down and his hair thin. Fortunately for him, fashion caught up to nature and now he shaves his head. Standing before his wife and me, he looks like an angry rodent. Or a pigeon. Of course, a pigeon is a rat with wings, so… I do the worse thing I can possibly do. I laugh. Derek clenches his hands into soft little woman fists and swings. I duck, he misses and Angelica catches him as he falls against the table. Her robe falls open and I notice her body, clad in insignificant pieces of satin, looks as good as the flash of leg I'd caught earlier. She pulls the robe shut, but not before Derek sees where my eyes had been. He turns on her.

"You whore," he screams and swings at her. I catch his arms behind his back and hold him.

"Derek, stop it. There's nothing between Angelica and me and you know it." If he hears me, there's no physical indication. He fights to get free, his body a vibrating mass of live wire.

"He's right, Derek," Angelica cries, tears trickling down her cheeks. "Any problems we have are just between us. Don't drag our friends into our hell."

"Your friend. Not mine," he says with a growl.

Angelica becomes statue-calm. "And that's one of the fundamental problems with our marriage."

"Me?" The word squeaks out before I can stop it. Angelica gives a sad smile and shakes her head.

"No. This isn't your fault, Rex. I mean the fact that our life has no us; it's partitioned too neatly into yours and mine. Right, Derek?"

The man quits struggling and I let him go. He straightens his shirt and throws his head back. I'm in a perfect position to kiss his shiny little pate. Or spit on it. I resist the impulse to do either.

"I won't interrupt your little adventure anymore," Derek says with an amazing level of dignity. "When you're ready to come home, we'll talk. I'll be waiting." And he's gone.

I put my arm around Angelica. "I'm sorry."

"Don't be," she says, her eyes bright but holding the tears

back. "My marriage has been in trouble for a while; at least with your situation there will be an end. And soon. Let's concentrate on fixing your hell first and then I'll go back to mine."

"Thanks. Just in case Napoleon comes back, don't you think you should put on something a little more socially acceptable?"

Angelica gives a wry grin. "Good idea. This wasn't bright, was it? That's what I get for entertaining before I've had coffee."

While she dresses, I sit and think about the past week. If the murders aren't solved quickly, I'll be in a world of hurt. My boss won't see the humor in me not being able to leave Yellow Springs, Mrs. Winthrop won't see the humor in me not being able to pay for another week of literary paradise and I don't see the humor in possible incarceration. We have to shake a villain loose.

"Uh-oh," Angelica says as she comes back into the room. She's dressed in jeans, a white polo shirt and sandals. I prefer the pink fluffy thing she was wearing earlier, but neither one of us needs the temptation. Or at least I don't.

"What do you mean, uh-oh?"

She shakes her head. "I recognize that look. What scheme have you devised?"

"The situation is becoming fairly desperate, wouldn't you say?"

"Ye-es."

"There are three, possibly four viable suspects, right?"

"Four?"

"John, Mr. Sharpe, Elmira and the Culbreaths."

Angelica frowns. "The Culbreaths?"

"They're creepy; they should be locked away."

"If creepy were a felony, the streets would be empty and the jails would be overflowing. Strike them off the list." Angelica's tone is not to be argued with. I reluctantly take them off my mental list. "Now," she continues, "why Elmira?"

"Jealousy in the first instance, self-preservation in the last. Once she'd already killed her lover, killing a blackmailer would be trivial."

A slow nod rewards this logic. "And Chase?"

"At this point, it doesn't matter," I say and watch Angelica's eyebrows rise. I feel a twinge of guilt, but shake it off. The girl is dead. Me accused of her murder will not bring her back or even clean up her memory. "Trying to figure out what happened in her apartment is only wasting energy."

Angelica taps her teeth. "I don't know. Without having the advantage of the forensic lab at our disposal, we need all the information we can get. There's something about Chase' death that's been bugging me. I just can't pinpoint it. Poirot never left a clue un-examined."

"As far as Chase is concerned, my little gray cells are tapped out. Let's concentrate on the real murders and ignore the questionable one. For the time being."

It's obvious that Angelica isn't convinced, but she relents. "Elmira is a possibility, but my bets are on the lawyer or the old man. Both have questionable pasts, solid links to each of the girls and reason to hate Dallas."

"That's my take exactly," I say. "But I wonder if the police have the same take on the situation."

"I don't see why not. They'd be idiots not to come to the same conclusion."

Angelica's indignation makes me laugh. "I'm glad you're so confident. Unfortunately, there's one reason the police won't see it our way."

"What?" she asks.

"Me."

"Good point. Not only have you been a central character in each of the deaths—"

"The last one is a stretch," I protest.

"Not only have you been central to each death, I don't think the police like you."

I can't argue her points. "That's why we've got to prove my innocence once and for all."

"I take it we're back to my original uh-oh."

I grin. "Exactly. I have a plan."

"And that would be?"

"Just be at the farewell luncheon and leave it at that. The less you know the better. It could be dangerous."

"I've eaten the food here, what could be more dangerous?"

The girl is smart as well as beautiful.

26

Convincing Angelica that she's better off not knowing my plan takes more persuasion than I anticipate. And more time. For some reason the girl doesn't trust me. Eventually I make her realize I'm holding fast and she concedes.

"I have to go; there are things that need to be taken care of before lunch. You be there at," I say and look at my watch. "Oh my god. I only have a half hour. The lunch starts at noon. Be there at ten till."

The frown on her cute little face makes my heart swell. "What if they don't let me in? You'll be alone."

"Just tell them you're with me. My name opens doors."

"I just wish they didn't have bars."

A kiss on the forehead and I escape. I have just enough time.

The pierced and painted Antiochians are running as late as I am and they welcome my help.

"How about if I set the tables?" I ask a bored youth with dreadlocks and a lightning bolt tattooed on his forehead.

"Sure man, knock yourself out," he says. His attention is fixed on a girl with a shaved head and a matching lightning bolt running down her scalp and ending at her neck.

Obviously a match made in heaven.

"I'll even put out these placards," I offer and take the box of nametags from him.

"Cool," he grins. "I don't know half these geezers. I might even put a vegan by an Adkins advocate."

"The horror... Why don't you go check on the eats? That young lady over there looks as if she could use some help."

"Cool," he says and saunters over to the lady in question. You can feel the electricity in the air.

Once the boy is occupied, I sort through the box. Vegetarians seated by carnivores are not my concern. Gathering the suspects in a tidy group is. There is room for eight at each table and that's perfect. Within minutes, seven placards are located and positioned. I pencil Angelica's name onto a blank one and put it beside my seat. I want her close for her safety and my peace of mind. The rest of the nametags go in whatever order they come up in the box. The kid with the dreadlocks would be horrified, but that's what he gets for trusting a strange geezer.

I wait for Angelica at the door and usher her in before her presence is questioned. Once seated at the table with her nametag validating her right to be there, I relax.

"Has your plan been put in motion?" she asks as she scans the growing crowd.

There's a heated discussion at the table with Ms. Hellstrom; as the guest of honor, she thinks it's beneath her station to be seated with the volunteers that drive attendees to the airport. The volunteers, two intense Mailer wannabes, are ecstatic and refuse to be relocated. It's fun to watch the mayhem, but my attention is required elsewhere.

"Yes it has and here it goes," I answer as the Culbreaths sweep into the room.

"Roger, here's our table," Rose shrieks. "How wonderful! I was afraid we wouldn't have a chance to socialize with our favorite friends before we left. Talk about luck." Before I can stop her, she swaps her placard with John's. Now she's by me and John is by Angelica. She repeats the switch with Roger and Sylvia. "There. Now it's boy-girl, boy-girl," she announces and plops onto the chair beside me. Her perfume cascades over me, suffocating with its flowery stench.

"Thank goodness you came. That was nearly a social catastrophe," Angelica says with a sunny grin. Retaliation for leaving her out of my plan. I grit my teeth and wait for the rest of the gang.

Sylvia and John show up as the salads arrive. John looks tired, but perks up when he sees who is sitting to his right. Sylvia stays tired. Mr. Sharpe arrives right behind them, and ignores his tag; preferring to sit beside Roger in lieu of Sylvia. Probably to distance himself from John. The elderly man looks every bit of his seventy odd years and then some. Insomnia may be contagious. Elmira shows up and confirms my suspicions. We'll all be glad to get back to a normal schedule. Vacations are murder.

"What's on the agenda?" Rose asks with a wink and a bite of her salad. I am not going to miss her one bit.

"The payment for lunch is listening to a series of heart felt, long winded good-bye speeches," Elmira observes. "Then it's good-byes all around and we're free to return to our lives."

"Amen," echoes around the table. This is as good a time as any to make my play.

"There's been an addition to the agenda," I announce and the answering silence is gratifying. Tension electrifies the air. "The little matter of—" the dramatic pause would make my namesakes proud, "—murder."

The lack of gasps or shifting eyes is disappointing. Thank goodness Angelica is here.

"What, Rex? Do you know something?" she asks with just the right amount of innocence.

"Yes. The identity of the killer."

Again, nothing. Until Sylvia laughs. "What could you possibly know that the police don't? They're still puzzling it out and they're professionals."

"Yes, but they weren't with Chase the night of her death.

The girl spilled secrets between the sheets that the police had no way of ferreting out."

It's satisfying to see the good humor drain from the judge's face. And everyone else at the table.

"If you know something important to the case, why don't you tell the cops? That's withholding evidence." John is gnawing on his right thumb. It's hard to picture him remaining cool in a courtroom setting. Maybe that's why he turned to writing.

"At first I wasn't sure who to trust. There's police involvement and I fear for my safety. And those around me."

"Oooh, how exciting," Rose says as she claps her hands. A server appears.

"Are you ready for your entrees?" he asks and gathers uneaten salads. He's not my friend from earlier, but he could be a cousin. Or brother. The youths are blurring together. Without waiting for an answer, he scurries off to return with plates of chicken breast and rice. Wine is absent and, for once, I'm glad.

"Go on, Rex," Rose urges as she shovels rice into her mouth and sprays most of it out in excitement. "What did the girl tell you? Was it a deathbed confession? Was she in cahoots with the villain? Did she kill herself because of the overwhelming guilt? And what about Kandi?"

"Kandi was also Chase' confidante, but the woman became greedy. She knew that it wasn't what Chase did; it was what she saw. Kandi tried to profit off the dead girl's information. And the fact that Chase' death wasn't suicide. No my friends, it too was murder." My melodrama is wasted. Nobody runs; nobody breaks down sobbing. They just wait.

"All right," Elmira says, tapping her fingers on the table. "Who did it?"

"That's information I'm saving for the police," I say. Elmira rolls her eyes.

"Then why did you even bring it up?" She picks at her congealing lunch. The rest of the table follows suit. Except for Rose.

"Well," she says and presses her meaty thigh against mine. "I think it's terribly exciting and I'm glad you shared all this with us, Rex. I feel as if I'm living an Agatha Christie whodunit. This has been the best vacation," she squeals. Her grin is decorated with bits of pepper.

Nausea sweeps over me and I turn to my own barely edible lunch.

Rose and Roger chatter, their heads close together, and stop only when the workshop director stands to give her long-winded good-bye speech. I don't hear any of it or even realize who herds me out of the banquet hall.

"That was the stupidest, most dangerous thing you could have done," Angelica hisses, close by my left elbow. The rest of the crowd dissipates, leaving us walking alone towards the Glen.

"The only thing stupid or dangerous about it is that now Rose is even more enamored of me than she was before. And I agree; that is dangerous."

"Be serious," Angelica snaps and shakes me. "Whoever this person is, they've killed two times for sure, maybe three. You're a prime target."

Still giddy from the success of my plan, I struggle to keep the excitement out of my voice. I don't want Angelica any more upset than she already is. "That's what I want. I'm disappointed that I didn't get more of a reaction, but the killer has already proven themselves to be a cool customer."

"Okay, Mr. Spade. What's the next step?"

"I wander around Yellow Springs with a bull's eye on my forehead."

"Forgive me. I thought the luncheon stunt was the extent of your stupidity. As always, you've proven me wrong." Angelica is shaking, from either anger or fear. My bet is on a combination.

"Ange, I've got to flush the killer out."

She calms down a little, but not much. "It's not too bad, I guess. Let's stay together. That's safer."

"No. I didn't tell you my plan so you'd be as surprised as the rest of the crowd. That worked just fine. Now, I'll wander around, alone, and you stay safely ensconced at the boarding house. Actually, I'd prefer you go home. I can handle it from here."

"No way," she snorts. "Derek is waiting for me and I'd rather face a murderer. I will go back to my room, but only if you'll take this." She shoves her cell phone into my hand.

"I've never used one of these."

The shock in her eyes is what I'd hoped for when I announced I knew who the murderer is. I have to work on my timing. She shakes off her disbelief and gives a quick tutorial. I hope I'll be able to recall the instructions when the time comes. Sam Spade never realized how good he had it.

A few minutes later, Angelica is gone and I'm wandering per plan. In my pocket, the phone's weight gives me the confidence I need to leave the safety of the village. I make my way towards Glen Helen. In spite of its mutant inhabitants and bizarre forms of self-expression, I feel as if I'm leaving sanctuary. My pace slows to a crawl as I reach the path leading into the dim forest. I take a deep breath and step forward. A harsh shrill draws me up short.

The phone is shrieking at me and flashing a wicked green light. I push buttons and finally hit on a valid combination.

"Hello?" I say into the miniature device. Angelica spills out.

"Rex, where are you? The police were here."

"Then it's a good thing I'm here."

"No, it's not. They're worried about you."

"That's a nice change of pace." I continue into the Glen. It's good to be out of the sun.

"Will you be serious? Sylvia told them about your luncheon stunt and they think you're in danger. Your plan may be a little too successful."

Panic oozes out of the phone. Tension builds along my spine. There's a presence in the Glen; pressing on all sides.

Hunting me. I pick up my pace.

"Do they have any idea whodunit?" I ask.

A crackle replies. I shake the phone, but it doesn't make any difference. I reach a clear spot in the trail and make out a frantic question. "Where are you?"

"The Glen. By the main hall."

"Get out of there." Her tone adds to the prickly sensation at the back of my neck. I swallow hard. "Get out now!"

Fear mounts and I turn to scramble back up the steep trail to safety. Sunlight dapples off the upraised bottle that swings at my head. I duck and the glass bounces off my skull. My balance goes and I grab Mr. Sharpe to break my fall. It fails and we tumble down the path, his skeletal body creating more bruises than the rocks. We come to rest at the base of a tree, me groaning from the fall and he sobbing. The sky, the path, the leaves, all swirl into a kaleidoscope just before I sink into unconsciousness.

27

When I come to, Mr. Sharpe is in a crumpled heap beside me. Déjà vu sweeps over me; I'm still groaning, he's still sobbing. His beer bottle is lying close by, glittering with evil intent in the blazing afternoon sun. Before the murderer can escape, I act. Scrambling to my feet, I approach the old man with caution. He ignores me. Obviously an act. He's responsible for the cold-blooded murders of at least two people, maybe three. I do the only thing I can. I sit on him.

Sitting on Mr. Sharpe is like trying to balance on a pile of kindling. He gives a dry "whump", squirms a little, and then goes still. For a second, I think I've killed the killer. Then I hear—feel—the sobbing. It's probably rage at being bested by a more intelligent foe. Visions of Sherlock and Watson facing down Moriarty dance through my head as I mull over my investigative skills. Maybe it's time for a career change...

After sitting for what seems like eternity, I consider my situation. Since Angelica knows I'm in danger, I assumed she and the Calvary would show up just as I apprehended the fiend. Hitchcock would have timed it that way. Instead, I'm uncomfortable, somewhat embarrassed and the climax is becoming anti. But then I hear them. Sirens. I affix a serious expression onto my face, assume a more macho position on the still weeping old man and wait for the authorities. And the adoration that is long overdue. Both aren't long in coming.

Angelica is the first into the clearing. She throws her arms around me and almost knocks me off my captive.

"Easy, I've got a criminal in custody. We don't want him to get away," I say and pat Mr. Sharpe. He moans. Angelica pulls away and smacks me on the shoulder.

"This is the stupidest thing you've ever pulled," Angelica says. She's smiling, but her eyes shine with unnatural brightness. I take her hand and squeeze it, assuring her with my grip, my gaze and my smile that everything is okay. A single tear slips down her cheek. And then the clearing explodes.

"All right, Mr. Barker," Lisa says, her gun pointed uncomfortably close to my family jewels. "You can get up now. We've got the perp covered." Harry is close behind, his gun drawn as well, but not matching her serious countenance. He is grinning wildly.

"Mr. Sharpe, don't make any sudden moves. We're prepared to do whatever it takes to perform our duties," he announces. His gun is pointed where it should be, at the murderer. But then again, Harry has always liked me better than Lisa does. I have that way with women. I ease up and away, grateful for Angelica's steadying arm when my legs threaten to collapse underneath me.

"You okay?" she asks.

"Yeah; I'm fine. My legs went to sleep."

In the background, Lisa is reading the Miranda to a handcuffed, weeping Mr. Sharpe. It's hard to envision him braining Dallas and then functioning normally. I point this out to Harry.

"I've seen this millions of times," Harry says, assuming a more serious air now that he's talking shop. In the last century, Yellow Springs has probably been the scene of two, maybe three murders. Until last week. Now, the sleepy little village is a regular hot bed of criminal activity. "A murderer will commit one, two, a dozen murders without an iota of emotion. But, faced with discovery and incarceration, they fall apart. Pathetic, but that's how the criminal psyche works."

Angelica and I grin at each other and don't comment. In my current frame of mind, if I say anything I won't be able to stop laughing. Lisa notices our exchange.

"Regardless of what you might think, Mr. Barker, we did not need your interference. Through careful investigation, my partner and I uncovered this man's past and his motive. We were merely awaiting the appropriate time to bring him into custody."

"Before or after he committed another murder?" The comment leaps out of my mouth before my brain engages. Angelica squeezes my arm in warning. Lisa is not amused.

"The only risk was your ridiculous stunt. And—don't quote me on this—some murders aren't necessarily bad."

Before I can ask any questions, Harry, Lisa and the perp march out of the clearing and my life. I start to follow, but a cool hand stops me.

"Let them go, Rex," Angelica says. "Let it all go."

I turn to my friend and give her a tremendous hug. She gives one back and we collapse onto each other with relief. Once we've laughed ourselves dry, we locate her cell phone and then make our way up the path, hand in hand.

"It'll be great to get back to life," Angelica says as we come out of the trees and onto Antioch turf.

"I'm not sure what that is anymore," I say, blinking in the sunlight.

"For you, there has to be a major shift in paradigm."

I stop and face Angelica. "Whadda you mean?"

"You came here to spark your literary muse, right?"

"Sure, but I failed in a big way," I admit. "I haven't written a thing since I got here."

Angelica grabs me by the shoulders. "But you've been handed an opportunity most writers would die for."

Maybe it's the bout of unconsciousness, but the girl is making no sense at all. I shrug and shake my head at her. She lets out an exasperated sigh and drops her hands.

"You've been at the heart of a real-life murder mystery. Regardless of what Tweedle-Dee and Tweedle-Dummy think, you were miles ahead of them in investigative talent. Now all you have to do is write it down. With the publicity this case will get, it's a ready-made best seller. Publishing houses will be climbing over each other to make you an offer."

Her eyes glitter and her chest heaves. Prickles run up and down my spine as I embrace her enthusiasm. "Ya think?"

"It's that kind of golden-tongued utilization of the English language that makes you a shoo-in." We both laugh and I give her another hug.

"What makes me a shoo-in is my support structure. Thanks for not giving up on me." We walk towards the boarding house. In no time, we are there. Even Mrs. Winthrop's scowling face doesn't ruin my mood. I wave and blow her a kiss as we stroll to the staircase. She sniffs and marches back into her den.

"How about a farewell/triumph dinner?" Angelica asks before entering her air-conditioned paradise.

"I'd even consider the Tavern. You buying?"

"Sure. But only if you show me an outline by the time we meet." She laugh at my expression. "Okay; the start of an outline."

I agree and head up my stairway, not even dreading the lurking heat. As soon as I enter my room, I grab a notebook and pen and stretch out across the bed. Ideas flow faster than I can write them down. I scratch on the lined paper at a furious pace for at least fifteen minutes. Then the heat and the excitement overcome me. I drift into sleep and don't even notice the pen slide out of my fingers, onto the floor and into oblivion.

In spite of my exhaustion, I wake up, take a shower and am somewhat alert when I meet Angelica in the lobby. I thrust my pages at her and she takes them with a grin.

"Unbelievable," she says as she scans them.

I bet she hasn't talked to Derek. She's fresh and animated,

her face radiating happiness at our success. In spite of the heat, the woman is cool and poised, her glow complemented by the silky rose dress she wears; a slinky sheath held up by spider web thin straps and forming to her body like cling wrap. It leaves little to the imagination and that's a good thing. Derek is an idiot. Silence interrupts my musings.

"What?" I ask Angelica, who is no longer reading and is now scowling.

"This is just a collection of disjointed thoughts."

"I was free braining."

The frown deepens. "Did you make that up?"

"No," I insist, the protest sharper than one expects from an innocent person. "This is one of the techniques I learned from the workshop. When you're starting with a book, write down whatever comes to mind, then gather them into logical groups and go from there."

Angelica's eyes narrows and she taps one lovely, sandaled foot. "I don't see how you can get anything out of this mess," she says and shakes the papers at me. I snatch them back.

"That's because you're an outsider. You can't possibly understand how the creative process works." Her eyes shift slightly. "Besides, you want me to start writing and I have. I expect support. Encouragement. If this is all I'm going to get when I try..."

Score. She crumples. "I'm sorry, Rex," she says and hugs me. Her breasts squish softly against my chest and I linger a little more than I should. She doesn't seem to notice. "You're right. I don't know much about writing, but I do know that everyone needs to find their own approach to creativity. Forgive me?"

I pull away from Angelica and pause, long enough to make her squirm, but not long enough to allow her to think. When I nod, her grin returns. Before she can speak, I hold up my hand, palm towards her. "But only if you buy dinner."

"You're on," she says and takes my hand, pulling me towards the back exit. A loud sniff from Mrs. Winthrop, lurking in the office, sends us on our way.

The journey to the Tavern brings back memories of when Angelica picked me up at the sheriff's office. As we drive, I try to reconcile the images of that night with the current panorama. Since then, the village has become more welcoming and more shrouded. Behind the eclectic buildings infused with history and culture, there is a roiling undercurrent of passion, creativity and individuality echoed by few other places. The result is that, much like earlier years, I am both repulsed and fascinated by Yellow Springs. I can't see myself living here, but I know it won't be long before I'm back. Especially now that I'm not facing long-term habitation of the local jail.

"That episode in the Glen was strange," I say. Angelica takes a little while to respond since she is maneuvering into the twisted maze of parking places behind the Tavern.

"In what way?" she asks after giving up on the parking lot and doing another turn around the block.

"I didn't think about it until now, but two of Mr. Sharpe's victims were killed by a blow to the head."

"Right," Angelica says, only half listening. The parking search is a daunting challenge. "That's why it's lucky you heard him come up behind you. If you hadn't ducked," the flash of taillights signals an empty space is becoming available. Angelica yanks her car around and waits, signal blinking, for the driver to back out of the space. She continues. "You'd be lying in state with a tag on your big toe. And I would still be explaining to the police why you had my cell phone and I let you run off and be a sitting duck. Oh, and I would have lost my best drinking partner."

The driver finally clears the space and we move in, a mere block away from the Tavern. Before meeting the crowd, I want to finish my train of thought. "But that's just the point. I didn't duck. He did hit me."

"Why didn't you say something? You might have a concussion."

"That's what's wrong. The bottle hit me square, but there isn't even a bruise. I've had worse bumps rolling over in bed."

"What's your point?" Angelica asks, making no move to get out of the car even though the engine is off. The temperature is rising and sweat is beading up on my forehead. She's not even glistening.

"How could he have killed Dallas or Kandi? I doubt he could squash a fly with that arm."

"There are plenty of documented cases of people gaining supernatural strength from rage or fear. You were just lucky." Angelica opens the door, the topic closed. I remain seated.

"Have you ever actually met someone that did?"

"Did what?" She pauses, one foot out.

"Lifted a car. Or pulled a girder off a trapped person."

"What are you saying? Do you think he's innocent?"

The question stirs up a mixture of emotions I don't like. "It doesn't feel right that he's the killer."

Angelica's impatient. "That's pretty flimsy. He had motive, a history of violence and opportunity. Maybe by the time he came after you he was worn down by stress. And guilt. After all, murder is hard work."

"True," I agree, hoping that my desire to believe what she's saying isn't grounded in self-preservation. I grin at Angelica and she grins back. "Let's celebrate a life without suspicion."

"And possible incarceration," she adds and hops out of the car.

"And great book potential." I follow her into the Tavern.

28

For the first time since Dallas died, I approach the Tavern without trepidation. The yeasty smell of beer soaked floors, smoke-filled air and the babble of drunken and soon to be drunk voices welcome me. Even the historical figures on the wall eye me benignly, now as assured of my innocence as the rest of the community. I'm not even put off by Rose waving us over to her table. She jumps up and envelopes me in a lilac tinged, beery embrace that isn't nearly as nice as the one I enjoyed from Angelica.

"Rex, isn't it too marvelous? You're free from the malevolent cloud of suspicion that darkened your days."

At least, that's what I think she says. Most of the words are lost as she crushes me between massive breasts. My ears buzz from the vibration and I struggle free. Once loose, I step back and catch my breath. I blink. Rose and her brother are once again dressed in English tweed, sweating and beaming ear to ear. I decide not to comment. Angelica chooses a seat beside Sylvia and pulls up a chair for me. Now that Mr. Sharpe isn't with us and Elmira most likely won't show, there's more room but I still have little choice. I take the seat, which is beside Rose. I sit and Rose immediately plops down beside me, her jacket scratching my arm as she scoots close.

"Help us, Rex dear." Rose waves at a half-full pitcher.

"Nonsense," John says and gestures to a girl hurrying past with a tray full of dirty dishes. She pauses, chewing on her lower lip, which is a near ebony shade of purple. "Bring a Jack on the rocks and," John pauses, raising his eyebrows to Angelica.

"Rum and Coke with a twist of lime. Morgan," she answers with a smile. John nods to the waitress.

"Sylvia," Angelica asks. "What's the latest on the investigation?"

"In all my years on the bench, I think this is the most twisted case I've seen. The old man admitted to beaning Dallas."

"Because of Kandi," I add.

Sylvia nods. "And because of the manuscript review. Mr. Sharpe followed him out of the Tavern and tried to reason with him, but Dallas laughed him off. In a rage, Mr. Sharpe grabbed a bottle and hit the victim as he walked away."

"Is that what Chase saw?" Angelica asks.

"Exactly. The poor girl must have told Kandi before ending her life. Kandi saw an opportunity to get more money out of her ex-husband and resorted to blackmail," Sylvia says and takes a deep drag on her cigarette.

"Which proves how stupid the woman was," John interjects.

"Which one?" Roger asks, "Chase or Kandi?"

John snorts. "Both, really. Chase for taking her life over an asshole, Kandi for trying to blackmail a known killer. A killer who's probably already tapped out. I mean, he is living with his daughter, isn't he?"

"That doesn't make sense," I say, but the arrival of our drinks interrupts me. John and Sylvia order another round and then attention is back to me.

"What doesn't make sense, dear?" Rose says, patting my hand with her plump sweaty one.

"Chase said she was afraid to go to the police. Why would she be afraid of turning in Mr. Sharpe?"

Sylvia's laugh ends in a coughing fit. When she can breathe again, she takes another pull on her cigarette and then stubs it out. "These will be the death of me," she rasps. "You have it wrong, Rex. Chase wasn't afraid of turning in Mr. Sharpe. She was afraid of the police. Given her history of drug use, it's understandable."

Memories tumble through my brain. "No, that's not what she said. She was specifically afraid because of the tie to the police."

This time it's John's turn to laugh. "And how drunk were you when she was spilling her guts, old man?" Everyone joins in, but it's Angelica that slices through me like a sword.

"Alcohol doesn't affect my hearing," I protest, which brings on even more laughter. I toss back my drink and wave for another.

Sylvia is the first to regain her composure. "Don't be upset, Rex. We're all just relieved this nasty business is over. Mr. Sharpe will be spending his last days in a cozy padded cell with a custom tailored jacket and we'll get on with our lives. Few cases are wrapped up this tidily."

"Don't you think it's a little too tidy?" I insist. "Life is rarely this neat."

"Now you're just being melodramatic; as if we're living an Agatha Christie novel. A bad Christie novel."

"Oh, speaking of mystery novels, I forgot to tell you our good news," Rose bubbles, her eyes sparkling with excitement. Her sibling's face is split in two by the grin he's sporting. We wait. They grin. Two Cheshire cats.

"Well, spill it," Sylvia orders as she lights another cigarette. Smoke hangs around her face, imparting a hellish taint.

"Oh, I'm sorry," Rose squeals. "We're just so excited. Our agent has gotten us a deal with a major publisher. We're going to write a fictionalized account of this sordid affair."

"What?" I nearly choke on my drink. I can feel Angelica's eyes boring into my neck, but I refuse to make eye contact.

"Is that why you dug out your Miss Marple and Sherlock Holmes outfits?" John asks with a twinkle in his voice. Rose and Roger nod in unison. Not cats; bobble-heads. If they're not careful, their skinny little necks will snap, causing their round heads to roll away like bowling balls.

"Exactly," Roger says. "Being in costume gets us in the mood."

"At our age, it's the best we can do," Rose says with a ribald wink and the standard thigh squeeze. I ignore it.

"What do you mean, fictionalized?" I demand.

"Instead of Mr. Sharpe, the perpetrator is actually a down-on-his-luck bartender. Full of rage at the way his manuscript is treated, he removes the source of his rejection."

Blood pulses in my ears. "And the two women?"

Roger takes over. "The first is another case of rejection; the second is blackmail. A brother and sister writing team solves the mysteries just as the killer is about to do away with another woman."

"The killer's beautiful friend?" Angelica asks with a wry smile.

"Exactly," Rose cackles. "Being close to the fiend, she realizes the depth of his rage. She promises she won't tell, but he's beyond believing or trusting. He turns on her and tries to choke her just as the police arrive."

"And everyone lives happily ever after?" I ask with as much sarcasm as I can infuse into one sentence. The group ignores me and showers the gruesome twosome with questions. They soak it up as quickly as I soak up whiskey.

"Your little book will be a lot more believable if you know the real story," I blurt into the din. The sound freezes mid-babble.

"The real story?" Sylvia asks with an arched eyebrow.

"Yeah," I say and meet her gaze without blinking. "Chase told me more than I've let on. As did Kandi." This warrants a cloud of smoke blown in my direction. I try to remain stoic but fail, first merely choking and then hacking from the bottom of my lungs. Nobody offers to pat me on the back. Out of the corner of my eye, I notice John snags a cigarette from Sylvia. Must be a special occasion.

"That's ridiculous, Rex," Rose says. "If you know something that has a bearing on the case, why haven't you gone to the police?"

"Like I said earlier. There's a tie-in that wouldn't be safe for the messenger." I'm feeling the whiskey. I warm to my story. "Judge, you know about informants. Their lives aren't worth a plugged nickel, especially if they're squealing on the foundation of the legal system."

Sylvia steadily meets my gaze. Her cigarette nearly burns her fingers and she flicks it away, lighting up the next before the embers die from the first.

"What are you going to do?" This question is from John, who looks like Sam Spade. Right down to the cigarette drooping off his lip. I wish I had something to add to the investigation. This is the most respect I've had in a long time.

"I'm not sure," I admit. "I'm going to think on it." Five pairs of eyes stare at me. I raise my glass in a toast. "To writers. May their brains never run out of ideas and their pens never run out of ink."

"We use a computer," Rose says in a deadpan voice. Nobody joins my toast, so I drain my glass alone. Angelica stands up.

"I'm ready to turn in; it's been an extremely long day. Come on, Rex," she says.

I remain seated. "I don't wanna go. I'm having a great time."

"Well I'm not," Sylvia says as she stands up. John follows, shoving back his chair.

"I have to pack. Morning'll be here before we know it," he adds.

Rose and Roger get to their feet as well. "Same here. We have to leave earlier than we'd planned. Monday morning we have to hand our agent an outline. There's a lot to do in the next twenty-four hours."

Within seconds everyone is gone except Angelica who is still waiting for me to get up. "You really know how to kill a party," she says, glaring at me.

"Didn't you hear anything? How can I write a book now that the Bobbsey twins stole my idea?"

"They don't have a lock on every version of the story. Just write a different one."

"You don't understand," I whine. "It's ruined. The whole idea is ruined."

Angelica is nearly purple with anger. Or maybe frustration. Or maybe angry frustration. Regardless, she loses her patience. "Fine. Don't even try. It's what you do best. Maybe the Culbreaths' take on the situation is the right one. The loser bartender who won't accept responsibility for his own actions. Always blaming the rest of the world for his failures. That's easy isn't it? That way you don't have to try. Failure isn't an option if you never start."

The server appears, her lips blacker than ever. "Staying or going?" she asks, bored with the answer before I give it.

"Staying," I say. "And I'll need a drink."

"Fine," the girl says and saunters off.

Angelica looks as if she's about to explode. "I told you I'm ready to leave."

"And I told you before we left the boarding house that I'm in the mood to celebrate," I say. Without another word, she stalks away, leaving me to my whiskey and self-pity. Eventually, the whiskey is all that's left.

It's hard to say how I made it back to my room or into bed. The next morning, I blame my pounding head on the heat. Jack Daniels has never turned on me like this. A shower helps and I'm able to pack my things and get downstairs in record time. Mrs. Winthrop has my bill waiting.

"What's this?" I ask, pointing to a twenty-five dollar damages fee.

"Scratching the floor. It's going to cost a lot more than that to get it fixed, but I'm giving you the benefit of the doubt."

I should protest and force the old bat to remove the unfair charge. But that takes effort. As I've mentioned many times before, I rarely take the difficult path. I clench my jaw and hand over the extra cash. She takes it with a witchy grin.

"Come back any time, Mr. Barker," and she turns to leave.

"Can you ring Angelica's room and let her know I'm here?" I ask her disappearing back. She stops and turns back, her grin even wider and more evil.

"Your nice young friend?" she asks with an air of innocence that sends chills down my skin.

"Yes. The one on the favored side of this house of horrors."

"She checked out early this morning. Left before daybreak. Most likely returning home to that charming husband of hers."

Without letting her see any more of my humiliation, I leave, struggling under the weight of my suitcases. In spite of the early hour, by the time I make it to my unair-conditioned car, sweat pours off my body. I decide to give the cafeteria one last try before slinking back to Dayton and every day life. The fact that Angelica left without saying good-bye worries me, but only a little. We've had tiffs before and our friendship survived. It will again.

The cafeteria is sparsely populated since most of the attendees left yesterday to get a jump on the trip home. For reasons unknown to me, the majority traveled long distances to be humiliated for a fee. Angelica would argue that they came to take advantage of the creative atmosphere, but what does she know? I help myself to the remnants of the breakfast buffet, watery egg substitute and meatless sausages, and make a beeline for a familiar table. The four remaining compatriots quit talking as I walk up.

"We have to get on the road," Roger says, picking up his tray. Rose grabs hers and follows him towards the exit. The mumbled good-byes are barely audible.

"In a strange way, I'm going to miss them," I admit and bite into one of the vegan sausages. The rubbery texture makes me doubt it's edible—more likely made of some petroleum byproduct. The coffee isn't bad, though, and I drink deeply.

"They've got the right idea," John says and rises.

Sylvia doesn't move. "Don't be silly. You have, what? An hour, hour and a half at most?"

"True," John agrees, but doesn't sit down. "But this way I'll have most of the day to unwind before work tomorrow." He laughs and flushes slightly. "Being a lawyer again will be tough. I like the writing life."

This cracks the judge's somber expression. She smiles. "I know what you mean. In spite of the murders, this has been fun."

"Aren't you heading out?"

"No," Sylvia says. "I'm going to enjoy the last moments of my literary adventure."

John shakes his head. "What about your dearly beloved? Isn't the honorable Mr. Anderson pining away? Counting the minutes until your return?"

Sylvia gives a cross between a snort and a cough. John pecks her on the cheek, throws me a cursory good-bye and then he too is gone. Sylvia watches him leave and scans the cafeteria. Except for a few trolls bustling in the back, we're alone. She opens her purse and pulls out a pack. She lights a cigarette and blows a perfect ring in my direction, her eyes narrowed with enjoyment and another emotion I can't identify.

"Should you be doing that?" I ask.

She shrugs. "What are they going to do? Throw me out? Make me go home?"

I look around. No one is paying any attention. I push fake eggs around on my tray.

"Mr. Anderson?" I ask, trying to place the name. It's familiar. Has she mentioned him at all this week? Of course, Angelica does everything she can to avoid talking about Derek. Sylvia echoes my thoughts.

"My husband. John thinks he's an insufferable prick. So do I, but divorce isn't good for public image," she says, letting the smoke leak out of her mouth in a lazy curl. Abruptly, she asks, "Where's your little friend?"

"Angelica?"

"Uh-huh."

"She left this morning. I'll catch up with her later."

Sylvia inhales deeply and blows another ring. "You don't have a lot of friends, do you Mr. Barker?"

"I have my share. I just haven't done very well this week. Out of my element."

The cigarette doesn't take long to burn down and Sylvia drops it onto her plate. It lies among the remnants of potatoes and bacon and smolders, a bright memory of wicked life. A smoke tendril drifts up and I stare at it, mesmerized by its lazy curls.

"Are you going to turn me in?" the judge asks with a brittle laugh. I jump.

"Wh-why?"

"For smoking. Some people see it as murder. Practically a felony."

Her tone chills; nauseates. I watch the cigarette burn, unable to look away, unwilling to meet her eyes. It finally dies; an ashy snake curled on itself. The memory percolating in my subconscious bubbles to the surface. I raise my eyes and meet hers. She knows.

"So tell me," she asks, lighting a new cigarette. "What haven't you told the police?"

My calmness surprises me more than it does her. "That you were in Chase' apartment the night she died. That you're the reason she was afraid to go to the police."

"That's interesting; why do you think I was there?"

"Because Chase was out of cigarettes and the next morning there were ashes in the ashtray."

Sylvia laughs but it's cold and biting. Humorless. "Lots of people smoke. Why does it have to be me?"

"Because there weren't any butts. And there aren't many people who smoke nonfilters. You do."

"All right. What about Dallas? What motive could I possibly have?" She's watching me intently; her words light, her gaze anything but.

"John."

"That's rich," she says, laughing again, her eyes steady.

"Some of this is supposition, but I assume Mr. Sharpe approached Dallas first, got into an argument and hit him with a bottle. Most likely ran when he realized what he'd done. You saw it or the old guy got a lucky swing in and Dallas was dazed or maybe even on the ground. Regardless, it was your opportunity to finish him off. That's what Chase saw."

"And I did this for John?" Her amusement is orchestrated, hollow.

"You love him. Will do anything for him." Another cigarette bites the dust only to be replaced with another. I am amazed that every fire alarm in the place isn't going off.

"How romantic," she says. "And Kandi?"

"Chase told her. Not that Mr. Sharpe had done it, but that you had. He didn't have any money and Kandi knew that. She'd drained him years before."

The judge claps her hands. "Bravo, Mr. Barker. You've learned a lot this week. Creative, imaginative, original. Unfortunately, there's one problem."

The temperature in the room plummets. I shiver. "And that is?"

"No proof. You just admitted it's supposition, which implies that Chase told you nothing. You merely put together an outrageous scenario based on the lack of butts. A lack of evidence doesn't win cases, Mr. Barker."

The last is a hiss and I almost lose my tasteless breakfast. She's right. "So why did you do it?"

Sylvia stares at a point somewhere beyond my left ear. "Why not?" she murmurs, almost to herself. "It's fitting that this mimic one of those dreadful English cozies where everything is tied up in a neat little package." Without blinking, her eyes meet mine. "All right. Because Dallas was a nasty bully who delighted in crushing other people's dreams. And he was a drug dealer that the local yokels hadn't been able to convict."

Another memory jumps to the forefront. A slippery drug

dealer let out on a technicality. Anderson. I was not only wrong; I'm stupid. John wasn't involved at any level. Except as an excuse. "Faun was your daughter." Not a question.

Sylvia freezes along with time. Even the planet stops revolving for one sub-arctic moment. Then the world starts turning again and one cigarette is stubbed out only to be replaced by another. "How did you know that?"

"It was in a newspaper article. I didn't make the connection at first. Is McMahan your professional name?"

She nods. Still stiff. Still frozen. Still dead. "My law degree was issued under my maiden name; it makes sense to keep it in a professional capacity. Faun was my only child and he killed her." It's strange that rage can exist inside so much ice.

"And you killed him."

"It took a while, but justice is served."

"Do you have the right to dispense justice as you see fit?" Sylvia meets my gaze with silence. "And Chase? Did she deserve the death penalty as well?" I ask.

"Her—demise is unfortunate, but she was a junkie that wouldn't have lasted another year before dying of an overdose or suicide. I just sped up the process."

"Chase was somebody's daughter."

Sylvia's eyes narrow. "Don't play at something you don't understand, Mr. Barker."

Terror is prickling down my back, but I have to know. Have to know everything. "What about Kandi?"

"She doesn't deserve explanation. Cheap, blackmailing floozy. Justice was served in all three instances."

"Why Mr. Sharpe? Why not me?"

Her smile is not attractive. "Don't think it was because of any latent emotional attachment. Mr. Sharpe was simply an easier target."

"But you've ruined his life. What's left of it."

"He'll do fine. He thinks he did it. He feels good about killing Dallas. Justified. They'll put him in a cozy sanitarium and he'll live out his days in comfort, away from the stress of real life. Even his family will be thrilled."

"And that makes it right?" I'm cold. Colder than I've ever been in my life.

Sylvia stubs out her last cigarette and laughs. "My dear boy, it's justice. And that's what I do. Of course it's right."

In another minute, I know I'll throw up. And Sylvia will laugh. I gather my things.

"Without evidence, you know you can't go to the police, right Rex?"

I pause and then nod, my head bent over my tray. Sylvia gets up and comes around to my side, lifting my chin with her hand. My eyes are forced to meet hers.

"If you get a case of conscience and feel you must talk to someone, talk to a priest. I assure you, the police will believe me before they believe you. And if they think you're harassing me, your life will become a living hell."

I nod again, held captive by her searching eyes. She studies my soul and finally releases me. I know how a mouse feels when it's pinned by a cobra. She smiles and it's a warm, caring smile.

"I have to thank you, dear boy," she says and kisses my cheek. The place where her lips meet my skin burns like a coal. There's no doubt I'm marked for life. "This is better than confession. Without this unburdening, I might have been tempted to blab to someone dangerous. Like John. It may not be obvious, but the idiot has a conscience. And a weak spine. Dangerous combination."

At least the nausea is fading. Unfortunately, a ringing in my ears replaces it. Now passing out is my main concern. I look around desperately, hoping an eco-Nazi has noticed the chain smoking and is coming with a fire extinguisher. Or a fire department. We are completely alone.

"Won't you just remove him, like you do all your problems?"

Her good humor disappears. "Don't match wits with me, Rex. You can't win. And if you lose, you may wind up in a very unlovely place."

"Or dead?"

The smile is back. "Good-bye, Rex. Stay out of trouble."

And she's gone; leaving me to my rubbery sausages and a truth that is equally impossible to digest.

ABOUT THE AUTHOR

E. Sabbag loves the drama and intrigue that exists at workshops almost as much as she loves writing. She lives on a sailboat in Boston Harbor and dreams of the day when she can write and sail the world without being tied to a desk.

http://www.triumphcharters.com/books.html